BURIED LIES

A DEAN LINCOLN LEGAL THRILLER

ALSO BY PETER O'MAHONEY

Dean Lincoln Series:

Reckoning Hour

Fatal Verdict

The Joe Hennessy Series:

The Southern Lawyer

The Southern Criminal

The Southern Killer

The Southern Trial

The Southern Fraud

The Southern Vineyard

The Tex Hunter Series:

Power and Justice

Faith and Justice

Corrupt Justice

Deadly Justice

Saving Justice

Natural Justice

Freedom and Justice

Losing Justice

Failing Justice

Final Justice

The Jack Valentine Series:

Gates of Power

The Hostage

The Shooter

The Thief

The Witness

BURIED LIES

A DEAN LINCOLN LEGAL THRILLER

PETER O'MAHONEY

This is a work of fiction. Names, characters, organizations, places, events, and incidents are either products of the author's imagination or are used fictitiously. Any resemblance to actual persons, living or dead, or actual events is purely coincidental.

Published by Thomas & Mercer, Seattle
www.apub.com

EU Product Safety Contact:
Amazon Media EU S.à r.l.
38, avenue John F. Kennedy, L-1855 Luxembourg
amazonpublishing-gpsr@amazon.com

ISBN-13: 9781662525414
eISBN: 9781662525421

Cover design by Dan Mogford
Cover image: © Edward D Crews ©elwynn © Suthin _Saenontad / Shutterstock

Printed in the United States of America

BURIED LIES

A DEAN LINCOLN LEGAL THRILLER

CHAPTER 1

The sky in the Lowcountry was enormous.

As I stepped into the open-air parking lot next to the Beaufort County Courthouse, I looked up and took it all in. The morning sky was drenched in a vivid blue, saturated in a color that seemed almost too intense to be real. The scent of the pluff mud carried on the thick, humid air, the horizon shimmered in the heat, and the breeze was gentle. A heron glided through in the distance, appearing timeless as it drifted over the ancient Southern live oaks. There were no clouds. No shade. Just the endless blue sky and the quiet presence of Mother Nature.

"Dean Lincoln," a voice called. "You're really going to do this?"

I turned and looked at the man waiting for me as I approached my car. I didn't answer as I took the keys out of my pocket. The sight of the man had ruined my sense of calm. And that was the problem with the South—the stunning beauty and the mesmerizing landscapes were ruined by the corrupt and powerful.

"Judge Newton was a great man." Stephen Freeman, a former circuit solicitor and now political lobbyist, stood beside my SUV. In his sixties, he was tall, tanned, and toned, with unnaturally white teeth. His suit was sharp, fitted, and he wasn't wearing a tie. He spat on the ground as I approached, grunted, and continued. "Judge Newton did so many great things for the people of this great state.

He dedicated his life to serving our community. He was proud of our city, proud of our state, and proud to be Southern. Don't you dare tarnish the reputation of a great man."

I stopped and turned to Freeman. "Judge Newton was accused of sexual assault many, many times."

"He was never convicted."

"Just because law enforcement didn't charge him, doesn't mean it didn't happen."

Freeman's fists clenched. His jaw flexed. His eyes narrowed. "This is about justice. This—"

"There was no justice for his victims. Judge Newton was a devious old man who touched every woman that worked for him. Five women had the bravery to come forward and speak their truth to power, to state that he sexually abused them, and the reason Judge Newton was never convicted was because he was so well connected. You and all your powerful friends protected that piece of scum."

"Don't you dare talk about him like that. He died without any convictions."

"His death doesn't mean he's exonerated."

"They should've given Malcolm Holt the death sentence. He was lucky to get life in prison." Freeman pointed his finger at my chest and stared up at me. "You think you can come here with your city attitude and use our system, but our justice is different than big-city justice. We don't let murderers walk back on to the streets just because they have a good lawyer. We have real justice here. True justice. And we protect each other from outsiders like you."

"Like you protected your son."

His eyes narrowed. "Paul got in an accident. That's all."

"A drunken accident that killed my sister." My teeth gritted. "Your son served five months of a ten-year prison sentence. You don't know anything about justice."

A smirk spread across Freeman's face, unable to contain himself. He reveled in the power he had over my anger, feeding on my pain. I turned away from him, struggling to control my fury, but a thought crossed my mind. I turned and stared at Freeman, then looked back at the courthouse. "You were waiting for me. How did you know I was going to be here?"

"I have friends everywhere, Lincoln. I know you had a 10 a.m. meeting with the court clerk and I know you asked to see the transcripts and files on Malcolm Holt's case. I know what you're trying to do, and I won't let it happen. You're trying to tarnish the good name of Judge Newton."

I squinted. Someone in the department had called him.

"Listen to me." Freeman pointed his finger in the air. "Malcolm Holt killed Judge Newton. The evidence is there. There's no doubt about it. Don't put his family through the horror of another trial. They already had to sit through one—don't make them do it again. Don't put them through that pain."

"I heard a rumor." I leaned close to him. "I heard you and Judge Newton were involved in many activities together, and you covered each other's tracks. And I bet if I dig deep enough, I'll find out what you did together. You don't care about Judge Newton's family. You only care about yourself and whether your corrupt behavior will be exposed in a new trial."

"You're not in the big city any more, boy. Judge Newton was my friend. I'll defend his honor, I'll defend his family, and I'll make sure his killer stays behind bars." Freeman gritted his teeth. "And I'll bury anyone who crosses me."

CHAPTER 2

The Broad River Correctional Institution had an imposing presence.

Rising above the pine-covered outskirts of Columbia, South Carolina, the institute loomed large, dominating the landscape with its harsh chain-link fences, spirals of barbed wire, and utilitarian brick buildings. The design, popular in modern-day prisons, prioritized function over aesthetics, and purpose over style. Simple lines, minimal enhancements, and a focus on concrete and steel.

Behind the layers and layers of perimeter fencing, behind the checkpoints and security screening, stories unfolded every day, some broken, some redemptive, and all tucked away from the outside world. The staff, hardened by their environment, worked to maintain the balance between authority and compassion, structure and disorder, succeeding sometimes, and failing others. There were headline stories of staff tempted by money and seduced by power, but the majority of staff were steadfast, focusing on their roles to deliver punishment or rehabilitation. The occasional scream of anguish drifted through the green surroundings, usually followed by an echoing gunshot and a prison lockdown.

I passed through the security checks and was guided to one of the attorney meeting rooms. There was little ventilation in the windowless room, causing the dampness to build on the concrete walls and saturate the air with the smell of mildew and body odor.

The sterile hum of fluorescent lights droned overhead, flickering every now and again, doing its best to give me a headache. I took off my tie, wiped my brow, rolled up my sleeves, and waited at the metal table.

Fifteen minutes later, Malcolm Holt was escorted into the room. The guard nodded to me, and I nodded in return. He removed Holt's cuffs and pointed to the white plastic chair behind the metal table. Holt sat without another word. For three years, Malcolm Holt had been languishing in prison after his conviction for the murder of Judge Stanley Newton and it showed in his stone-cold interaction with the guard.

Dressed in an orange jumpsuit, Holt was a solid man, with dark skin and short-cropped gray hair. Strong jaw, broad shoulders, rough hands. Despite the hard years in prison, he still looked younger than fifty-five. He waited until the door slammed shut behind him before he looked at me.

"You're a lawyer? You're big enough to be a bouncer," he said as he looked me up and down. "Thank you for coming."

"It's good to finally meet face to face," I said. We shook hands. His grip was firm. I respected that. "I've read your court transcript, the written appeal, and all the briefs you lodged, and it feels like I know you already."

"It's been a long process and I've put a lot of work into that, but then, what else have I got to do?" He rested his elbows on the table and clasped his fingers together. "So, Mr. Lincoln, what's wrong with you?"

"Wrong with me?"

"No other lawyer in Beaufort would touch my case. As soon as I said who I was, they all hiked their prices five times over, because they knew I couldn't afford it. And every other pro-bono lawyer rejected my requests for representation for the appeal."

"And you rejected a court-appointed lawyer in favor of self-representation."

"I had to. Look where the court-appointed lawyer got me last time. The man was a complete mess." He shook his head several times. "So, tell me, why are you the only lawyer in Beaufort who would even look at my case?"

"There's a lot of noise around your case, and most people in the justice system are connected to each other." I nodded. "Although they see me as an outsider now, I was born and raised in Beaufort but spent most of my life working in Chicago. I've been back in Beaufort around ten months now, working in criminal law in the Law Office of Bruce Hawthorn. My wife and I came back so she could look after her mother, who's going through a tough time with her health right now."

"Sorry to hear about your mother-in-law, but I'm glad you're here. I've worked hard all my life, raised a family, provided for them, and this is what the system does to me. As soon as I was arrested, it was me against the establishment." He looked at the table for a few long moments before he shook his head several times. "I couldn't afford a lawyer, so the court gave me Chris Tomlinson, but that was a mistake. I should've defended myself. Even first thing in the morning, Tomlinson showed up to court stinking of alcohol. In one of our first meetings, I told him to use toothpaste instead of vodka, and he never forgave me for that. The guy hated me and pushed so hard for me to take a deal, but I refused. I wanted my day in court."

"I don't know Mr. Tomlinson, and I can't comment on his approach. The one thing he did do well was convince the jury not to impose the death sentence, due to mitigating factors."

"But I still ended up with life in prison. You've read the court transcript, right? You know how Tomlinson fell asleep most afternoons, and the judge had to call out to him to wake him up. Even then, I knew he was drinking at lunch, but now I have the proof. The bar across the road from the courthouse sent through the security footage—he went to the bar every single lunchtime for three weeks and ordered several Jack and Cokes. On one day, the footage shows him having five drinks in the hour before coming back to court. That's what this appeal is based on—his failure to do his job and represent me. I should never have been convicted."

"In a direct appeal in South Carolina, we can't present new evidence. That's reserved for a post-conviction relief motion. An appeal can only look at the court record, and the judges will base their decision on law, not evidence. But even without new evidence, given the information you've put forward as part of the briefs, you have a strong case to win the appeal."

"I have a strong case because I didn't shoot the judge." His fists clenched and he tapped his hand on the table. "And I mean it. It's not prisoner talk. I wanted to kill the judge after what he did to my daughter, but I didn't do it."

I opened my briefcase, removed a file, and placed it on the table. "Your biggest mistake was talking to the police the day after the shooting."

"I know." He threw his head back. "I know that now. I've thought about that so many times, and I was under all sorts of pressure, and I hadn't slept, and I thought that maybe, if I told the truth about what I saw, the police would need to believe me. I thought telling the truth was my way out, but they used it against me. I should never have trusted them. They had it in for me right from the start."

"The day after the shooting, the police asked you to accompany them to the station for questioning. You went with them voluntarily. You told the police you went to Judge Newton's home with the intention to kill him. You told them you wanted to put a bullet in his skull. You—"

"I was going to stop him from assaulting another girl." He stood and started to pace the end of the room behind the table. "I got a phone call that night, and the person said the judge was going to drug another young woman and assault her, just like he did to my daughter. I went there to stop it from happening again because the police wouldn't stop him. Someone had to put an end to it. Someone had to save those young women." He rested against the wall at the back of the room and folded his arms across his chest. "If my daughter was white, we would've got justice. The judge picked my daughter because he knew we didn't come from money. That filthy animal used his connections and brushed her statement aside. And it wasn't the first time, either. Once my case hit the courts, several women came forward and said they were sexually assaulted by the judge. Judge Newton invited the girls to work late at his house, and he'd drug them. They'd wake up without a clue as to what happened to them. And he kept doing it because he could get away with it. Don't tell me the system isn't rigged. Don't tell me he didn't use all his power to get away with it." He expelled a large sigh. "I mean, what was I supposed to do? The courts couldn't protect my family, so I had to. I wanted to kill him. I needed to do it. My job as a father is to protect my children, even when they're adults. And we tried to do it the right way, we tried to do it through the justice system, but they brushed us aside like we were nothing. The judge laughed in my face when they dropped the charges of rape. He laughed in my face. He thought he was untouchable."

"I hear you. I can't imagine the pain and suffering your daughter, and your family, went through because of what Judge Newton did to her. You did the right thing by going to the police about the assault and the system failed you. That must've been heartbreaking."

"The system failed my family twice. I know it sounds stupid now, but I talked to the police that morning because I thought they'd believe me if I was honest with them. I should've known they wouldn't help me. I shouldn't have trusted them. The only reason I'm locked up is because I'm Black."

"No. The reason you're locked up is because you made death threats against the judge, admitted you were at the scene of the crime, and you were seen throwing a gun into the Beaufort River moments after the murder."

Holt paused for a few moments and nodded. "I like you, Lincoln. You're straight up. You don't get a lot of that around here." He rubbed his forehead as he wandered around the far side of the meeting room and then sat back down. "I'll be up front with you—I don't have a lot of money. With a fancy suit like that, I imagine you charge a lot. I don't want to put my family in debt."

"Lawyers in South Carolina are encouraged to give back to the community by taking on pro bono cases, which means you don't have to pay anything for my services. But that's not why I'm doing this. I'm doing this because I believe in your case."

He raised his head and studied me with suspicion. "But there's something else driving you, isn't there?"

"Justice."

"Justice? In Beaufort?" He scoffed and didn't seem convinced by my answer. But he didn't push the idea any further.

"We'll get to the finer details if we win the appeal." I opened the folder in front of me. "Right now, our focus needs to be on the upcoming oral arguments."

"Listen, if I did it, if I killed the judge, I would've taken it on the chin and stayed in prison. And it would've been worth it. I would've loved to have shot him. That would've been real justice. But I didn't get the chance to do it."

"After your guilty verdict, you lodged the appeal on ineffective counsel, and as a pro se defendant, you've prepared a brief for that appeal. Your written argument is very solid."

"Tomlinson stank of alcohol all day, every day. I knew he was drinking, and I told him to sober up. The judge even warned him to stay awake or he risked a mistrial. That's on the court record. It was almost like Tomlinson was trying to lose the case. And that wouldn't surprise me. All the judges, lawyers, and cops were protecting each other. They're the real criminals. They're the ones who've committed so many offenses, yet they're untouchable. They're above the law."

I nodded but steered the conversation back to the details of the appeal process. I spent another fifty-five minutes with Malcolm Holt, detailing the process and focusing on where we had the best chance of winning during oral arguments.

As a pro se defendant, he had compiled a good written argument for the appeal, but instead of approving the appeal outright, the appellate court had arranged an additional hearing for oral arguments.

As the meeting finished, Holt looked at me. "Do you think we can win?"

"You've got a great argument for appeal." I stood. "There's a chance the judges will find in our favor and demand a new trial."

But I knew that would only be the start of our problems. This wouldn't just be a legal battle—this would be a fight for survival.

CHAPTER 3

"How was your mother this morning?"

My wife, Emma, offered a half-smile and blinked back a tear. She bit her lip, swallowed hard, and looked at the basket to her right. We lay on the picnic rug as a fresh coastal breeze blew off the May River, bringing with it the salty scent of the ocean, strong enough to overpower the smells of the fresh produce laid on paper plates between us. Forty-five minutes from Beaufort, the Wright Family Park in Bluffton was drenched in calmness, perfect for a quick romantic escape. Moss-draped live oaks stood strong and tall, the grass was luscious and green, and the slow-moving tidal river shimmered in the late-afternoon sun.

"It's her last round." Emma blinked fast, fighting back the tears. "That's eight in ten months. Of aggressive chemotherapy. It's worn her down, and she's a shell of herself. She's still the same woman—that fiery, happy, cheeky, and loving woman that I've always known, but it's taking a toll on her body. Ovarian cancer is brutal. The doctors aren't sure how much more her body can handle. And the risk of infection is high." She looked at me. "She needs us to stay another twelve months, Dean. I need to be here and look after her. She's either going to go into recovery, or . . ."

I reached across and held her hand. "It's okay."

She swallowed hard and took a moment. Then she looked at me. "Did you call your firm in Chicago?"

"I did. I talked to them this morning about my role. They tried to convince me to go back. They presented lots of different ways for me to manage a split life between here and Chicago. They even suggested I fly out Sunday night to Chicago and return Friday night."

Emma's face tensed. "And?"

"And they've asked me to resign," I said. "I told them we needed to stay, and they said if I wanted to stay in Beaufort for another year, then they couldn't hold on to my position. I was lucky to get twelve months in the first place. There was no chance they were going to extend it. They added that if I want to return to Chicago in the future, they'll happily look at open positions and reemployment, but now, if I don't go back within the next two months, my position is gone."

"What are you going to do?"

"I said I would talk to you first." I looked at her, but the answer was written all over her face. "I'll call them on Monday and let them know we'll stay in Beaufort for another twelve months."

Emma reached across and held my hand. She squeezed it. "Thank you, Dean. I know how much that job means to you."

My job in Chicago had defined my identity for so long, but after almost a year back in South Carolina, I was starting to let go of it. I was accepting that my worth wasn't tied to the value of my suit, it wasn't tied to my job title, and it wasn't tied to the firm I worked for. "Staying here means I'll need to dig up a bit more work. I've already talked to Bruce, and he said he'd be happy to have me around as long as possible. He's got more work than he's ever had, and he wants me to stay."

"Including the retrial of Malcom Holt?"

"If we win the appeal, yes."

"There's a lot of talk around town. Lots of people praised Holt for what he did. It was an open secret that Judge Newton was abusing those girls, and nobody would do anything about it."

"He was connected to some very powerful people who made sure that he didn't have any charges pressed against him." I drew a breath and sighed. "Including Stephen Freeman."

Emma's head snapped around. "Not again."

I nodded. "He's connected to everything. I can't let that family keep getting away with so much. Someone needs to stop them."

"It doesn't need to be you." Emma sighed again and then turned away. A ball rolled over from a group of young children playing nearby. Emma's eyes lit up. She bounced to her feet, picked up the ball, and passed it to the little girl who came running over. The girl gave Emma the loveliest smile.

Emma sat back down, and the silence hung over us for a while. Emma leaned back and looked at the sky. "I've been thinking about . . . trying again." I gave Emma all the time she needed to continue. "But I'm scared of another miscarriage."

I reached across and held her hand. "Me too."

We didn't talk for a while and listened to the sounds of the children giggling nearby. It was a mesmerizing sound, and one that I hoped to have in my house one day.

But if I was going to stay in Beaufort, if I was going to raise a family here, I had to deal with the past.

And that meant confronting my grief—and the family that caused it.

CHAPTER 4

Bruce Hawthorn, the principal attorney of the small firm I was working for, was in a cautious mood as I walked into his office on Monday morning.

Bruce was a Beaufort man with a Southern drawl and a love for telling stories that grew wilder each time he told them. A Lowcountry man through and through, he was thick in the chest, broad across the shoulders, and had hands that looked like they could crush a watermelon with a single squeeze. He was calm but vibrant, strong but caring, and when he smiled, which he did often, it came with an easy charm.

"You'd better tell him," Kayla Smith said to Bruce, while nodding toward me. Kayla was Bruce's assistant. She was petite, but not fragile. Toned but not muscular. Middle-aged, but with a youthful vigor. She was always well dressed, and a glow of good health surrounded her. Her blonde hair was tied back, her blue dress hugged her frame, and her heels looked new and expensive. "He needs to know."

Bruce groaned as I sat down. "Dean, I got a call over the weekend."

"From whom?"

"The attorney general."

I raised my eyebrows. "What did he want?"

"To chat."

"About?"

Bruce groaned again and leaned back in his chair, rubbing his hand on his brow. His office had the weight of history, of someone who had spent decades in the space. His hefty mahogany table was filled with files and notes, with a closed laptop to the side. A bookshelf took up most of the right wall, filled with legal volumes that hadn't been touched in years, and a leather couch sat to the left. "He wanted to talk about my firm's decision to represent someone who's been convicted of murdering a local judge."

"He warned you off the case?"

"He didn't warn me off it, but he said he needed to ensure I knew what I was getting myself into. He thinks there's going to be a lot of pressure coming with this appeal, and he needed to ensure that my firm was up to the task." Bruce stood and walked to the window. He clasped his hands behind his back and looked out at the large oaks covered in Spanish moss, studying the rhythm of the trees for a few long moments. "Before you started here, I would've said yes sir, no sir, and everything in between sir. I was very happy to do my job, play some golf, and enjoy my final few years' work before retirement."

"And now?"

"And now, I'm playing less golf."

I waited for him to continue, and when he didn't, I added, "And?"

"And, I'll admit it, for the first time in decades, I feel like I'm doing my job. I'm not pandering to the wills and ideals of others. I have that spark I had back in college, like law and justice mean something." Bruce turned back to the table. "But on the flip side to that, I've now got some of the most powerful people in the state checking in on me."

"What does that tell you?"

"That feathers are being ruffled. Someone powerful is making calls about this case, and if we keep pushing, then they'll do what they can to stop us. This isn't a run-of-the-mill case. This is the murder of a sitting judge we're talking about. The judge was shot in his own home, sitting in his own living room. And we're busy, Dean. Because of all the publicity over the past few trials, I've got more work than I've ever had. I don't know if we can take on another case, especially one as big as this."

"No other cases are making the attorney general give you a call."

Bruce sat back down and sighed. "Who do you think got in his ear?"

"Stephen Freeman."

"What's his involvement here?"

"He confronted me outside the courthouse after I requested the files on Holt's case. He said Judge Newton was his friend, and he doesn't want to put the family through another trial, but there was something more to it. There was a rumor that Freeman and Judge Newton had a falling out. Freeman didn't want the details coming to light, and he might've shut Judge Newton up for it."

"Freeman is a ticking time bomb, Dean. There are rumors circulating that he's starting to lose his influence in Beaufort County, and he doesn't like it. He's starting to lose his grip on power, and he's the sort of guy who won't go down quietly."

"I've heard he's having some mental health problems," Kayla added. "A friend told me he lost it in a restaurant last week. Started yelling at the server for getting his order wrong. Word is that it was a complete meltdown, even to the point where other diners had to restrain him from yelling any more obscenities at the staff."

"What's causing the breakdown?"

Bruce looked at Kayla, and Kayla looked at me. "Some people don't like having their behavior questioned," Kayla explained. "Especially when they've got a lot to hide."

"I, for one, don't want to be around when he explodes," Bruce added. "What was Malcolm Holt like?"

"Stoic."

"Believable?"

"If he does the right thing."

"Which is?"

"Keeps his mouth shut."

"That's always the best advice. Tell me about the appeal."

I took out the file from my briefcase and placed it on the table. Bruce flicked it open and scanned his eyes over the pages, studying the lines with focus and making small expressions of approval.

"The appeal is based on ineffective counsel," I explained. "Chris Tomlinson was the court-appointed lawyer, and he was drunk most afternoons during the trial. Holt suspected Tomlinson was purchasing alcohol during his lunch breaks, and with some help from his family on the outside, they gathered evidence of those purchases. Once the court granted the subpoena for footage from the bar across the road, the security tapes were handed over to the court, and it clearly shows Tomlinson drinking during his lunch breaks. Then, there were several times where he fell asleep at the defense table. The judge even stated, on the court record, that Tomlinson needed to stay awake or there could be a mistrial."

"Sounds like a clear violation of his right to effective counsel, and if we don't win the appeal, we can file a post-conviction relief motion," Bruce said as he continued to read the pages. "I know Chris Tomlinson. He's had some troubles over the years, gambling and drinking mostly. He's always been a mess. I see him now and again at various functions, and you can tell what he's been drinking from his breath—either bourbon, rum, or vodka."

"He didn't do his job and a man is in prison for it."

"Let's not get two things confused here—just because Chris was drunk doesn't mean Holt is innocent. I knew Judge Newton, and never liked him. There was something off about him. He was good-looking, fit, and charming, but he had a thing for younger women, even though he was in his fifties. Married twice, but that didn't hold him back. There were even some rumors that the girls he had interest in might've been underage."

"His murder was big news around here," Kayla added. "Everybody in Beaufort followed the case when it was going through trial—and from what I read in the papers, it was clear Holt was guilty. Nobody even doubted it. Holt talked to the police, and he admitted he went to the judge's house on that night to kill him."

"He also said he heard gunshots as he approached the home, and then ran away. All Holt did was park near the judge's multimillion mansion home on Spanish Point Drive. That's not a crime."

"Let's deal with the appeal, and then see where we go after that." Bruce nodded, closed the file, and leaned back in his chair. He rubbed his eyes and looked at the ceiling. "Did you talk to your firm in Chicago?"

"I did. They've said if I'm going to stay here for another year, then I'll have to quit. If you need me for another year, then I'm happy to stay."

"Good," Bruce stated with a smile. "Because I need your help. I've got people calling me from all over and I've taken on more than I want to. I've been knocking back work, but last week an old friend called me. I've got too much on my plate at the moment, so I need you to help her. I'll help you with Malcolm's case, if you take the Julie Steinberg case for me."

Kayla passed a file to me, and I flicked it open. "What's the charge?"

"She's been charged with assault and battery in the second degree. She hit a young man who visited her bar. She owns a dive bar on Boundary Street, and the guy was drinking all day, mouthing off to various people. He said something that riled Julie, and she slapped him."

"Second degree for a slap? Must've been a hard slap."

"The police claim she hit the young man so hard that he ended up in hospital, and his ears have been ringing ever since." Bruce leaned forward, watching for my reaction. "The kid's name is Casper Remington."

"Remington? Any relation to John Remington, the real-estate developer trying to buy up half of the Lowcountry?"

"The very one. John is well connected with just about every law enforcement and government official around here, so you're going to need to tread carefully. He's got deep pockets and he wants to protect his son. He doesn't like that Casper was hit by a bar owner." He drew a breath. "Now, I don't want to be a conspiracy theorist but if Julie is charged with assault, there's a good chance she'll lose her liquor license. And if she loses her liquor license, then she would need to put her bar up for sale. And if she put the bar up for sale . . ."

"Then it would be open for John Remington to swoop in, buy it, and develop the land." I nodded. "Is Julie open to a deal for a lower charge?"

"She could be. The people handling the liquor license, the Department of Revenue, would look more favorably on a third-degree assault than second. I've let her know that you'll talk to her this week," Bruce said. "And Dean, I'm getting too old for all this risk. Don't go stirring up too much trouble."

"I'll do my best, Bruce," I said as I closed the file. "But trouble seems to follow me like a shadow."

CHAPTER 5

I parked out front of Laughing Jack's as the sun warmed the morning air, long before the place would be filled with people drinking, laughing, and much later, fighting.

Off the main thoroughfare of Boundary Street, the outside of the dive bar had cracked and faded paint, a boarded-up window, and a flickering neon beer sign. It was a standalone building with a gravel parking lot, and although it was empty now, at night it usually filled with well-loved pickup trucks.

When I was nineteen, I snuck into the bar a few times with a fake ID, fueled by young enthusiasm and stupidity. I remembered the place well—there were seats out back looking over the marsh, but not many people sat outside—the energy was inside, where the air was thick with the smells of beer, sweat, and old cigarette smoke that clung to the wooden panels. The music was almost always country or eighties rock, the pool table was always in use, and the regulars nursed their drinks with the patience of people who had nowhere else to be.

I stepped inside the bar and noticed the place still looked the same—the same dim lighting, the same décor, and the same outdated signs. The pool table in the rear of the room was still there, there was a bar along the right side of the room that was unchanged, and the small wooden tables with upturned wooden chairs resting on top looked like the same ones I had seen nearly twenty years ago. Despite the recently mopped floor, the smell of beer and bourbon was still strong in the air.

Julie Steinberg was wiping glasses behind the counter as I walked in. She was tall, perhaps six foot, broad in the shoulders, and solid in the arms. Her jaw was square, her skin weathered, and her hands were large. She was former Army, and it showed in the way she held herself. Despite her tough exterior, there was a calmness to her smile, and a softness to her eyes.

"Dean Lincoln," I introduced myself, reaching across the bar to shake her hand. She shook it solidly. "Bruce has asked me to take over the assault case."

"Bruce said you were a better person for the job than he was. He said you were some big shot from Chicago and you've handled more assault cases than I've slapped young men."

"Do you make a habit of slapping young men?"

"No, but I slapped that Casper Remington kid as hard as I could. The little prick deserved it after what he said to me." She shook her head and led me to a wooden table at the rear of the bar. The bar was empty, and we had another hour until she opened it for lunch. "What's the world coming to when you slap a kid for inappropriate behavior, and you're the one who gets charged? Come on. I'm fifty-five, and they think I want to accept a plea deal for an assault charge? No way. I'm not pleading guilty to that."

I placed my briefcase on the ground, took the upturned wooden seat off the table and sat opposite her. "You told the police you slapped him because he threatened to hurt an innocent girl."

"Someone told me that Casper Remington was seen taking photos of girls as they left school. He was a semi-regular here at the bar, and one night he comes in, already drunk. He orders a bourbon and then starts trying to talk to everyone else. Starts telling people how he's an amateur photographer of people and places. I asked him if that was his cover for taking photos of girls leaving school, and he said there was nothing illegal about that. And it might not have been illegal, but it was morally corrupt. I wanted to slap him at that point, but I resisted. I think he could see he was making me angry, so he kept talking. That's when he started bragging about 'up-skirting.'"

"Up-skirting?"

"Yeah. He said it was when your camera is down low, and you take a photo up the skirt of the girl that walks over the camera. Disgusting. How could he even say something like that? There's something wrong with that boy's head. He was always causing trouble, always mouthing off to people, and it was time for someone to rein him in. He told me he'd love to upskirt me, and that's when I slapped him."

I nodded. It seemed like a reasonable response to me. "Did you ask to see the alleged photos?"

"Not the up-skirting ones. But I saw the photos he took outside the school. They were only of girls. And young ones as well. I told the police about the photos, but they did nothing. Why didn't the police arrest him? Why did they come after me?" She paused when I didn't answer the question. "Actually, you don't need to answer that. I know why he wasn't charged."

I looked around the bar. Things were tidy, looked after, but nothing was new. "Had any offers from real-estate developers recently?"

"I have. Remington Red Rock, the property development business owned by Casper's father, put an offer on the table in front of me. They said they wanted to build a whole lot of units along the back of the marsh here. It was a low-ball offer, way less than the place is worth, and I said no. I have no interest in selling this place. I've owned this bar for twenty years now, put my heart and soul into it, and I'm not letting go of it." She nodded. "So, I told them all where they could put their offers."

"And where was that?"

"Where the sun doesn't shine." She smiled. "Which works unless you're a nudist, then I guess the sun shines everywhere."

I smiled with her. She had a tough but likable presence. "Tell me what happened after he showed you the photos."

"He said it wasn't against the law to take photos of people in a public place, and I told him it was. I told him I'd report him to the police, but then he said his dad was connected to everyone important, and he'll never be charged with a crime. So, I got close to him, pointed my finger in his face, and told him to stop taking photos of schoolgirls. That's when he said he'd love to upskirt me, and that's when I slapped him. And I have to admit, I enjoyed it. I enjoyed watching his scrawny little body fall to the floor."

"Don't repeat that to anyone," I cautioned her. "He says you used a clenched fist."

"I didn't. It was an open-hand slap." Julie raised her right hand for me to look at. It was calloused and hard. "I do a lot of gardening," she explained when she saw my surprise. "Every night, I'm out in the greenhouse I have in the back of my yard. I grew up poor, and my parents couldn't afford gloves for us kids, so my hands have always looked like this."

I reached down and grabbed my briefcase. I unclipped it and removed a file. "Firstly, you've been charged under Section 16-3-600 (D) of the South Carolina Code of Laws, which defines second-degree assault. Remington claims you hit him so hard that he needed to go to hospital, and he's had multiple medical appointments since that day. He claims he's had ringing in his ears ever since, and that's very hard to disprove."

"I hope he can't sleep because of the ringing in his ears."

"As there are witnesses and video evidence of you hitting him, we can't argue that you didn't do it. The video isn't helpful. I've reviewed the footage taken by a patron in the bar, and the actual hit was obscured, so the video doesn't prove whether it was an open-hand slap, or a closed fist. On the video, it appears like you're both talking calmly before you lash out and slap him. He then tumbles to the ground."

"That wasn't me being calm, that was me holding in my anger."

"Even with the video, we do have a few options."

"Is one of them defense of others? Because that's what I was doing."

"Unfortunately, the law stipulates there needs to be an imminent and immediate threat to another person to justify the use of physical force. If Casper had said he was going to assault a particular person at a specific time, we could argue for the defense of others, but given the situation, we can't. But we do have several options—one, we can argue that it was sufficient provocation and you acted in the heat of passion. The provocation needs to be at a level where a reasonable person would react. This would be good because we could talk about what he told you. That information would then be on the public record, and I'm sure his father doesn't want the headline, 'Developer's son talked about taking sexual photos of schoolgirls.'"

"That's good. I like that."

"Our second option is to push for a reduction in the charges," I continued. "You've been charged with second-degree assault, which leaves us room to negotiate down to third-degree. To show the prosecution is being heavy-handed, we'd need to throw doubt on the level of harm that was caused to Casper, since second-degree assault is defined as involving moderate bodily injury. We'll review his medical records, and I'll have my investigator look into his behavior over the past few weeks, and over the coming weeks as well. We'll be looking for anything that contradicts his medical claims. Ideally, we'd catch him going to a loud bar, which could suggest the ringing in his ears could be from somewhere else. Even if we had footage of him listening to loud music in his car, it would help our position."

"Who do you use as an investigator?"

"Sean Benning. Know him?"

"I've heard of him, but don't know him. One of the regulars at the bar is a private investigator around here. I could give him your name. He'd do me a solid and help us out for free. Do you know Wayne Cascade?"

I nodded slightly.

Julie smiled. "I see you do know him. Listen, I know some of his tactics might border on illegal, but he's good."

"Wayne and I have had a run-in or two."

"Ah." Julie acknowledged my reluctance. "Say no more."

"Our investigator will also look at the links between the witnesses and Casper Remington. If they're connected, we could argue they're embellishing the story to help their friend. You would still plead guilty, but the penalty would be $500 or a small amount of prison time, which I'm sure would be suspended, if you haven't had any trouble with the law. Have you been arrested in the past?"

She grimaced.

"What happened?" I asked.

"Assault in the second degree."

"That's not good. When and why?"

"Twenty-five years ago. My abusive ex-husband, who used to slap me regularly and never let me control any money, showed up to our anniversary dinner with an escort on his arm. I told him the dinner booking was for two people, so he kissed her goodbye and then walked to the dinner table like it was nothing. I lost it. I hit him several times, and the staff had to drag me off him. The prosecutor offered a deal with no prison time for an early guilty plea, and I took it."

"Due to the time passed, we should be able to argue that information is kept out of any potential trial. Hopefully, it doesn't get that far, but that's good to know."

Julie hesitated in response, before she leaned forward. "I'm sure Bruce told you what my theory is."

"He did."

"The Remington family wants this bar, so they bring in Casper, and he baits me until I react." Julie lowered her voice. "The witnesses, who I've never seen in this bar before, then testify about how bad it is, and I get an assault charge. Once I've got the charge, John Remington calls his contacts in the Department of Revenue, and I lose my liquor license. And once I lose my liquor license, I need to sell the bar, at which point, John Remington swoops in and buys it for cheap. He then develops it into a new set of poorly built townhouses and makes a big profit."

"That's hard to prove."

"Doesn't mean it's not true."

"If you find any evidence that supports that theory, send it to me," I said, and then diverted the conversation back to the process. "In the coming weeks, we'll meet with the prosecution, and we'll discuss options for the way forward. They'll present us with a deal, and we can negotiate further with them for an early guilty plea. They won't want a case like this to go to court, and we can leverage that in the negotiation."

I chatted to Julie about the process for a while longer, and one thing became clear—this wasn't going to be just a legal fight. This was going to be a fight against people with money, power, and connections.

CHAPTER 6

The boardroom in the Law Office of Bruce Hawthorn was a busy space. A whiteboard was to the side of the room, filled with scribbles and notes, a potted plant sat in the corner, and a long wooden conference table ran down the center. A painting of Hunting Island State Park hung on the left wall, the air conditioner hummed low and steady, and a smell of lavender filled the air, thanks to the occasional squirt from the air freshener at the end of the room.

Kayla had organized Malcolm Holt's files into neat stacks, covering most of the boardroom table. There were court transcripts in one pile, evidence documents in another, and notes on potential precedents in a pile nearest the window. Several sheets of paper were laid out with information about Chris Tomlinson, and reports about the judges for the appeal in the center of the table.

Sean Benning, the firm's investigator, sat at the far end of the room, closest to the door. Tanned, toned, and scarred, his appearance spoke of a life exposed to the ruthlessness of Southern weather. His eyes were blue and narrow, always scanning his surroundings, and his fingers were constantly twitching, tapping on a table, chair, or anything in reach. He lived a humble life on a houseboat, going from one dock to the next when he felt the need, drifting through the rivers around Beaufort County with the contentment that only life in the Lowcountry can bring.

"I did some work for Tomlinson once, about five years ago, and I vowed never to work for him again," Benning said. "Everything about the man was a mess. His office was a mess, his car was a mess, and his whole life was a mess. He was going through a hard time in his marriage, and he just kept digging a deeper hole for himself by drinking every day. It's a demon, drink. Some people can handle it, but others, well, they don't have an off switch."

"You never know what happens behind closed doors," Kayla added.

"How did we do with his alcohol purchases?" Bruce asked.

"According to his credit card receipts subpoenaed after the trial, he made purchases of alcohol at lunchtime on fifteen of the twenty-five days of the trial," I replied. "There are court bailiffs who are willing to testify they smelled alcohol on him, and there's court staff who will testify he appeared drunk on several occasions during the trial."

"Tomlinson is known to treat the staff of the courthouse terribly," Bruce added. "Always talks down to them, yells at them, and generally treats them like dirt. They would leap at the chance to testify against him."

"It goes to show you that it's important to treat everyone nicely," Kayla said. "Politeness goes a long way. As my grandma always used to say, 'Kindness doesn't cost a cent, but it affords you so many things.'"

"Sounds like a smart woman," Bruce said. "Being drunk isn't enough to prove lack of counsel. We need rock-solid evidence, on the court transcript, that he failed in his duty to represent Holt."

"There are many instances where he failed his duty." I looked at my notes and continued. "He failed to ask a question on cross-examination to ten of the twenty-five witnesses, and even when he did cross, he failed to ask even the most basic questions. And then there's his lack of objections." I flicked a page in my notepad. "After looking at the court transcript, there are 115 possible objections he didn't object to, and a further twenty-five instances where he absolutely should have. There were so many instances where the prosecutor led the witness, testified in his questioning, and asked questions with no basis in fact, and Tomlinson said nothing. During the testimony of the eyewitness who states they saw Holt throw a gun in the river, which was essential to establishing the case against him, the judge told Tomlinson to wake up or there would be a mistrial. That alone shows Holt was without significant representation at times during the trial."

"But we're skipping the elephant in the room." Benning leaned forward. "Even a drunk like Tomlinson could've landed a guilty verdict in this case. Everything about it points to Holt's guilt. He admitted he went to the judge's house around the time of death, admitted he made death threats against the judge, and then police found Holt's gun in the river. There's not much to dispute."

"We're focused on the appeal," I stated. "We've got to win that first."

"But then what?"

"Malcolm Holt deserves a fair trial. That's a constitutional guarantee—the Sixth Amendment doesn't make exceptions for people with a strong motive. Holt had the right to competent counsel, the right to confront his accusers, and the right to a defense that stood up in court. He got none of that. What he got was a defense attorney who barely stayed awake, who missed critical objections, who didn't challenge the state's witnesses, and who let the prosecution run unchecked. That's not justice."

We heard a ding from the front desk, and Kayla got up to answer it. She returned a moment later with a concerned look on her face.

"Bruce," she whispered. "It's Chris Tomlinson."

"What's he doing here?" Bruce groaned.

"He said he's heard you're taking on the appeal for Malcolm Holt."

Bruce looked at me.

"I'm leading the appeal." I stood. "Let him talk to me."

"Or I could give him an appointment time?" Kayla asked. "Tell him to come back tomorrow? He seems quite angry right now."

"No. I'll meet him now. I'll take him to my office."

Bruce avoided eye contact. I stepped out of the meeting room and greeted the lawyer waiting next to Kayla's reception desk.

Chris Tomlinson looked a mess. He was average height and overweight, with a protruding stomach, and he had little brown hair left. His skin was pale, his face appeared swollen, and the whites of his eyes were tinged with yellow. His shoes were scuffed, his white shirt was half-untucked, and his collar had food stains on it. I would almost feel sorry for the man if his failures hadn't sent Malcolm Holt away for life.

"Mr. Tomlinson." I offered my hand. "My name is Dean Lincoln."

"Where's Bruce?" he snapped and ignored my offer to shake hands. "I need to talk to Bruce."

"I'm here." Bruce stepped out behind me. "Chris, always a pleasure. How can we help you?"

"You can help me by not trashing my reputation, Bruce!" Tomlinson flung his arms around like a petulant child. "You're going to destroy me! Your appeal makes it look like I should be disbarred! This is absolutely ridiculous."

"If you did your job, we wouldn't need to do this." I stepped forward, towering over him. "You didn't defend your client."

"My job! I did my job!" It looked like Tomlinson was about to cry. "My job was to defend Malcolm Holt. I did that and made sure he didn't get the death penalty. That's what I did for him. I can't help it if he shoots a judge five times in the chest. A judge, for crying out loud! What does he expect?! Who shoots a judge?"

"Malcolm Holt claims he's innocent."

"How could he be innocent! Did you even look at the evidence?" Tomlinson began to pace the reception area, but quickly tired himself out. He leaned one hand on the counter, huffed, and squinted his face in an attempt to look angry. It wasn't convincing. "Malcolm made death threats against the judge days before the murder, and then he went to the judge's house, at the time of death, and a witness says they saw him throw a gun into the river as he left. That gun was later proven to be Malcolm's! Come on, what was I supposed to do? Claim that a burglar shot the judge and Malcolm was there by coincidence? I did the best I could with the situation we had."

"You failed to defend him," I stated. "You didn't do half the amount of work you should've in that courtroom. There were so many objections you failed to raise."

"Shall we discuss in my office?" Bruce offered. "We can talk about the case and see if there's any way you might be able to help Malcolm."

"No, no, no." Tomlinson's demeanor changed in a heartbeat. When he saw that anger wouldn't work with us, he went from angry to whining. "Don't do this to me. Please, Bruce. We've known each other for years, and we've always been nice to each other. I've always said good things about you. You're a good Southern man, Bruce. So, please, I'm begging you. Not now. Don't throw me under the bus. I'm going through a divorce, and this will just about knock me out. You're kicking a man while he's down."

Bruce offered him a half-grimace.

"Come on, Bruce," Tomlinson pleaded. "I have debts to pay, and a case like this will ruin my reputation. I need the work."

"Gambling again?" Bruce asked.

"I've been good. I really have, but I've just had a bad run. That's all. It'll get better. I'm sure it will. The change is coming. I can feel it. My turn is coming."

"I'm sorry, Chris. We won't make any unjust accusations against you, but we need to do our job."

"Please, Bruce. Keep my name out of it. Make the appeal based on prosecutorial misconduct, or evidentiary errors. I'm sure you can find something to dispute this. Take my name out of the document and make it about something else."

"Can't do that, Chris."

Chris bit his lip and turned for the door. His anger returned. He clenched his jaw and curled his fists into balls. His tone dropped. "You'll regret this, Bruce. I'll bring Stephen Freeman in. He owes me a favor, and he'll make sure the appeal doesn't get up."

"What does Freeman have to do with this?" I asked.

"He has something to do with everything," he scoffed and looked at Bruce. "This guy doesn't get it, does he? Freeman controls everything around here."

"Not any more." Bruce stood up straighter. "Things are getting cleaned up, and I suggest you do the same."

"How dare you." He gritted his teeth and lurched toward Bruce in anger. I stepped forward.

He looked up at me, and then grunted and walked toward the door. He stopped and turned back. "Watch your step, Lincoln. You've rocked the boat, and now everyone's watching. And not all of them play fair."

CHAPTER 7

I drove two and a half hours inland to meet with Malcolm Holt the day before the oral arguments for the appeal. The Broad River Correctional Institution was fifteen minutes away from the Court of Appeals, where I would be arguing on Holt's behalf the following day.

The conference room in the administrative wing of the prison was cold and emotionless. The brick walls were painted in a dull, institutional beige, the smell of bleach hung heavy in the air, and the white Formica table looked older than me.

Holt sat at the table, leaning forward, arms crossed, his leg jiggling up and down, trying to disperse the nervous energy running through him. The appeal was his chance to try again. This was his moment. And he had no control over it.

"I'd love to be there," he whispered, more to himself than me.

"I understand, but as the appeal focuses on legal errors made during the trial, your presence is not required, and in fact, the appellate court discourages the presence of the defendant, due to security issues."

"What if I'd represented myself? They would've had to let me in."

"They wouldn't have invited you to present oral arguments and, instead, would've used the written briefs alone to make their decision."

He sighed and rubbed his brow. He looked close to tears. To distract him, I took him through the process. "The Court of Appeals involves arguing before a panel of three judges, and the purpose of the oral arguments is for attorneys to clarify legal disputes in regard to the trial and respond to judges' questions. It's not a new trial and no new evidence will be presented. The appellant, which is us, and the respondent, the State, will present separate arguments, which typically last five to ten minutes. I'll summarize key issues and emphasize how Tomlinson's mistakes affected the trial, and why these errors meet the Strickland v. Washington standard for deficient performance and prejudice, and I'll also present legal precedents supporting our claims of ineffective assistance."

"What can the State even argue? They can't deny he didn't do his job."

"They'll argue why the conviction should be upheld. Most likely, they won't deny Tomlinson's errors, but they'll argue the errors did not affect the trial outcome, nor did his deficient performance affect the jury's decision. We'll then have a chance at a rebuttal, and the judges may interrupt at any time to ask questions. After oral arguments, the judges deliberate and issue a written opinion weeks or months later. The possible outcomes are that the conviction is reversed and a new trial granted, the conviction is upheld and the appeal denied, or they may remand for further proceedings and ask the trial court to review specific issues."

"There's all that evidence he was drinking." He rocked back and forth as he spoke. "Why won't they look at that?"

"The direct appeal doesn't consider new evidence, including his credit card records. If we lose this appeal, then we can raise the new evidence of his drinking in a post-conviction relief motion."

He nodded but didn't respond. I spoke to him for another fifteen minutes, but it was clear his mind was elsewhere. After we shook hands, I went to my hotel for the night and reviewed my oral arguments, rehearsing line after line, and trying to anticipate the questions the judges might ask.

The following morning, after a long night of preparation, I was standing outside the Calhoun Building in downtown Columbia, which housed the Court of Appeals. The limestone building, built in a Renaissance Revival style, was named after John C. Calhoun, a nineteenth-century Congressman, Secretary of State, Senator, and Vice-President, who had used his final political speech to argue for South Carolina's constitutional right to secede in response to northern suppression.

With the fate of a convicted man hanging on my shoulders, I entered the building, passed through security, and walked through the quiet hallways. Jason Neville, an experienced attorney from the South Carolina Attorney General's Office, greeted me in the corridor outside our courtroom. Neville was a fit man in his forties, clean-cut, religious, and had a wide smile. With his smooth charm, family connections, and deep voice, he was destined for a future in the minefield of Southern politics, but right now, his focus was on defending the State and the courts' processes.

He wished me luck as we stepped inside, passing the only other people seated near the front. I recognized the faces from the files we had on the Newton family. Judge Newton's sons, Kane and Robert, watched me closely as I walked by. On the other side of them sat Stephen Freeman. None of them offered a greeting.

Neville spoke to them in a hushed tone while I reviewed my statements before the court clerk entered and asked if we were ready. When Neville and I confirmed we were, the clerk called the case and the judges entered from the door near the back left of the room. Once the judges had settled, Judge Jackson, the presiding judge, invited me to begin the argument for appeal. "Good morning, counsel. You may begin your argument, Mr. Lincoln."

"May it please the court. Good morning, Judge Jackson, and members of the court. Thank you for this opportunity for oral arguments in the appeal of Mr. Malcolm Holt. The appellant, Mr. Holt, was left without representation many times during his trial. The conduct of his court-appointed attorney was incompetent, inept, and, at times, useless. This left Mr. Holt without his constitutional right for representation in court and violated Mr. Holt's Sixth Amendment right to effective counsel. Mr. Tomlinson was drunk at various times during the trial, he attended bars at lunchtime on most days of the trial, and he repeatedly fell asleep in the afternoon when the prosecution presented witnesses, leaving Mr. Holt without representation."

"This feels like a personal attack on another lawyer, Mr. Lincoln, and I need to ask what the central issue is here," Judge Jackson interrupted. "Is it Mr. Tomlinson's behavior, or Mr. Holt's lack of representation?"

"The central issue is Mr. Holt's lack of representation; however, we can't talk about that without highlighting Mr. Tomlinson's behavior. There was a failure to provide a meaningful defense, as a sleeping and intoxicated lawyer cannot effectively question witnesses, object to improper evidence, or provide a sound legal strategy. The defendant was prejudiced because key arguments were not made, and no real defense was presented."

"Fair enough." The judge shrugged. "You can continue."

"In our written briefs, we've highlighted that Strickland v. Washington established the standard for ineffective counsel under the Sixth Amendment, and Mr. Tomlinson's performance fell well below the objective standard for reasonableness. He failed to cross-examine ten of the twenty-five prosecution witnesses and failed to object to twenty-five questions that were clearly leading the witness, were speculative, and were not based in fact. Mr. Tomlinson failed to call crucial witnesses that would've assisted the defense case, and he failed to ask even the most basic of questions to some of his witnesses."

"And do you have precedents that support reversal?" asked Judge Garrison, sitting to the left.

"Yes, Your Honor. We cite State v. Burton, 2005, where the conviction was overturned because the defense lawyer was asleep during key moments of the trial, and State v. Gold, 2015, where the defense attorney was intoxicated, leading to ineffective assistance of counsel. These cases establish a clear precedent that extreme attorney misconduct automatically warrants reversal. In our written brief, we've highlighted the many times that Mr. Tomlinson was asleep, where he failed to cross-examine crucial witnesses, and how he failed to call even the most basic witness in his defense case."

"Do we have concrete proof the lawyer was intoxicated, or is this based on speculation?"

"Concrete proof can be provided, Your Honor."

"And perhaps that's why this argument would be better suited to a post-conviction relief motion, Mr. Lincoln, because as you know, we can't consider new evidence here. Now, your brief says Mr. Tomlinson had two drinks during one lunch break. I don't know how drunk you think a person can get off two drinks, Mr. Lincoln. It's below the standard for drink-driving."

"Your Honor, after one drinking session—"

"I'll stop you there, Mr. Lincoln. Two drinks doesn't constitute a drinking 'session.'"

"After one lunchtime, where Mr. Tomlinson consumed alcohol in a bar, he failed to cross-examine all three State witnesses that afternoon. He was asked by the judge whether he was asleep, as evidenced on the court transcript, and failed to object to questions that were leading, not relevant, and speculative. There are affidavits from court staff that state they could smell alcohol on Mr. Tomlinson's breath in the morning, well before his lunch break at the bar. We don't know how much alcohol Mr. Tomlinson consumed in private; however, his credit card statement shows he went to the liquor store every second day and purchased over five hundred dollars' worth of alcohol during the trial."

"Again, that evidence is why this argument is better for a post-conviction relief motion. We're here to review the court record, not consider new evidence," Judge Jackson said. "Did the trial judge notice and take action when the lawyer fell asleep?"

"On one occasion, the trial judge warned Mr. Tomlinson that it could be a mistrial if he continued to fall asleep, and on another occasion, he asked Mr. Tomlinson if he needed a break for coffee, but Mr. Tomlinson denied the request, and on a third occasion, the trial judge recommended Mr. Tomlinson needed more sleep in the evenings."

"Is there direct evidence the lawyer's incompetence changed the verdict?"

"The very fact that Mr. Tomlinson failed to cross-examine ten crucial witnesses is evidence enough. Mr. Tomlinson also failed to call the witness who provided a police statement that she had seen a suspicious pickup truck with two men drive off moments after hearing the gunshots. She's listed on the defense witness list; however, Mr. Tomlinson did not even call her to the stand as he presented no clear legal strategy. His closing statement was a ramble with no clear direction."

"Thank you, Mr. Lincoln." Judge Jackson turned to the prosecutor. "We'll hear from Mr. Neville in reply."

Neville gathered his notes, checked his pens, and walked to the lectern. "May it please the court. My name is Jason Neville and I'm appearing on behalf of the State in its case against the appellant Mr. Holt. Moving to the real issue at hand is that Mr. Tomlinson's behavior did not change the verdict in this case. The evidence was strong, the facts were indisputable, and any jury would've found the defendant guilty, given the evidence available. The defense had no clear strategy, because there was no other option. The facts were overwhelming."

"Do you believe the trial judge's behavior was reasonable in warning Mr. Tomlinson?" Judge Jackson asked.

"Absolutely. Mr. Tomlinson's behavior was unprofessional, but it was not prejudicial. We acknowledge he liked a drink at lunchtime, and we acknowledge there were occasions where he dozed off, but the overwhelming evidence of guilt means the outcome would have been the same, regardless of the lawyer. There isn't a specific moment where the lawyer's absence harmed the defense."

"What about his failure to cross-examine several witnesses?"

"There was no use. It was clear the witnesses' facts could not be disputed. The jury still reached a fair verdict despite the lawyer's issues. If the problem was so bad, why didn't the trial judge declare a mistrial? He didn't because it was clear the case was still fair. And our question is, if the defendant noticed, why didn't they raise concerns during trial? There were many remedies to this issue before now, and it's our belief the conviction should be upheld."

"Does a sleeping lawyer inherently mean the defendant was denied representation?"

"No, Your Honor. The lawyer had read the statements from the witnesses and there was nothing to dispute. The statements were factual."

"If the lawyer was intoxicated daily, how can we be sure he was competent at any point?"

"As you've pointed out, the defendant's level of intoxication was likely below the legal threshold for operating a motor vehicle."

Judge Jackson leaned forward, his hands clasped. "And are there any cases where a conviction was upheld despite clear attorney misconduct?"

"We've listed several precedents in our briefs, Your Honor, where attorney error, although serious, was not deemed prejudicial enough to warrant reversal. Each case turns on its own facts."

When no further questions were asked, Neville thanked the judges for their time, closed his folder, and sat back down.

I stood for the rebuttal.

"This is not a close decision," I began. "This is a case of incompetence. A lawyer who is intoxicated and unconscious during trial proceedings is ineffective. The Sixth Amendment guarantees more than just a physical presence at counsel's table, it guarantees a meaningful representation. The fair and just remedy is a new trial, one where Mr. Holt has a competent attorney and a real chance to defend himself."

No further questions came from the bench.

Judge Jackson offered a courteous nod. "Thank you, counsel. The matter is now under advisement, and we will reserve our decision for later. We're now in recess."

And with that, we had thrown our best punch. Now we had to wait to see if it landed.

CHAPTER 8

In the foyer of the courthouse, I called Holt at the prison and told him how the session went. I could hear the nerves in his voice when he asked how long until the decision was made. It could take weeks, or months, I told him, and the line went silent for a while. He thanked me and that was the end of the call. He sounded more worried than ever. This was his shot. This was his chance. This was the moment where he could change his future, and now he could do nothing but wait.

After the call finished, I spent a moment to gather my thoughts before I stepped out of the courthouse into the bright midday sun. The humid air clung to me as I walked across Sumter Street toward my car parked on the side of the road. The cicadas were buzzing in the trees, and the horizon was simmering with heat. By the time I had crossed the road, sweat had already built on my forehead.

As I approached my car, I noticed Judge Newton's sons waiting for me. They were standing with their arms folded in front of a new pickup truck. Behind their vehicle was an older blue truck, the engine rumbling as it idled. I'd seen the truck before when I was at the courthouse in Beaufort. It had a dented fender. Oversized tires. Rusted paint. There was someone in the driver's seat, but I couldn't make out who it was.

Kane and Robert Newton were sizable men. Both broad-shouldered, both square-jawed, and both appeared to shop at the same store—wearing blue jeans with black boots, although they wore different-colored flannel shirts. The older brother, Kane, had a trimmed beard, gray hair, and wore thin-rimmed glasses. I had read that Kane was a successful day trader in New York, while Robert had started a deep-sea commercial fishing business. His father's political connections had helped him secure licenses, permits, and quotas that seemed otherwise impossible to obtain.

"You're scum," Kane growled. "Our father was a great man, and you're determined to destroy his legacy with some legal tricks. And we won't stand for it."

"Can you hear us, city lawyer?" Robert added. He was rougher than his older brother. Unshaven, messy brown hair. The scar on his right cheek hinted at a history of explosive anger and bar fights. "We said leave our father alone. Let his killer rot in prison."

I didn't respond and continued toward my car. Robert grabbed my shoulder. I turned and pushed him, shoving my hands hard into his chest. He stumbled backward.

"You touch me again and I'll break your jaw." I pointed my finger at Robert.

He puffed his chest up, lifted his chin, and flayed his arms out wide. Kane held his hand out for Robert to calm himself. "Watch your step, Lincoln. You never know when someone might jump you."

I eyed him for a long moment until I turned back to the car. Stephen Freeman, hands in pockets, stood next to my car door, looking satisfied with my interaction with the Newton sons.

"Not a bad legal argument, Lincoln." Freeman's voice was laced with arrogance. "But let me warn you, if this case goes to a new trial, then things are going to fall apart for you. Those men will do anything to protect their father, as will the many people who were connected to him."

"Why?" I stepped up to face Freeman. "What are you scared of? What's going to be exposed in a new trial?"

"I've got nothing to hide."

"I don't believe that. The closer I get to the truth; the more concerned people seem to get. What were you and Judge Newton up to?"

"Careful, Lincoln. If you keep pushing, people won't just be concerned. They'll become dangerous. Believe me, this is just getting started. If you defend Malcolm Holt, you're going to find out how protective our community can be."

I wanted nothing more than to smash a left hook on to the jaw of Freeman, but I knew that wouldn't solve any problems. I took a deep breath and opened the door of my car.

As I started the engine, I looked back at Freeman and the Newton family. They were all glaring at me.

But they weren't just staring. They were calculating. And I realized I wasn't just battling one man.

I was battling an entire system.

CHAPTER 9

Rhys Parker's Sundance skiff drifted slow and easy on Lake Warren.

The morning air was fresh, carrying the quiet hush of dawn as a golden glow spread over the glassy surface. Mist rose from the water, with dragonflies hovering just above it, and birds were starting to wake, singing their beautiful songs, symphonies full of grace and wonder.

A hidden gem around an hour inland from Beaufort, Lake Warren was edged by towering pines, thick underbrush, and the occasional weathered dock reaching into the stillness. Rhys knew one of the rangers and he had opened the park up early for us, allowing us to fish in solitude. I cast my line using a Carolina rig, letting the weight settle on the lakebed, searching for the slow pull of a largemouth bass. As we fished, we said little, enjoying the moment of stillness, rocking gently as the water pushed against the hull. It was meditative and calming, a moment surrounded by the splendor of the south.

Rhys Parker was a big man, solid, hard-working, and a family-first type of guy. He had been widowed by my sister's death, leaving him as a single father to raise their children, Zoe and Ollie, both under ten. Emma had offered to look after them overnight, allowing Rhys and I a chance to drive up to the lake. We didn't say much for the first hour, but when we saw another boat on the shore, our conversation began.

"It's been good having you back, Dean. You remind me so much of your sister." Rhys looked out at the water. "Have you and Emma made a decision on whether you want to stay or go back to Chicago?"

"It's been good to be back. There's something about Lowcountry life that gets to you," I said. "Emma and I have confirmed we're here for another year. Her mother still needs her around."

"Is that right?" Rhys smiled. "You still got a job in Chicago to go back to?"

"They'll fill my position but said I can reapply when I get back. They understood why Emma needs to stay, and they still expect me back in another year."

"And if Emma wants to stay in Beaufort long-term?"

I considered the question for a long moment before I admitted, "I miss Chicago. I miss the heartbeat of the place. There's a rhythm of life there, a pulse of something great. It's loud, it's bold, and it's in your face, and I love that."

"It ain't loud around here. Here, it's a world of whispers instead of shouts."

I nodded, and his statement sat with me for a while, running through my head.

"Charleston, Savannah, Atlanta. None of them are far away," Rhys continued after a few minutes of reflective silence. "Just make sure you get out for a weekend every now and again, and you'll get your fix of the bigger city. You get used to the slower pace, less traffic, more free time, and suddenly, the bigger cities will start to make you angry. I've seen it happen to people. There's something about slowing down."

My line tugged. I stood, bracing against the sway of the boat, and gave my rod a sharp pull. The fish wrestled back, strong, and we locked in a quiet tug of war. The fish dived deep, trying to dislodge the hook, and I kept the pressure on. After a moment, the large bass was pulled to the surface, and Rhys was ready with the net.

"That's dinner sorted for a few days." He patted me on the back as he brought it on board.

Between the two of us, we'd reeled in six bass in an hour, reaching our daily limit, and Rhys almost looked disappointed. I imagine he wanted to spend most of the morning on the water. Slowly, he drifted along the lake, heading back to the dock as the world came alive. Two more boats were pulling in. The birds were singing louder. The breeze was picking up.

We spent the next half an hour getting the boat out of the water and back on to his trailer.

"You look like there's something on your mind, Rhys," I said after we'd tied the boat down. "What is it?"

Rhys bit his bottom lip before he ran his tongue along his front teeth. He leaned against his truck, folded his arms, and stared out at the water. "Paul Freeman has been calling me."

"Paul Freeman?"

"Yeah." Rhys nodded and screwed up his face.

"Was it about the restraining order?"

"I have no idea what he's calling about. I haven't answered his calls or read his messages. I'm trying my best to hold it together, and he's baiting me. He wants me to explode and tear him apart. He knows what I'll do if I see him, and it'll mean I end up in prison. It's bad enough he killed my wife in a drunken car accident, and now he wants to take me away from my kids as well."

"Rhys, holding on to the anger isn't healthy for you."

"Aren't you angry? She was your sister."

"Of course, I'm angry. But I also know that beating up Paul Freeman isn't going to bring her back."

Losing a loved one in the prime of their life is not an easy thing.

It's confusing, puzzling, baffling. It leaves behind so many questions. Why now? Why her? Why not me? The burn of grief, the clawing in your chest, the cloudiness in your head, stays for so long. There at breakfast, there at dinner, in the quiet moments and the loud, in the moments where you think you've dealt with it, in the moments where you feel you've left it behind.

Over the years, the intensity lessens, the sharp edges of pain ease, but the confusion still remains. None of us really know what happens when we die. Does the soul continue on and leave clues behind? Are the signs I've noticed messages or coincidences? Is there anything at all after death? Nothing highlights the lack of answers like the loss of a loved one. We try to make sense of it, try to understand, try to perceive the unperceivable. We look for evidence that can answer the questions, evidence that this theory or that theory is real, but we never know for certain. People with after-death experiences talk of a bright light, they talk of an afterlife, they talk of a collection of souls, but they never come back with evidence.

And when there's no justice, without answers in the real world, the emotions fester, they irritate, they change. The sorrow becomes rage. The heartache becomes fury. The grief becomes wrath.

For Rhys, the rage was growing stronger with each passing month. I had suggested counseling, but he wasn't the type to sit down and spill his emotions. I suggested boxing, a way to release his pent-up anger, but he injured his shoulder. There was only one path that would work for Rhys.

What he wanted, what he needed, was justice. Or, perhaps, revenge. I wasn't sure.

"How about his father? An eye for an eye. That would be fair."

"That's what I would love," I agreed. "Bruce thinks Stephen Freeman's losing his grip on power and he's going to go down swinging. Stephen Freeman is going to explode."

"Good. I hope he takes his son down with him." Rhys gripped the edge of the boat tight. "I can't get Paul's smug face out of my head. Sitting there, smiling as his sentence was read out. He knew his father would get him out early. He knew he could use the system to his advantage. He knew the courts couldn't stop his family. He served five months of a ten-year sentence, Dean. How can that be right?"

"The prisons were crowded. They either let him out early or let a violent felon roam the streets again. The sentence was suspended, and he's on probation."

"That's just legal talk trying to cover up the real reason—it's because Stephen Freeman pulled strings behind the scenes. It took two years to get Paul to court, and he was given a ten-year sentence, but he got out in five months. Five months, Dean. That's not right." Rhys's jaw clenched and then he turned to me. "You've got to stop that family, Dean. You need to take them down. They're taunting me. Teasing me. Trying to bait me into acting out so I end up in prison. Paul killed Heather, but I'm going to be the one who ends up in prison. Where's the justice in that?"

I didn't respond. Rhys was right. There was no justice in that.

Something had to change soon, because I wasn't sure how long Rhys could contain his anger.

CHAPTER 10

Sundays moved slow in the South, especially once the heat set in.

Mid-morning, the roads were quiet, the church lots had cleared, and the only sound was the occasional squawk of the seagulls drifting overhead.

Emma and I walked to my grandparents' place at eleven. Still dressed in their Sunday best after church, my grandfather's shirt was unbuttoned at the collar and his sleeves rolled up to the elbows, as if to prove he hadn't fully surrendered to his age in his eighties. My grandmother welcomed us with tight hugs and many kisses on the cheek, so happy to see us.

While the women set up in the kitchen, discussing lunch plans, Granddad changed his shirt and put on a pair of jeans, before leading me out back to the tidy yard. He handed me the clippers without a word and pointed at the bushes that apparently needed taming. I trimmed, he chopped, and together we tamed the bushes. Around 1 p.m., when the sun started to burn, we called it.

Grandma Lincoln set up a folding table under the shade of a tree out front, and Emma followed with chairs. My grandmother returned, carrying a tray of sandwiches, a tin of cookies, and a pitcher of something sweet. They always made a production out of these things—like it wasn't just lunch but a tradition worth preserving.

After a hearty lunch, we cleaned up and then returned to the table to play cards. Emma won most hands, and I called her a cheat. Granddad slapped me on the shoulder with a backhand and told me to treat my wife better. Grandma barely looked up from her hand, treating every round like it was a test of mental fitness. When she hadn't won in a while, I played a soft hand and let her take it. She knew it. She smiled anyway.

After the final hand, another narrow win for Emma, two of my aunties showed up, and the women retreated inside for sweet tea and local gossip.

I packed up the table and chairs, and by the time I wandered back outside, Granddad Lincoln already had two camp chairs set up in front of the open garage door. The cicadas hummed in the trees, and the air was thick, but the shade was a welcome retreat.

"Catch," Granddad Lincoln said, tossing me a cold beer, and I caught the errant pass just above my knee. "Good catch."

"Bad throw."

"Ah, nobody's perfect." He shrugged. "You know, I once told your grandmother to embrace her mistakes, so she gave me a hug."

"She's a very wise woman." I smiled.

"But I caught up with a friend of mine at the bar yesterday." Granddad Lincoln's grin was broad. "And he looked a bit down, so I asked him if everything was okay. He said, 'My wife and I got into a huge fight, and she said she wasn't going to talk to me for a month.' And I said to him, 'Well, maybe that's a good thing. You could get a little peace and quiet.' And he says, 'Yeah, but today's the last day.'"

I chuckled with Granddad Lincoln, more than the joke warranted. It was hard not to laugh when he did.

"So, I asked him what the fight was over," he continued, "and my friend said his wife was standing in front of the mirror, and she says to him that she feels old and ugly, and would love a compliment. So, he says to her, 'Your eyesight's perfect.'"

Granddad Lincoln was a storyteller, born and bred. He'd grown up in an era when front porches doubled as stages and the best entertainment came from rhythm. Over time, he'd honed the craft—timing, tone, a right pause at the right moment—and his delivery was effortless.

The smile lingered on his face for a long time as he sipped his beer. When the jovial moment had passed, he asked, "How's the appeal on the murder conviction going?"

He never let go of his interest in the law. He had practiced criminal defense law when records were kept in paper boxes, secretaries typed memos on typewriters, and trial strategies were hashed out over ashtrays. When I was living in Chicago, he'd call after big hearings and ask for a full breakdown. He gave advice if I asked but never stepped on my toes.

"We've got a great shot at a retrial," I said. "His first lawyer failed in so many ways. And if we don't get this one, then we'll try again in a post-conviction relief motion."

He nodded, taking a slow sip. "Everyone around here thinks he's guilty. And nobody blames him for what he did. Was manslaughter on the table during the original trial?"

"If the victim was a builder, or a schoolteacher, or an office worker, manslaughter would've been on the table from day one. But he wasn't. He was one of the most connected judges in the region."

"You mean corrupt."

"I didn't say it."

"As C.S. Lewis once said, 'Good and evil increase at compound rates.' Every little action you take moves to the next action. Every little decision affects the next decision. Every little moment matters. Judge Newton was a terrible man, and every time someone looked the other way, that evil compounded. If someone had stopped him at the start, if someone had stood up to him, he never would've gotten away with so much abuse."

"Money, family, connections and power," I quipped. "That's how he got away with it."

We spent the better part of an hour on the front lawn, beers in hand, watching the afternoon shadows stretch across the yard. Conversation drifted between legal tactics and the old cases Granddad had tried back in his day. He still followed the court bulletins, still read the dockets, still had opinions—most of them sharp. When mid-afternoon hit, I thanked him for the beers, stepped inside, kissed Grandma on the cheek, before Emma and I walked the short journey home.

After I snuck out to the gym, I returned to the scent of fried chicken filling the house. Real, home-made, the kind that makes you stop at the front door and smile. A vanilla candle flickered in the hallway, trying to compete. I almost blew it out.

Emma was in the kitchen, apron on, in her element. I leaned in and kissed her. "Go and shower," she told me off. "And brush your teeth before you kiss me again. All I can smell is those protein shakes you drink."

"Yes, ma'am." I smiled and disappeared to the shower.

When I returned, I sat on the bench and watched her move through the kitchen. I offered to help, but she waved me away.

She talked as she cooked—about her mother's chemo, the side effects, the optimism. Jane believed she'd beat it. Emma did too. Her brother was still stuck in California, flying in when he could, but Emma had stepped up for the day-to-day help. And she was okay with that. Grateful, even.

She told me about the library where she was volunteering, the retired teachers, the kids who needed someone to read with, the quiet joy of shelving books. It suited her. She'd been good at HR in Chicago, but she'd hated everything about the corporate machine, especially the part where she had to fire people she barely knew. Life in Beaufort, with her mother, her cousins, and her old friends, suited her so well.

And I saw that. I loved seeing her at peace.

The plan had been to stay for a year, maybe less, long enough to help her mother through chemo. Long enough to be present. But the longer we stayed, the longer we settled into life here, the harder it was to imagine leaving.

When dinner was ready, Emma served it hot and didn't let me touch a thing. We ate at the kitchen bench, careful not to make a mess.

"This is incredible. You know this is my favorite," I said, leaning in again to kiss her temple. The smile didn't leave Emma's face as I sat back down. "What are you grinning about?"

She reached behind her and set a small plastic stick on a tissue on the table in front of me. A pregnancy test. Positive.

"Again?" I said, staring at it. "So soon?"

She nodded and took my hand, pressed it gently to her stomach. Her fingers trembled.

"We've been here before," she said. "But I'm ready. I want to try again."

Her voice didn't waver. Not once. And in that moment, I wasn't thinking about Chicago or the courthouse or the world I'd left behind. I was thinking about what came next.

And whether we were ready to face it.

CHAPTER 11

While we waited for the appellate court's decision, Bruce and I discussed the potential retrial.

Strategy mattered, and the earlier we committed to a course, the stronger our position would be. Every move we made, every decision we weighed, could shape how the jury saw the case. But no matter our approach, no matter our tactics, one thing was clear—we couldn't allow Holt to testify again. Not after last time.

"It was a terrible decision to allow him to take the stand," Bruce said as he read over the court transcript. "Holt looked like a fool up there."

"The prosecutor destroyed him, and he was avoidant of every second question," I said. "It's never a good idea to allow a defendant to testify. Everything else goes out the window. Jurors stop questioning the evidence, they stop questioning the eyewitnesses, they forget about everything the experts stated. They focus on one thing—do I believe this guy? And up against a skilled prosecutor that could make the Pope look like a liar, most often, the answer is no."

"A complete failure from Tomlinson. There's no way he should've allowed that to happen."

"Holt probably felt like he didn't have a choice. Tomlinson was failing at every turn, and he had no hope left. But it's rarely the right decision." I leaned back in the chair. "He failed so many times, and not just in the courtroom. He also failed to investigate the call that was made to Holt on the night of the murder. I have a contact who worked for the FBI in their CAST team, and—"

"CAST?"

"Cellular Analysis Survey Team. They analyze cell phone data, cellular network information, and geolocation data to pinpoint where and when calls were made. My contact retired several years ago but got bored of golf courses and swimming pools, so he now works as a private consultant out of Charleston. If this makes it to trial, I'll contact him, and he'll follow up the call for us. We'll know who called him."

"That could be a game changer." Bruce tapped his hand on the table. "And Alannah Drew, the witness who wasn't called?"

"Lives down the street from the judge. Filed a police report that said she saw a pickup truck parked outside her home on the night of the murder, and it appeared to be deliberately parked behind a row of bushes. She watched two men dressed in black get out of the pickup and walk through the bushes that lead to the judge's house. Then she heard the gunshots, and the two men came sprinting back to their vehicle before speeding off."

"Not a clear win, but it does raise suspicion that other people could've been involved."

Kayla entered the boardroom, balancing three mugs, with the rich scent of coffee trailing her. She placed the mugs down, then left and returned, this time carrying a large plate full of cookies.

"It's the fuel required for brilliance." She winked at me. "But I'm not sure there's enough to help Bruce."

"Hey, that's not very nice." Bruce chuckled and took a bite of a cookie. His eyes lit up in delight. "All is forgiven. I can't be angry with someone who can bake like this. These taste like they were baked in heaven."

I took a sip of the coffee, then sampled one of the cookies. Sweetness burst across my tongue. "Kayla, these are amazing."

She gave a modest shrug, but the glow in her expression showed how much the praise meant to her. "It's an old family recipe," she explained. "And I'm taking the secret ingredient to my grave."

For a long, serene moment, the room was quiet except for the soft rustle of paper and the comforting hum of shared company. The appeal, the court, the outcomes—none of it seemed to matter.

"How'd it go with Julie?" Bruce drew the focus back to work as he sipped his coffee. "Does the case have much hope?"

"She admits she slapped the kid, and you've seen her hands—they're like baseball mitts."

"She must've slapped him hard," Kayla added. "From the police photos, the kid had a black eye, and bruising on his cheek. If what Julie said is true, she shouldn't have been charged in the first place. Casper Remington was talking about schoolgirls and taking photos up their skirts."

"He deserved it," Bruce agreed. "Think it'll go to trial?"

"I don't think it'll make it that far," I said. "If we can present someone to convince the prosecution to deal low to a third-degree charge, I'm sure Julie will take it. I'll call Sean Benning and ask him to do a deep dive into Casper Remington's behavior. If he can find anything that might suggest his ears weren't as damaged as he suggested, we can make him look like a liar. If we can find some evidence of him listening to loud music, or using power tools without ear protection, then we can expose him."

"Thanks, Dean." Bruce nodded. "Julie is a good woman. She doesn't deserve to be charged because some kid wasn't raised right."

"Hear, hear," Kayla added. "She's done so much for the community. You won't find a veteran in Beaufort who hasn't been helped by that woman."

My cell phone buzzed. I checked the number. It was the courthouse. I looked at Bruce. He nodded. Kayla drew a breath.

"Dean Lincoln," I answered, and put the call on speakerphone.

"Mr. Lincoln, it's Lisa Worthington, Clerk of Court at the Beaufort County Courthouse." Her tone was flat. "The appellate court has made a decision on the matter of Mr. Holt's appeal. The written decision will be provided to you later this afternoon, but I thought I'd give you a call and let you know the outcome."

"Hello, Lisa. Thanks for the call."

There was silence on the other end of the line for a long moment. I could feel the beat of my heart against my chest. I could feel the weight of the decision hanging heavy on me.

And then she delivered the news.

CHAPTER 12

I drove north to talk to Malcolm Holt in person.

After clearing security at the Broad River Correctional Institution, I was shown into a small attorney-client meeting room and left to wait. The room was hot, with little ventilation, leaving the air stale, thick with the smell of sweat and body odor.

After fifteen minutes, Holt was brought in, shackled and silent. He looked broken. His head hung forward, his shoulders were slumped, and he avoided eye contact. He sat across from me without a word, hands trembling enough to notice. He looked like a man on the edge—ready to break down or blow up, and it wasn't clear which would come first.

"How are you, Malcolm?" I asked.

"Terrible. I haven't slept in so long. Every night, these nightmares come back." He bit his lip. "Have they made a decision?"

"They've made a decision."

Holt stared at the table, his face vacant of expression.

"Go on then," he whispered. "What is it? What did they say?"

"They ruled in our favor."

The breath caught in Holt's throat. He sat up straight and looked at me. "What does that mean?"

"All the judges found Mr. Tomlinson erred when he showed up to court drunk on several occasions. They couldn't prove he was drinking every day, but there was clear evidence he was drunk and asleep during important moments of the trial. They determined there were many times where you were effectively left without a lawyer during the case."

"Give it to me in plain English."

"Malcolm, there'll be a new trial."

Malcolm chuckled, once, twice, and then smiled. His chuckling became louder as the news sank in. "I can't believe it." He stood and the smile grew wider. "Is this even real?"

"This is real."

"Thank you, Dean. Thank you." He reached over and shook my hand so hard that it felt like he was trying to rip it off. "Thank you."

"You did most of the heavy lifting, Malcolm." I released the grip before he squeezed my hand any further. "Your written arguments were strong, and your legal precedents were good."

His smile broadened, and he chuckled to himself again, shaking his head. "I can't believe it."

"We'll get you transferred to Beaufort County Detention Center as you're no longer serving an official sentence here," I stated. "You can say goodbye to Broad River for now."

"I can leave this place?"

"Until a new jury gives a decision, yes."

"And they could find me not guilty, right?" His eyes widened. "You can work some sort of legal magic, and I can get out of here. Man, I never thought the day would come. You start to lose hope back here. After three years, it had started to sink in that I might never be free again."

"There'll be no legal magic. We need to work hard to win the new trial," I said. "There was a lot of evidence against you, Malcolm. We'll work hard to have some of it excluded from the trial, but there's still a lot of it. Which brings me to the next point—we need to start to prepare for another trial."

"Start with Jackie Florence." His voice was exasperated. "She was one of the main prosecution witnesses and she was lying from day one. She said I told her that I was going to shoot the judge, but I never said that to her. I never said it. And when she was giving her testimony, I told Tomlinson to ask her about her husband, but he refused. He didn't ask her a single question, even though she was lying. He refused to do anything during the trial."

"Why would she lie?"

"My wife and Jackie had a beef going back years. They're cousins, but you wouldn't know it. They had a falling out over their grandmother's will. The grandmother left my wife some money, but not a dime to Jackie. Said she was a good-for-nothing drug addict. And that's why Jackie lied. She wanted to hurt my family."

"Seems like a stretch."

"No, it's true. The cops got her to talk because her husband was locked up. And guess what? He got an early release the week after her testimony. That's not a coincidence." He shook his head. "She was lying. She was lying straight up to the court. If Tomlinson wasn't such a failure, he would've had her testimony thrown out. It was clear she was dishonest, and Tomlinson didn't do anything about it."

Malcolm and I went over the process for another twenty-five minutes, covering what we needed to. When the meeting was done, he stood, extended his hand again, and I shook it. He had a broad smile—tired, but genuine.

After he was gone, I gathered my notes, packed the file, and exhaled.

It was time to start again.

CHAPTER 13

It took Sean Benning two days to track down Jackie Florence.

She had moved to Jacksonville, Florida, after her husband was released from state prison, and she was living in cheap accommodation, working as a cleaner for a large factory. I hit the road again, enjoying the long stretches of land as I drove south.

From what Benning had gathered, Jackie's entire life seemed to be overshadowed by the curse of illegal drugs. Her parents were addicts, her siblings were addicts, and at various times in her life, she had been an addict. Between her and her husband, there had been many arrests, complaints, and struggles. They had periods of holding down jobs, periods of getting their life together, before these were followed by periods of incarceration and homelessness.

I would never judge anyone for their addictions.

As a criminal defense attorney, I'd seen enough to know that addiction wasn't the problem—it was the easy fix the individual sought out. Addiction was the language of old wounds, of unresolved pain, of unsettled trauma. It was an escape from the burden of suffering, an escape from the agony of the past, and once a substance had a person in its grip, it didn't let go gently. There were better ways, much better ways, to deal with the wounds, but substance abuse was the easiest answer.

Jackie was working, she was trying, and she was moving forward. Nobody could ask for more. In a world where so many fall, praise should be given to those who continue to push forward.

Parking outside the address Benning had given me, I drew a breath and sighed. The apartment looked like it was barely standing upright. The brickwork was chipped, the main window had a large crack down the middle, and there was trash sitting outside the front door. I imagined the rent was cheap, and it was safer than sleeping on the street.

I checked my watch: 10:05 a.m. Jackie Florence should be on her way home from her night shift as a cleaner. The loud huff of a bus blustered on the street nearby, and I watched several people stagger off, including my target. She was a skinny woman with dark skin, dark hair, and dark clothes. Her braided hair ran down her back to her hips, she wore no make-up, and her eyes were dull.

"Jackie Florence," I stated as she approached her front door.

"I ain't done nothing wrong, mister." Her tone was strong, not stopping to talk to me. "You've got the wrong person. You can't arrest me for something I didn't do."

"I'm not a cop." I raised my hands in surrender and gave her my best Southern smile. It eased her reluctance. "And I'm not here to arrest anyone."

"Then I ain't buying whatever you're selling." She took her keys out of her purse and went to her front door. "You're talking to the wrong woman."

"Not selling anything." I stepped closer. "I'm a lawyer."

"Who for?"

"Malcolm Holt."

She stopped. She looked around before she answered. "What do you want?"

"I want to know why you lied to the court."

She put the key in the lock. "I ain't speaking to you."

"Malcolm Holt won his appeal, and that means he's going to have another trial in court. You'll be called as a witness, and there'll be a subpoena out for you. That means more lawyers, more police, and more court cases."

"They can't make me testify."

"You testified in the last trial."

"Yeah, well, they can't make me do that again."

"Why not?"

"Because they threatened my husband."

"With what?"

"More prison time."

"And why won't that work this time?"

"Because he was shot a year ago. I spread his ashes along Hunting Island beach. They can't touch him now."

"I'm sorry to hear that." I paused for a moment before I continued. "Jackie, what did Malcolm really say when you saw him that day? Did he talk about the judge, or did he talk about Rachel, his wife?"

"He talked about my cousin Rachel." She paused, dropped her head, and looked at me. "Rachel didn't deserve the money from my grandma's will. Rachel told my grandma lies about me, saying I was on drugs and this and that. She lied all the time, and then my grandma left me out of the will."

"And you saw this as a way to get back at her?"

Her head snapped at me. "It had nothing to do with that. I saw it as a way to get my husband out of prison. That's all. I needed to look after my family, because nobody else would."

"And now?"

"And now I want nothing to do with it. They can't force me."

"They'll subpoena you."

"If they try to drag me back to court, I'll tell 'em the truth. If they put me on the stand, I'll tell the court that the cop told me what to say. I was so high I couldn't remember what Malcolm really said that day anyway. All they knew is that we had an argument in the supermarket, and that's why the police talked to me. They suggested my husband would get a reduced sentence if I admitted that Malcolm talked about shooting the judge, and I went along with it. If they force me back into the courtroom, that's what I'll tell 'em."

"They could fine you for contempt of court and perjury for lying in the first trial."

"They've got to find me first." She leaned on her door. "I don't even know why you're picking on me. Everyone lied in that case to put the judge killer away. The cops put the squeeze on all the witnesses."

I squinted. "What do you mean?"

"I know the dashcam footage was changed."

"Go on."

"In one meeting, I overheard the prosecutor say the dashcam footage was altered. That's all I know. The rest you'll need to find out for yourself." She turned away. "But don't come here again. There ain't no way I'm getting involved this time."

CHAPTER 14

The farm on St. Helena Island was hidden behind a row of large live oaks draped in Spanish moss. Behind the trees, rows of collard greens and okra stretched in neat lines across the soil, and several tractors worked their way back to the sheds as the working day came to an end.

I leaned against an older blue pickup and waited. The registration plate had been listed in the court documents for Holt's first trial, and I had no problem tracking down Nigel Impala. He seemed like a man driven by routine and repetitiveness, locked into a daily rhythm he had no desire to get out of. As he stepped out of the sheds, Impala spotted me. He appeared hesitant as he approached.

He was a tall man, slightly taller than me, and his lack of width made him appear even taller. His face was thin, with a long nose and long forehead, and he held his chin pointing toward the sky, even when he was looking at the ground. As he approached, he wrestled with his safety vest, pulling it off his skinny frame, and holding it in his left hand. "What do you want, pal?"

"To talk about your dashcam footage."

"If you're talking about the accident last week, then it's all sorted. The other driver was at fault, and I've sent him the footage.

It's all on my dashcam. You insurance lawyers don't rest, do you? Harassing me at work. I should put in a compliant about you."

I ignored the comment and continued with the conversation. "And your dashcam is accurate?"

"The best."

"It doesn't change dates?"

"Why would it do that?"

"Because it's happened in the past."

He squinted, still with his chin pointed upward. "What are you talking about, man?"

"Malcolm Holt's trial."

He stood up straighter, seemingly gaining another inch in height. "You're not here for the accident from last week, are you?"

"No."

"Are you even a lawyer?"

"I am."

He groaned, leaned against the truck, folded his arms, and clucked his tongue a few times. "I heard Malcolm Holt won his appeal." He shook his head. "But everything I did was legal."

"The dashcam footage you used should have a date and time stamp in the bottom left. It comes standard with that model." I nodded toward his truck. "But the file you presented to the court didn't have a time or date stamp on it. Why did you alter the footage?"

"It wasn't altered."

"There was no time and date stamp on it."

"It wasn't altered, just . . . clarified." He shook his head. "Listen, it was the right date, and the right time. When my footage was set up, the wrong date was entered, so everything was a day behind. So, the footage said the fourth of May, but it was really the fifth of May."

"And the prosecution changed it."

"They didn't change it. The cops suggested I take off the date so things didn't get confused. It was easy to do. All I had to do was click an option before the download and it removed it. Listen, it was the right date, on the right night, but it was recorded as the wrong date on my dashcam. That's all. It doesn't change the footage. The footage was still real."

"That evidence never would've been admitted to court if the date was wrong."

"We put away a killer."

I looked at him. It was time to appeal to his masculine side as a father. "Do you have daughters, Mr. Impala?"

He looked away. "Two."

"And if a man sexually assaulted one of them, and then was not charged by the cops, what would you do?"

"I'd beat him to within an inch of his life, but I wouldn't shoot him."

"And if the man who assaulted your daughters was about to assault another woman, would you stop him?"

"I'd call the cops. That's what the law is for."

"You and I both know law and justice don't work like that around here. And do you think Malcolm Holt, who was doing his duty as a father, deserves a fair trial, or a trial that's tainted by evidence that's been altered?"

He didn't respond.

"I'll answer for you—Malcolm Holt deserves a fair trial." I stepped closer to him. "The truth about the dashcam footage will come out whether you like it or not. If you want to say it wasn't altered, then you'll be charged with perjury. Do you want to spend time behind bars for perjury?"

He scoffed.

"Unlike in the first trial, Malcolm Holt now has a capable lawyer. And if you testify about the footage, I'll expose it, and you'll go to jail for perjury."

He stared at the horizon for long moment, before he turned and stepped into his truck, not saying another word. But he didn't need to say anything.

The message was received loud and clear.

CHAPTER 15

I left the farm with a knot in my stomach.

Nigel Impala struck me as a decent man—quiet, deliberate, hard-working. When he had testified about the dashcam footage during the first trial, he had believed he was doing the right thing. He had believed he was helping put a murderer away. He had believed he was helping his community. But belief was a dangerous entity in the courtroom. The courtroom needed facts, not theories. Convictions had to be based on the truth, not assumptions.

And I felt Nigel knew that. He knew it was wrong, and he knew he was providing an incomplete version of the truth. He had told himself the small change didn't matter, that his omission was helping, not hindering, the justice system. I understood why. He had seen Holt that night, even if the footage was changed, and he wanted to consolidate his version of the truth. But the justice system isn't built on good intentions, and it isn't built on convenience. If the courts picked and chose which parts of the truth to tell, the system would rot from the inside. Its foundation was reliant on integrity—integrity of the witnesses, integrity of the evidence, and integrity of the lawyers, judges, and staff involved. It was my job to hold the prosecution to that standard.

The road alongside the farm was long, and after I passed the line of oaks, the landscape opened up on both sides to wire fencing and dry pastureland.

I caught the pickup in the rearview mirror about two minutes after I left the farm. It came fast. Too fast. A cloud of dust kicked up behind it.

No plates.

My stomach sank.

Even before I could make out the shape, I knew the truck. It wasn't Impala's. It was the same one parked outside the courthouse last week. Same dented fender. Same oversized tires.

I flicked on my indicator and eased toward the shoulder, assuming he'd blow past.

He didn't.

He closed the gap. The first hit came soft—a tap, almost polite, nudging the back of my SUV like a warning. I tightened my grip on the wheel.

The second hit wasn't polite. It was deliberate. The rear end bucked hard, my tires squealing against asphalt. The steering went light for a second, and I fought it, yanking the wheel to stay straight.

Another push—this one grinding. The truck was riding me now, nose tucked into my bumper like he meant to lift me off the road.

I swerved, trying to shake him, but he stayed tight. Then my tires caught the shoulder. The dirt gave way beneath me, and the SUV skidded sideways, wheels fighting for traction.

I spun. Full rotation. Dust and gravel everywhere. When I came to a stop, the front end of the SUV dipped into a shallow ditch. My hands were still locked on the wheel. My pulse thundered in my ears.

I threw the door open and jumped out, half-expecting the truck to stop.

It didn't.

It tore past me, engine growling, dust kicking up like a tail of smoke. I didn't get a look at the driver, but I didn't need to.

This wasn't road rage. It wasn't a mistake.

It was a message.

The Freeman family didn't play by the rules. They never had. And if I wanted justice, it wasn't going to come easy.

It was going to come with a fight.

CHAPTER 16

The double garage was Rhys's man-cave, his escape from the pressure of being a single parent to two young children. The concrete floor was stained by years of grease and sweat, the benches were covered in tools, and the smell of oil was strong. A brightly colored toy set of tools sat in pride of place at the end of the garage.

Rhys wiped his hands as he checked out the bumper on the SUV. He unscrewed the bolts and clips, disconnected the lights and sensors, and then gave the bumper a solid shove to detach it from the vehicle. He placed it on the bench, used the heat gun to warm it up, and then pushed the dent out from the inside.

"I've done this hundreds of times," he said, referring to his upbringing as the son of an autobody repairman. "The guy just ran you off the road?"

"Didn't even give me a chance." I picked up one end of the bumper as Rhys grabbed the other end. "And didn't stop after he hit me either. I got out of the car and he sped off into the distance."

"Then you need to get rid of this city car and buy a pickup."

"Not yet. Emma doesn't want to drive a pickup. She wants a family car."

"You've got to get a pickup eventually," Rhys said as we placed the bumper back on the raised SUV, clipping it into place. Rhys got under the car and screwed the bolts back on. "You can't live in the Lowcountry without a pickup."

I knew it was true.

Out here, a pickup wasn't just a truck for appearances. It was for hauling goods, or towing boats, or helping neighbors move. It was for carrying coolers for oyster roasts, dogs with freedom, and lumber for the family renovation project. It was for Christmas trees or busted fence posts. It was for ferrying kids during summer parades, loading up with fishing equipment, and muddy boots. It was for late-night drives with the windows down, for makeshift beds during drive-in movies, for tailgates that turned into seats. When the storms hit, and they always hit hard, a pickup was the first responder before the sirens arrived, pulling trees from roads, navigating flooded streets, and bringing hot meals to those without power. The pickup wasn't about horsepower, it wasn't about showing off, it was about showing up when it mattered. It was a symbol of practicality, of willingness, a vehicle that was as much a part of the Lowcountry as pluff mud and porch swings.

"What did the police say?" Rhys asked.

"That it was an unfortunate accident. There are thousands of blue pickups in this area, they said. I told them it belonged to one of the Newton sons, and they called around. Both sons were out of the state when the accident happened, but it wouldn't surprise me if Robert had sent one of the workers from his deep-sea fishing company out to do it. The cops said they'll keep the file open, but there isn't much chance of a resolution. They said it was most likely to be some drunk who accidently clipped the back of the car."

"Well, you're lucky it wasn't worse." Rhys checked the bumper was in place by pressing down on it. It didn't budge. "Cars like this are designed to squash in and squash out."

"Thanks, Rhys. I appreciate you."

As I patted Rhys on the shoulder, a brand-new white pickup pulled up at the end of the driveway. Rhys and I looked at the vehicle, waiting for the driver to exit. When the front door opened, my mouth dropped open in shock.

"Is that . . ." Rhys's words trailed off as he watched the young man step out of the truck. "Paul Freeman?"

Paul Freeman, dressed in a pink polo shirt tucked into his black shorts with boat shoes, looked like he'd never done a hard day's work. His thick brown hair was full of bounce, his skinny arms were flung wide as he walked, and his skin appeared smooth and soft.

Rhys squinted and as he confirmed who he was, his expression changed from one of confusion to pure anger. His fists clenched, his jaw tightened, and his face squished together. I could sense the rage seeping off him.

"Wait." I stepped in front of Rhys and put my hands on his chest. "We don't need any more violence."

Rhys's breathing rate increased as Paul approached us. Paul had his head bowed and held up his hands in surrender.

"I know I'm not the person you want to see," Paul said as he came up the driveway. "But I need to talk to you."

"Not today. Not ever." Rhys's teeth gritted together. "Get off my property."

Rhys pushed forward. I held him back. Paul Freeman came closer. "Listen, I wanted to talk about Heather—"

Rhys moved fast. I had no chance to stop him. He threw a solid right hook, connecting with Paul's jaw. Paul was sent sprawling to the ground.

Rhys stepped forward for another shot, but I caught him by the shoulders and pulled him back. It was taking all my strength to stop him from turning Paul Freeman into roadkill.

Paul scrambled to his feet, dazed, holding his hands up.

"Never say her name!" The anger surged through Rhys. "Never say her name!"

I held my arm across Rhys's chest, bracing him, trying to stop another punch.

As Paul retreated, he tried again. "I'm—"

"Get away from here!" Rhys continued. "Get off my property!"

Paul took the hint and stumbled back. Rhys's anger continued to rage long after Paul had driven away.

And I wasn't sure how long he could keep it contained.

CHAPTER 17

The morning mist hung over the golf course.

The Spanish moss swayed in the live oaks off to the left of the fairway, and the marsh, full of wildlife waking for the day, was to the right. The perfectly manicured green grass was damp with dew, and the sun, soft and golden, was casting its long rays across the course.

Bruce lined up his first tee shot, took two practice swings, and then hit the ball straight down the middle of the fairway. He didn't say anything about the shot. He didn't want to jinx himself. Instead, he smiled and nodded. It was the perfect start to a perfect morning.

My tee shot swung left, out-driving Bruce's ball by a few yards, but sitting in the rough near a large tree. Bruce's smile widened further. He didn't say a word until he hit his next shot, and it landed in the rough to the left of the green. He tapped his five-iron on the ground. His perfect morning was perfect no longer.

Despite the occasional expression of frustration, it was a gentle start to the weekend, an easy way to enjoy the slower pace of life in the Lowcountry. As we played the first few holes, the conversation flowed freely. We talked about life, about the city, and about the heat. Bruce talked about his current wife, his ex-wives, his children, and his grandchildren. He talked about his dream of sailing in the crystal-clear waters of Fiji, of seeing the Alps in

Austria, and watching the sun rise over the vast savannahs of Africa. His retirement dream was to travel, to see the world, to experience different countries and different cultures. Only a few years away from retirement, he was already starting to plan. At the fifth hole, Bruce caught me daydreaming, staring at the oaks as they were bathed in the morning sun.

"Thinking deeply?" he asked.

"Thinking about how it would be to raise a family around here," I said.

"This place teaches you more than any school in the city could." Bruce placed his tee in the ground and took a practice swing. "This place teaches you how to be at one with nature, how to calm yourself, and how to be still."

I nodded and watched Bruce send his shot into the trees on the right. He mumbled to himself about the shot for a while, telling himself to be better. We continued playing, but eventually, like always, our conversation moved on to more serious things.

"Think Rhys will snap?"

"If pushed."

"A better question is whether Rhys or Stephen Freeman will snap first." Bruce shook his head as my shot went straight down the fairway. "This court case has Stephen all riled up, much more than the first time."

I agreed, but steered the conversation elsewhere. Out here, it was too calm, too peaceful, to be thinking about Stephen Freeman. "Did you know that humans see less than one percent of the light spectrum available?"

"Is that right?"

"The spectrum of light includes ultraviolet, infrared, and x-rays, among others. There's a whole range that we can't see. Bees can see ultraviolet, butterflies can see polarized light, and some birds of prey see colors we can't even imagine due to their number of receptors. Humans can only see a tiny part of the light available, and it makes you wonder what we don't see."

"Like the jury in a court case."

"Exactly," I said. "They see what we want them to see. They hear what we want them to hear. And they don't ever see the full picture. Tomlinson showed them nothing. They were blind when they made their decision."

"Because Tomlinson was blind drunk." Bruce scoffed and swung his club. "What are we going to do about the video footage from the dashcam?"

"The prosecution will still try to use it, but we'll dispute it. There's no way it'll be used in the court case."

"Do they know you know the truth yet?"

"Not yet."

"The lack of footage and a missing witness weakens their case, but they've still got his confession that he was near the scene of the crime at the time of death."

"And as soon as the prosecution finds out about the footage, they'll panic." I swung hard. "They'll be starting to put together the case, and they'll find out we've talked to Florence and the dashcam owner. They'll come to us with a better offer, but unless it's for time served, Holt won't take it. Unless they find new evidence."

"What do you mean?"

"I'm sure the prosecution has something else. They're too confident. They've still got another play to make."

Bruce didn't respond and we played the next fairway in silence, the rhythm of the game matching the pace of our thoughts.

"Another murder case," Bruce said as he lined up a putt. "I hadn't done any in thirty years, and then you show up, and now I'm on my third."

"Are you thanking me?"

"All this stress is going to send me to an early grave, Dean." Bruce stepped back, reassessed the line, then tapped in the ten-footer. "But I don't mind the extra money it's bringing in with all the publicity we keep getting."

As we played the next hole, I could tell Bruce wanted to say something else about the case, but I kept steering the conversation elsewhere.

After we hit our tee shots on the ninth hole, Bruce laid it out. "Stephen Freeman called me late last night."

I didn't answer, keeping my eyes on the horizon, looking down the fairway.

When I didn't respond, Bruce continued. "He's furious about what Rhys did to Paul. Paul ended up in hospital, but his cheek isn't broken. A large bruise, and he'll have a black eye for a while, but no long-term damage."

"What charges is Rhys looking at?"

"None."

I turned and Bruce continued.

"Paul is refusing to speak to the police. He's found God, apparently, and is not saying a word." Bruce chuckled. "Paul told his father that it was God's plan for him to be punished by Rhys. That he deserved it, given his past mistakes."

"A member of the Freeman family is repenting for the family sins? That's going to be a lot of repenting. There are generations of corrupt Freemans."

"Stephen Freeman hates it. I could hear the anger in his voice as he spoke about Paul. Paul is going around and apologizing for all his past sins and putting Stephen in a precarious position. Stephen asked me to tell you that if a member of your family attacks his son again, he'll come after you personally." Bruce chewed the inside of his mouth for a long moment. "But it got me thinking about why Freeman seems so desperate. He can feel the walls closing in on him. And when a man like Freeman can feel things are about to go down, he starts swinging. He's going to explode, Dean, and he's going to go down fighting."

"I'm looking forward to the day."

"I'm serious, Dean. A man like Freeman won't go quietly. He'll use every play in the book to stay in power."

I shook my head. "Why are you even friends with Stephen Freeman?"

"I'm not, but this is how small towns work. Everyone is connected in some way, somehow. You need to shake hands with people you don't trust. It's not friendship. It's survival."

As I putted the final ball from fifteen feet, it dropped into the hole. Clean. Precise.

But I was sure nothing connected to Stephen Freeman was going to end that way.

CHAPTER 18

The morning sun drifted through the windows of our rented home in the Old Point historic district of Beaufort, creating a calm atmosphere, only disturbed by the sounds of Emma trying to vomit.

I was preparing a peppermint tea for her when she came into the kitchen looking queasy. She stood at the end of the bench, resting one hand lightly on her belly, and offered me a half-smile. Once the stovetop whistling kettle had boiled, I poured her a cup and let the tea steep for a few moments before passing it to her. I put one arm around her as she blew the steam off the top of the tea, and pulled her in close. I learned long ago that love was not all about the grand gestures, the roses, or the presents. It was about standing quietly, holding space, being supportive in times of need. It was about growing, building something, experiencing the ups and downs of life together.

Emma settled after a few minutes and walked out to the swing chair on our front porch. She took her book and curled up in the seat, letting it sway gently beneath her. I returned to the kitchen and checked the emails on my laptop and looked over the electronic files for Holt's case, reviewing line after line of information, before Emma came back inside for her phone. She took it outside and called her mother, talking for twenty-five minutes before returning to the kitchen.

"How is she?"

"She's . . ." Emma swallowed hard and looked away. I stood and drew her into a hug, and she held me tight for a moment. I held her for as long as she needed. When she was ready, she drew away and wiped her eyes with the back of her hand. "She's trying, but her body is struggling. They put her off in a special ward because her risk of infection is very high. The doctors aren't sure if her body will take the final round. There's almost nothing left of her. She's just skin and bone now."

"She's one of the toughest people I've ever met."

"I know, but this is pushing her past her limits."

"Did you tell her about the pregnancy?"

"I did. Her voice lit up. She's so happy for us."

"It's something to fight for."

Emma nodded. "I want to raise our child in Beaufort, Dean. I want them to grow up here in these streets and have the upbringing we had. I want them to know this part of the world, like we did."

I nodded. I wasn't convinced about it, but there was no way I was going to argue with a pregnant woman who was so often on the verge of throwing up.

Emma and I spent the rest of the morning together, tidying up the house and rearranging things. It seemed her nesting instincts were kicking in early. Under her instruction, I gave the house a deep clean. We laughed together as we moved things around, sharing the type of inside jokes that come with being married for over ten years. As I cleaned, Emma sat nearby, directing me and filling me in on everything in her world. She talked about her friends, about her cousins, and their kids. She told me about the latest social media trends, and I shook my head most of the time. She talked about the latest dance steps and performed a few moves for me. When I tried to join in, it was clear her dance skills were well above mine. She laughed at my attempts, and I smiled as I listened to the beautiful sound of her laughter. She talked about the right time to tell her friends about the pregnancy, about what star sign the child could be, and the early candidates for names. I cleaned, I listened, and I laughed with her. I told her some names had to be taken off the list, and she agreed with my veto calls. Emma helped clean when she was feeling better, before making lunch for both of us.

After a morning of dusting, mopping, and wiping, I was happy to sit down to a fresh, home-made Reuben sandwich, full of pastrami, sauerkraut, and Swiss cheese.

Once lunch was finished, Emma prepared a bath for herself and I wandered over to my grandparents' place, a short stroll away. Granddad Lincoln put me straight to work in the yard again, and I spent two hours weeding, pruning, and cutting branches off trees.

When I had finished, I packed the tools back into the shed, and I could sense Granddad Lincoln was itching to tell me something. He stood at the end of the garage, leaning against the wall, looking out to the yard.

"Dean," Granddad Lincoln said without a hint of emotion. "Paul Freeman came past here."

It took me a few moments to process that thought. "Paul Freeman came past here?"

Granddad Lincoln nodded but didn't look at me.

"What did he say?"

"Before or after I pushed him off the porch?"

"Did you?"

He nodded. "And I was about to punch the kid as well until your grandmother stopped me."

"What did he want?"

"He wanted to apologize."

My mouth hung open.

"Apparently, the kid has found religion," Granddad Lincoln continued. "He said he didn't want to say her name and disrespect her, but he talked about the accident and how sorry he felt for what he did. He's going around apologizing to all the people he hurt in the past."

"People he hurt . . ." I shook my head. "That's an understatement."

"I said to him, 'Don't tell me you've changed. Show me how you treat others, show me how you respect the community, show me how you live, and then I'll tell you if you've changed.'"

"You used to say that to me when I was young."

"It's still as true today as it was then." Granddad Lincoln sighed. "Paul said he was trying to live a good life. He was righting the wrongs of his past since getting sober."

"AA meetings?"

"Looks like that was the start of it for him. He said his AA sponsor had taken him to church and he found love and peace there, something he never had in his life. Given who his father is, I don't doubt that. He said his AA sponsor was Terry Wallace, an old school friend of yours."

"And now a Beaufort police investigator."

"That's the man," Granddad Lincoln said. "Your grandmother listened to Paul with an open heart and then invited him inside for a sweet tea, but I had to draw the line there. I wasn't ready for that. I wasn't ready to let him into my house. The kid killed my granddaughter, and I couldn't let him inside. I don't think I'll ever be at that point."

I didn't respond, looking out at the horizon for a long moment. Much like my grandfather, I didn't know if I could find forgiveness in my heart for what Paul did. I didn't know if I could let go of the anger. And I didn't even know if I wanted to.

CHAPTER 19

The Beaufort County Detention Center was better than Broad River Correctional, but not by much. The place was a temporary holding facility, where hope still lingered, where cases were pending and futures still undecided, but the anguish of incarceration was still present.

Bruce and I waited in the unsympathetic attorney-client meeting room for fifteen minutes before Holt was escorted in. He looked lighter. Freer. Almost happy. His shoulders were pulled back, his chin was held high, and he had a small bounce in his step.

"It's a different world back here," Holt stated as he sat down. "You don't have lifers in a detention center. They're the ones who've lost hope and accepted that prison is their whole world. There's a different weight to people. The system hasn't destroyed them yet. People have confidence, and that changes everything. Like me, I'm a different man since being back here. I've got hope about the case, and I've got hope that I'll see the outside again. I can't wait for this trial."

"You'll need to wait at least five weeks," I said. "In that time, there's going to be some media pressure. The first trial gathered a lot of attention, and the solicitor's office will feel that burden. They'll hear the public say it's a waste of public money to keep pushing this case. Everyone acknowledges Judge Newton did some terrible things, and everyone accepts your actions. Even during the first trial, there were calls for you to serve a light sentence and not spend life behind bars. The public will see you've already served three years, and given the circumstances, some people may accept that as enough."

"When I was first convicted, I received a lot of letters from fathers saying they would've done the same thing, and some people even sent me money to say thanks for protecting their daughters from a slimy predator like the judge. So many people have thanked me for preventing the judge doing it to another girl and getting away with it."

"That works in our favor," I said. "We can use that to pressure the prosecution into a better deal. Our best hope right now would be a lower charge to manslaughter and offer a deal for time served. Would you be interested in a deal?"

"One that gets me out of here? Absolutely. Tell me where to sign."

"Good," Bruce noted. "It's what we'll push for. In the meantime, we'll prepare for trial, but I need you to take me through what happened that night. Tell me, in your own words, what you remember about the night Judge Newton was shot."

"It's what I told the police. I tried to be honest with them, but they wouldn't listen," Holt said. "I went to his mansion on Spanish Point Drive to stop him from hurting another young woman. Someone called me and said the judge had another girl at his house and was going to assault her like he did my daughter. I called the police, but they told me there was nothing they could do. I stewed on it for a while, thinking about the poor girl, and I worked myself up into a frenzy. I grabbed my gun, and I went to his house to make sure he didn't do it again."

"You told the police you didn't grab your gun."

"Yeah, well." He shrugged. "I lied to them about the gun."

"Did you recognize the number that called you?"

"It was an anonymous call. It came up as a private number on my cell phone."

"We can still access the phone," I said. "Even if a number is private with no caller ID, the phone companies still keep a log of that information. We'll subpoena your phone company, and we'll retrieve the number and trace it."

"You can do that? Then why didn't Tomlinson do it? Ah, don't answer that. I know why—he was too busy drinking." He shook his head for a moment before he continued, "But why didn't the police do that?"

"They didn't see the need. In their eyes, they had their killer, and an unknown caller might've complicated things."

"The police had it in for me from day one. They never listened to my daughter, they didn't listen to me, and they didn't listen to the other women who made complaints against the judge. When I called the police the night of the murder, they laughed at me. They literally laughed at me and said it wasn't illegal for the judge to have an adult woman in his home. The judge hadn't been convicted of any offences, so they said there was no solid ground to even question him."

"What did you do after you left your home?"

"I drove to the judge's house to ensure real justice was going to be delivered to that predator." Holt's tone firmed. "I parked down the street and walked the block toward his house. As I approached, right outside his property, I heard the gunshots. Five of them. They were so clear. I wasn't certain they came from the judge's house, but it was close by. I was rattled as soon as I heard those shots."

"And what did you do next?" Bruce asked.

"I went into shock. I turned around and walked back down the street, and when two cars passed me, I knew I'd be identified. So, I panicked and ran close to the river, and threw my gun away.

I thought if I was caught with a gun nearby, the cops would pin it on me. After doing that I ran back to my car and drove away."

"You didn't call the police?"

"No way. I knew they'd try to pin it on me the second I heard those shots. My first thought was the girl had done it in self-defense. I thought she'd snapped and shot the judge before he assaulted her."

"The evidence they have against you is that you were seen walking away from his house after the gunshots, and you were also seen throwing a weapon into the river. You made threats against the judge earlier that week, which established motive. Although the gun they recovered was damaged by heat and humidity, they were able to match the bullets and shell casings to a Glock, although they weren't able to say if it was a Glock 17 or 19. It was too damaged to match the gun to the bullets and casings." I paused and sighed. "Despite all that, our main problem is your discussion with the police the next day."

Holt groaned and threw his head back. "I know, I know. I should never have talked to them without a lawyer."

"You told the police you went there to stop the judge from assaulting another girl, but you heard gunshots. You then told them you walked away. The next day, when the police questioned you, you told them you didn't own a gun any more. However, the gun that was recovered from the river was registered to you."

"I thought if I was honest with them about going to his house, they'd believe me."

"But we do have some good news. The dashcam video footage from one of the cars that passed you on the street is likely to be thrown out in pretrial hearings, and I've spoken to Jackie Florence. She's unlikely to testify this time."

"She was always lying." Holt exhaled hard. "So, we have a chance?"

"It's a small one," I agreed. "But we have a chance."

CHAPTER 20

I met Julie Steinberg in the parking lot of the Solicitor's Office Headquarters in the community of Okatie, twenty-five minutes outside of Beaufort. She pulled up in a beaten-up F-250, complete with rusted rear bumper and scratched paintwork. When she stepped out of the truck, she had a concerned look on her face.

"Julie, thanks for coming," I greeted her. "What's wrong?"

"Dean, I'm stressed." She shook my hand and leaned against my SUV. "I have an old friend at the Department of Revenue, and he called me and said my license has been flagged. Because of my prior conviction, there's a chance I'll lose my license for the bar, even if I accept a deal for a lower charge." Her voice trembled. "I can't afford another conviction. There has to be another way out of this."

"Do you think Remington had a hand in flagging it?"

"Without a doubt."

She didn't need to say anything else. I believed her—every word of it.

I led her inside, nodded to the receptionist, and gave our names. She pointed us toward a meeting room near the entrance and told us Angus Blessington would be with us shortly. Julie and I stepped in and took a seat. The room was beige and lifeless. No art, no plants, no signs of warmth or personality. The whiteboard looked untouched, possibly for years. The table was generic—clean, dull, and forgettable. The smell of bleach and disinfectant hung in the air, sharp and sterile. It was the kind of room where conversations were meant to be short, and nobody stayed longer than they had to.

Five minutes later, Assistant Solicitor Angus Blessington entered.

"Mr. Lincoln, it's good to see you again." We shook hands. His handshake was weak and limp. I hated that. "And you must be Ms. Julie Steinberg."

Julie shook his hand, and her hand engulfed Blessington's.

Blessington had an unnerving presence. Pale, pudgy, and unappealing, he presented himself with a false confidence, trying hard to be the leader in the room, trying to assert himself, but there was no weight behind his bravado, no feeling of strength, and no sense of conviction. His skin was soft. His smile was unsettling. His breath stank like he hadn't brushed his teeth in a week.

Bureaucrats like Blessington weren't born cruel. They began life as normal children, searching for their place in the world, searching for the best job they could get, but somewhere along the way, they found themselves knee-deep in a world of rules and guidelines and decrees. Not all bureaucrats were horrible, not all bureaucrats were soulless robots who only did what they were told, but there were many heartless ones in offices around the country. Those were the workers who had forgotten that people existed, that there were faces to the names, that every signature had a story. Those were the workers who were trained to believe the system triumphs over common sense, that the rules could not be broken, that the process must come before the people. They didn't see the damage they caused because they were trained not to see it. They didn't see the pain their rules imposed because they didn't look for it. In their world, a world of spreadsheets and documents and meetings, empathy was nothing more than an inconvenience.

The real tragedy, of course, was that these people believed they were doing the greater good for the community, forgetting that communities were made of people, not rules. They had forgotten, or perhaps never learned, that mercy was required in all systems, and that compassion was required in all structures. And worst of all, they forgot that they, themselves, still had souls.

"Thank you for coming into the office today. I understand your eagerness to get this issue resolved, Ms. Steinberg. So, let's not beat around the bush and get straight to the point. Considering the impact of the assault, and this is deemed assault in the second degree, we're willing to negotiate. If you agree to an early guilty plea to second-degree assault, we're recommending five months in the county jail."

"No chance," Julie snapped. "The Remington kid had it coming."

"You can't assault people because of their thoughts, and nobody else heard what was said. To be justified in your actions, you would need sufficient provocation, and you don't have it." Blessington turned to me. "There's a video of them talking calmly before Julie slapped him."

I held my hand out for Julie to settle her anger. "The video was taken by someone with connections to Remington. We know this is a set-up."

"There was no set-up, and this is not some great big conspiracy theory."

"You're right—there's no conspiracy here. John Remington makes no secret that he wants Julie's land."

"But the land has nothing to do with this case. This is a case of a grown woman slapping a young man."

"He said he was going to take pictures up the skirts of schoolgirls, and that he'd love to take a photo up my skirt." Julie pressed her hand into the desk. "That's provocation."

"You can't prove he said those words." Blessington smirked a little and looked at me. "And the only way that information will be presented in court is if Ms. Steinberg testifies, which we would welcome."

"You want me to testify?!" Julie gritted her teeth and pointed at Blessington. "I'll testify and I'll tell the court that you're a conniving little prick."

"Julie." I held my hand out again to calm her down. "Angus, if you want to take this to trial, then we'll be forced to subpoena Remington's phone records, his phone data, and all the pictures he took."

"The problem there is that the phone has been lost."

"What a surprise," I scoffed. "Of course, without a phone to confirm his actions, we'll need to subpoena for his computer, and any associated cloud storage to verify his actions. And then, because we couldn't be sure which computer he uploaded the photos to, we'll need to subpoena all the computers in his house." I watched Blessington sit up a little straighter. "And considering he lives at home, I'm not sure you want that subpoena to be granted."

"No judge would approve the scope of that subpoena." Blessington was trying to sound strong, but it wasn't working. "Perhaps you'll get one for his personal computer, but it'll never be granted for his entire residence. There would be too many privacy concerns."

"Are you scared of his father?"

"This has nothing to do with who Casper Remington's father is."

"You've got a woman who slapped the son of a powerful real-estate developer, and you want to charge that woman with assault," I stated. "This is all about who his father is."

"Are you suggesting this office is influenced by family names?"

"Yes."

Blessington sat back, stunned that I would be so direct. "We're not used to that type of language in the South. Perhaps you've forgotten where you are. This isn't Chicago."

"You've forgotten where you are. You represent justice, not family names."

"None of that matters." He waved me away. "This is assault. The victim had a ringing in his ears for weeks."

"No jury will see it that way."

"I think they will." Blessington closed the folder. "The offer will be on the table for another two weeks. Think it over."

"No chance, you smug little prick." Julie's anger rose. "I should slap you as well."

"Julie." I shot her a hard look. Assaulting the prosecutor wouldn't help the case. Once she'd calmed down, I turned my focus back to Blessington. "The reputation of the people involved will take a hit if this case goes public."

"Ha," Blessington chuckled to himself. "This case is about the slapping of a young man. The only way you can present evidence of what Julie thinks was said is if she testifies." Blessington looked at me. "And you and I both know that if she takes the stand, she'll be fair game. We might even ask her about what else happens in her bar that doesn't require a slap. Say drug deals by the Rebel Sons, a one-percenter motorcycle gang, or whether she's aware of the underage drinking that occurs on her premises. If we can do that, it'll be goodbye to your liquor license, and goodbye to the bar."

Julie's mouth hung open for a long moment. She was between a rock and a hard place. Either way, she was going to lose her liquor license.

"That's what I thought." Blessington couldn't contain his smile. "Early plea for five months, some of which would be a suspended sentence. That's the best we've got."

Blessington left with a pep in his step, a smile on his face, and an arrogance that seemed to linger in the room. Julie was in shock, trying to process what she had just been told. She didn't say another word until we were back in the parking lot.

"The Remington family thinks they can get away with anything." Julie gripped the door of her car. "And I bet this isn't the first time he's done something like this. There'll be a long line of people who've been done wrong by him and his family. Who's going to stop them?"

"We are."

She squinted at me. "And how are we going to do that?"

"We need to influence their negotiation," I stated. "Right now, they won't negotiate with us because we have no leverage. We need to change that."

"Any ideas how?"

"We need to start by getting as many powerful people linked to this case as possible."

"Why?"

"Because Blessington won't take a weak case to trial if influential people are tied up in it," I said. "I'll look for links between Casper and anyone powerful that we can use, and I need you to gather a list of names of anyone similar who would've frequented your bar over the last year."

"Then what?"

"Then, just before we go into pretrial hearings, we send a questionnaire to all the potential witnesses and threaten to send out a media release with all their names linked to the case of a young man taking pictures of schoolgirls. Blessington will panic and may withdraw the case. It's a risk, and we're bluffing, but it's a risk we should take."

"They think they're untouchable." Julie stared at me. "Let's prove them wrong."

CHAPTER 21

Prosecutor Andrew Harley called and asked for a meeting for Holt's case.

He stated he had received a call from Nigel Impala about the video dashcam footage and had also talked to Jackie Florence. Like we expected, a new deal was coming. They would start with ten years, maybe five years, but Bruce was sure we could get them down to time served for voluntary manslaughter. Together, Bruce and I walked into the Beaufort County Government Center building off Ribaut Road, next to the courthouse, passing the title of the Fourteenth Circuit Solicitor, which was displayed proudly on the wall beneath the Seal of South Carolina.

Assistant Solicitor Andrew Harley was waiting near the reception area, talking on his phone. When he saw us, he ended the call and welcomed us with handshakes and a smile. Something didn't feel right. Harley was too happy, too jovial, for someone who looked like he was about to offer a low deal. As he led us to the meeting room, he made a few comments about the weather, the heat, and the value of a good air conditioner.

Harley was a plump man who carried his weight like someone who hadn't broken a sweat in years. His pale skin had the type of softness that came from a life lived in climate control and good insulation. What passed for a chin faded right into his neck, and his light brown hair was stuck in place with enough gel to make it shiny.

I was guarded as we entered the meeting room. A long wooden conference table took up much of the space, with a pitcher of water and several glasses placed in the middle. There was a potted plant in the far corner, and a picture of the Beaufort River hanging on the wall. The whirl of the air conditioner in the ceiling was loud, bringing with it a smell of plastic and stale air.

Harley was comfortable, lounging back in his chair, and chatting about the weekend, his new car, and the latest sports results. He talked about his investments, about his rental properties, and about the new developments on Hilton Head. He mentioned a large storm was due to hit Beaufort that afternoon, with drenching rains and flooding predicted. Bruce entertained all the information with a smile and joke. He was better than me at that.

"What's the new deal?" I asked when the conversation between them started to wane.

"Straight to it then," Harley quipped, and leaned forward. He flicked open the file on the table. "Fifteen years for an early guilty plea for manslaughter, including time already served. He'll be out in twelve years, perhaps earlier for good behavior."

"You've got to be kidding," I scoffed. "We know about the video footage, some of your key witnesses won't testify again, and you won't be able to ask half the questions you asked last time. The only weight this case has is his discussion with the police the day after the murder."

"You mean his confession."

"There's no confession and any suggestion that his discussion with the police is a confession will result in a mistrial."

"I can see you're a lot more capable than Tomlinson." Harley smiled. "And I'll admit Jackie Florence's refusal to testify does weaken our case. As for the video footage, we'll fight to have it still included." Harley was smirking as he took a sheet of paper from the file. "But we do have this."

He placed the paper in front of Bruce. We leaned close and looked over it.

"What is this?"

"It's a witness statement from James Dalwick, who was one of Malcolm Holt's cell mates from the Broad River Correctional Institution. They shared a cell, and discussed what they were in for. That's when Holt confessed to Mr. Dalwick that he killed Judge Newton. Mr. Dalwick has provided a lengthy statement about what was said."

"A jailhouse snitch." I laughed at the absurdity of it. "That's what you're building your case around? You can't be serious."

"On top of his 'discussion' with the police, we now have a rock-solid confession where Holt told the cell mate about things that were never released to the public. It's a very detailed, and very accurate, confession from a murderer. The only way this person could've known these details is if Holt told him."

"Come on." I leaned back in the chair and threw my hands up in the air. "That's ridiculous and you know it. This is laughable."

"This is the murder of a sitting judge who had served this court for decades. There's nothing laughable about it. The best deal is fifteen years for manslaughter, including time already served, and we're not budging on it. The court needs to be strong and protect the people that serve it. We'll take this back to trial because we know we'll win. We'll protect our people, and we'll ensure justice is done."

"Justice? Where was the justice for Judge Newton's victims?"

"That's a different issue." Harley brushed my question aside. "Holt made death threats to the judge in the days before the murder. He admitted he was there on the night of the murder. His gun was found in the river nearby. This isn't some great big conspiracy. This isn't some great big cover-up. This is murder. Plain and simple." Harley adjusted himself. "The public will praise us for being strong and sending a message that vigilantes aren't what this county needs. We don't need people taking the law into their own hands."

I shook my head. "You won't win this in court."

"What other play do you have? That someone else was coincidentally there, at the same time, on the same night, to kill the judge?" Harley stood and shook hands with Bruce first, and then me. "I implore you to encourage your client to take the deal. Don't take this to court. Because if you do, then there are interested parties that might become very dangerous."

CHAPTER 22

"A jailhouse snitch?!" I slammed my fist on the table of the boardroom in our office. "This isn't the 1970s."

"I've seen cases built on less, and I've seen people convicted on nothing more than a snitch's confession. They don't need him to be credible, they just need him to sound convincing," Bruce stated as he leaned back in the chair. The chair struggled under his weight. "Prosecutors love them, juries believe them, and judges usually let it slide."

"If the court wanted the truth, they wouldn't rely on guys negotiating for a lighter sentence. This isn't right."

"They do it because it works, Dean. And you're not going to win that fight. No judge is going to stop the snitch from testifying."

I groaned and sat down. "What do we know about our snitch, Mr. James Dalwick?"

"In and out of prison most of his life," Kayla read off the laptop in front of her. "Currently in prison on a fifteen-year sentence for the brutal assault of a gas station attendant he was trying to rob. Previously served a five-year sentence for the very public assault of his girlfriend. She ended up with five stitches in her nose after he smashed a plate over her face in a diner. And this was the fifth time he'd been arrested for assault, including three ex-girlfriends."

"Terrible," I said. "And no doubt his current fifteen-year sentence will be reduced for this 'honest' testimony."

"No doubt," Bruce added. "What does Mr. Dalwick say happened?"

"He says he shared a cell with Holt last month—"

"After Holt's appeal was lodged?"

Kayla paused and nodded. She knew what it implied. Dalwick was planted. "Dalwick shared a cell with Malcolm last month and that's when Malcolm admitted he killed the judge. The statement from Dalwick is quite detailed, going into how Malcolm described walking into the judge's house via the side door, how he found the judge in his armchair, and how he shot him five times in the chest. He goes on to add that Malcolm said the lights were out in the house, with a candle burning in the sitting room where the judge was found. He also says Malcolm told him where the judge was sitting and what he was wearing. And Malcom admitted he picked up three of the bullet shells, but two rolled away and he couldn't spend any more time looking for them."

"That's ridiculous. No prisoner would say that." I clenched my fist and pressed it against the table. "It's too detailed."

"Mr. Dalwick goes on to say that Malcolm was proud of having shot the judge and proud he was protecting other young women from the judge's predatory behavior."

I thumped my fist on the boardroom table again, stood, and moved to the window, looking out as the drenching rains arrived.

The Spanish moss outside whipped around in the wind, the hefty rumble of thunder rolled over the city, and the rain pelted down with aggression. A bolt of lightning cracked, startling Bruce. The lights flickered in our office. The sound of rain echoing in the room became louder. It was coming down in sheets, blowing hard against the window, testing the strength of the glass.

"Was this predicted?" Bruce asked.

Kayla checked her phone. The internet connection was slow. She nodded, and then checked the weather radar app on her laptop. "It should blow over in fifteen minutes," she said. "There's nothing behind this front of clouds."

Bruce stood and came to the window, checking his car in the gravel parking lot next to the building. "And I just washed my car. I should've known it was going to storm today." He went back to the table and sat down. "What do you need, Dean? How can we deal with the snitch?"

"I need every police file that was written by the investigators," I stated, bringing the focus back to work. "I need access to every note they've ever written."

"What are you looking for?"

"The information they've fed to the snitch. I need to know when it was put together."

CHAPTER 23

The Beaufort County Courthouse was deserted first thing in the morning. When it was empty, it almost felt friendly and welcoming, a well-designed building to be admired, but it stood in stark contrast to what was delivered inside.

I stopped outside the front steps and let the early sunlight hit my face. It had been over a decade since I first walked into a courtroom as lead counsel. Back then, I was a fresh-faced kid in Chicago, still clinging to the belief that the justice system worked the same for everyone. Ten years in the Cook County justice system had broken that idea for me. I learned how the machine worked. How it ground people down, case by case, crime by crime, quietly and efficiently sucking the hope from its targets. I became a part of the machine, and the machine became part of me.

I had never planned on coming back to a small-town system, I had never planned on leaving the intensity of Chicago, but here I was in a courthouse where gossip echoed louder than justice. I took a deep breath of humid Lowcountry air and stepped inside. The guard gave me a nod, and I returned it. He didn't say much as he scanned my briefcase. Moments later, my footsteps were echoing down the corridor as I made my way into the courtroom.

At the defense table, I unpacked my laptop, a few files, my legal pad, and a pair of pens. I sat, took one more breath, and nodded to myself. I was ready. Five minutes later, the court doors swung open. Andrew Harley entered with his usual confidence, dressed in a tailored gray suit and a crisp red tie that somehow made him look even more soft. His assistant followed a few steps behind, wearing a complementary shade.

There was a shift in the room as the doors opened again. Tension rose. I turned and saw Stephen Freeman walking in. He eyed me and sat in the first row behind the prosecutor's table.

The bailiff called the court to order, and Judge Jessica LeBlanc entered. From the fifth judicial circuit, she was the closest judge available without a personal or professional connection to Judge Stanley Newton.

Judge LeBlanc was a stern woman in her sixties. Her brown hair was tied back, her make-up was minimal, and her glasses looked like they hadn't been updated in the last twenty years. Despite her words and appearance, there was an understanding to her tone, and a sense of care and compassion to her voice. "We have several motions to work through today, so let's not waste anyone's time and get straight to the point. I don't want any grandstanding, and no preaching to the choir. I need both of you to be upfront, direct, and blunt. Is that understood?"

"Yes, Your Honor," Harley and I said in unison.

"Mr. Harley, we'll begin with the State's pretrial motions." Judge LeBlanc moved a file in front of her. "You've submitted a motion to add twenty-five names to the witness list. Please explain."

"Thank you, Your Honor. We understand this is a late change; however, there are no surprises in this updated list. Among others, we've added ballistics experts, specialists in forensic science, and another two law enforcement officers who were involved in the search for the murder weapon."

"Any objections, Mr. Lincoln?" Judge LeBlanc stared at the file in front of her and didn't look in my direction.

"We have no objections to the expanded witness list, Your Honor."

"Then we'll move on." Judge LeBlanc turned another file over in front of her and looked over her notes. "And now the defense motions," she said, lifting her glasses as she glanced down at the stack in front of her. "Mr. Lincoln, care to begin with the request for a change of venue?"

I stood. "We believe the jury pool in this county is tainted, Your Honor. The media saturation has created an environment where a fair trial is nearly impossible. Public opinion has already been shaped."

Harley leaned forward without missing a beat. "That's exactly why we have *voir dire*, Your Honor. To identify and eliminate bias during jury selection."

Judge LeBlanc didn't flinch. "Motion for change of venue is denied. This court has every confidence in the *voir dire* process to ensure impartiality."

I tried again. "Then we request the jury pool be selected from an adjacent county. Somewhere less exposed to the coverage."

"You're still making the same argument, Mr. Lincoln," she replied flatly. "And I'll give you the same answer—that's why we have *voir dire*. The motion is denied."

She flipped to the next page. "Motion to exclude evidence. You're referring to the interview footage, correct?"

"Yes, Your Honor," I said. "The footage must be excluded. The defendant believed he was under arrest. There was no Miranda warning. He was misled about his rights."

"He was informed multiple times that he was free to leave," Harley interjected, his voice rising slightly. "The transcript reflects that clearly. There was no custodial interrogation."

"He wasn't formally in custody, but the pressure applied by the officers created a coercive atmosphere," I pushed. "Perception matters, and the defendant's understanding of the situation is key."

Judge LeBlanc gave a slight shake of her head. "The law deals in facts, Mr. Lincoln. Not feelings. The transcript is clear, and there's no evidence of coercion. Motion denied." She moved on without pause. "Next, we have a motion to compel discovery."

I stepped forward. "We never received the original police file, Your Honor. What we have is labeled 'version five.' We're concerned the first files contained material that may have been altered or omitted."

Judge LeBlanc looked over the rim of her glasses. "And do you have any proof that version one and version five are different?"

"No, Your Honor," I admitted. "And that's exactly the problem. Without version one, we have no way of knowing what's missing."

She turned to Harley. "Are the original files present?"

Harley nodded and tapped the folder beside him. "They are, Your Honor. We provided the files to the previous lawyer; however, it appears his record-keeping was not up to scratch. We're prepared to hand over the files to the defense now."

"Good. Then hand them over. No more delays. Motion is moot." She sighed, flipping another page. "Anything else, Mr. Lincoln, or are we finally ready to proceed with the trial?"

"Yes, Your Honor," I said, rising slowly. "The defense has filed a motion *in limine* regarding the proposed testimony of Mr. James Dalwick."

Judge LeBlanc gave a subtle nod. "Proceed."

"We believe Mr. Dalwick is clearly fabricating elements of his statement," I said, pacing a step toward the bench. "There are inconsistencies in what he claims he was told, and more importantly, the risk of prejudice to the defendant is undeniable."

The judge leaned slightly forward. "Go on."

"If the prosecution calls a jailhouse informant—especially one currently incarcerated—then the jury will inevitably speculate as to why Mr. Holt was also in custody. Mr. Holt has not been convicted of any crime. Introducing testimony obtained while he was behind bars plants the dangerous assumption of guilt." I let that settle for a second before adding, "The prejudice is inherent. The setting alone creates bias, regardless of any instructions given to the jury."

Harley stood, hands clasped behind him. "With all due respect, Your Honor, this can be addressed with a limiting instruction. The jury can be directed not to infer anything about the circumstances of Mr. Holt's incarceration. We've seen it work before."

Judge LeBlanc considered both sides in silence. Then she spoke with calm authority. "Mr. Harley is correct. The risk of prejudice is real—but so is the responsibility of the court to provide clarity. A limiting instruction will be issued to the jury, making it explicitly clear they are not to speculate on why the defendant was in custody." She glanced down at the motion in front of her, then back at me. "Motion to exclude the witness is denied." Judge LeBlanc turned to the next file. "Mr. Lincoln, I see you've also lodged another motion to suppress. Can you please explain this?"

"Yes, Your Honor." I cleared my throat. "The State has made it clear they intend to present evidence that's incomplete, inaccurate, and altered from its original state. We've lodged a motion to suppress the submitted video footage evidence, supported by an affidavit, under Rule 901(a) of the South Carolina Rules of Evidence. This evidence has been altered, and in its altered state, the evidence is prejudicial against the defendant. The prosecution has admitted the watermark date has been removed from the original video. The removal of the time and date from the footage eliminates a key identifier that helps verify when this alleged incident occurred. This new evidence is inadequate and deceiving."

"And the State objects to this motion?" Judge LeBlanc looked at Harley.

"We do, Your Honor. The date was removed for clarification."

"Clarification?"

"That's correct, Your Honor," Harley said. "When the owner of the footage set it up, he entered the wrong date. He thought it was best to remove the date so there was no confusion. The evidence in question is dashcam footage which clearly shows the defendant near the scene of the crime at the time of the murder. It was footage taken from a passing motorist named Nigel Impala."

"Thank you for the context," Judge LeBlanc stated. "And on what grounds are you objecting to this evidence, Mr. Lincoln?"

"Your Honor, the video footage has been tampered with. The date has been removed. We cannot possibly verify when the footage was taken."

"Understood, Mr. Lincoln." Judge LeBlanc adjusted her glasses as she looked over the affidavit before glancing back at Harley. "Can you please explain why the footage was altered?"

"Yes, Your Honor." Harley nodded over his shoulder to the person seated behind him. "The State would like to call the owner of the dashcam footage, Mr. Nigel Impala."

Impala wore jeans and a suit jacket that was a size too big in the shoulders. He took long strides as he approached the witness stand, keeping his eyes forward and avoiding eye contact with me.

"Mr. Impala," Harley began as he moved in his seat. "Can you please explain your footage?"

"I can." Impala's voice was deep and raspy. "It was taken the night of the murder. I set the date incorrectly, and the footage was not otherwise altered."

"Were there any changes to it?"

"Yes, but I programmed the incorrect date. The version you have has had the date removed. I removed it before I gave it to the police to save any confusion."

"Thank you, Mr. Impala," Harley said. "No further questions."

"Defense?" Judge asked.

I stood. "Did the first version you provided to the police have the date attached?"

"Yes."

"And then you changed it?"

"I thought it was best to not have the date on the footage to save any confusion, so I downloaded another version without the date watermarked on the bottom. Nobody asked me to do that. I did that myself to save confusion."

"Mr. Impala, how can we be certain of the date of the footage if the footage says it occurred on the previous date?"

"How can you be certain of anything?"

"That's not an answer, Mr. Impala."

"It's true, because it happened. It's a watermark. It doesn't change anything. The footage is real. I entered the wrong date when I set up the dashcam. That's all. It's all fixed now."

I glanced at Judge LeBlanc and raised my eyebrows. She nodded her understanding in return. I turned to Harley, but he avoided eye contact.

"I put it to you that the date is incorrect."

"It's not."

"How can we be certain?"

"You have my word."

"Your word that you altered the footage?"

"Ah, no. That the footage is real."

I looked at the judge and stated, "No further questions."

"Redirect?" Judge LeBlanc asked Harley, who shook his head. "Then you may step down, Mr. Impala." Judge LeBlanc looked back at the lawyers. "Are there any other witnesses?"

"No, Your Honor."

"And any final arguments before I make a decision?"

"Yes, Your Honor." Harley stood again. "While we acknowledge a minor element of the footage had been altered before it was received by the Circuit Solicitor's Office, the footage is conclusive in what it presents. The change in the watermark date is nothing more than an innocuous misstep."

"This is not a misstep, Your Honor." I also stood. "This is a blatant and deliberate attempt from the prosecution to mislead the court. If this evidence is admitted, then it's a clear reversible error. The video owner has admitted he deliberately altered the footage. We cannot be sure what else has been altered in this footage."

"Your Honor, Mr. Lincoln is using every trick in the book to save his weak case," Harley said, raising his voice. "This is nothing more than a pitiful attempt to discredit clear evidence of the defendant's behavior."

"Mr. Harley, I'm here to make a judgment on the law, not to make a judgment on Mr. Lincoln's behavior," Judge LeBlanc stated. She glared at Harley for a long moment before he nodded his understanding. "Mr. Lincoln, do you have anything to add?"

"No, Your Honor."

"Then it's clear to me the original footage had been altered before it was received by law enforcement, and considering there is no way to confirm what the original footage contained, I find it biased and deceptive to present this to the court." Judge LeBlanc paused before she continued. "However, it's clear that Mr. Impala witnessed the person walking past, so I will allow him to testify about what he saw that night. Do we have any objections to my decision?"

"No, Your Honor," I responded.

"Nothing from the State, Your Honor." Harley shook his head.

"Good," Judge LeBlanc said.

When she confirmed there were no further pretrial motions, she tapped her gavel and rose from the bench. She strode out of the room without another word. No fuss. No drama. Direct and to the point.

The case was on.

CHAPTER 24

After leaving the courthouse, I drove aimlessly for a while, my mind racing.

I passed Judge Newton's Spanish Point Drive residence, a multi-million-dollar home steeped in prestige. The stately, colonial-style home had no fence, a wide porch, and a dignified feel. Backing on to the river, the mansion was shaded by moss-draped live oaks and oozed Southern charm. It was five minutes' drive from downtown Beaufort, and an equal amount of time to the courthouse. Despite the location, it felt tucked away from the city in its own quiet enclave for people who appreciated tradition, status, and power.

Three years after the murder, the house had been sold for much less than it was worth—a public murder tends to drop the house price—and a new family had moved in. Life has a way of moving on. There were new cars in the driveway, new trees planted, and a swing set visible in the rear yard.

I kept driving, not wishing to disturb the family living there, and stopped at the nearby Cypress Wetlands in Port Royal. The Wetlands were a hidden pocket of wilderness tucked away from the houses nearby. It felt wild, natural, and untouched. Bald cypress trees rose from the still waters, and the place was alive with the sounds of herons, egrets, and red-winged blackbirds. A wooden boardwalk cut its way through the marsh, allowing people to catch glimpses of turtles or alligators. Stepping out of my car, I was met with thick humidity, the type you could taste. The earthy smell of the marsh was strong.

I walked to the start of the boardwalk and stopped at a bench beneath one of the larger oaks, its branches sprawling like arms, offering shade from the unforgiving sun. I sat down, tilted my head back, and stared up at the endless blue sky, my eyes unfocused, lost in thought about the case.

I sighed, loosened my tie, and undid the first few buttons of my shirt. Rolling up my sleeves, I watched the river pass by, shimmering in the sunshine. I sat there and looked at nothing for a while. Under the spell of the South, the anger, pain and stress began to melt away. Just a moment in the beauty of the Lowcountry, watching the moss wave in the gentle breeze. The birds chirped, the bugs hummed, and the Lowcountry rolled on like it had for centuries. It was a reminder that, no matter how stressed I was, no matter how many worries I had, the world continued to keep moving.

After fifteen minutes in solitude, feeling the anger subside, I stood and accepted that I needed to return to work. I drove, blasting the air conditioning in the car, and was soon back inside the office.

"Good afternoon," Kayla said as she sipped her coffee. "You look calm?"

"It's the Lowcountry. It takes the edge off."

"Well, it's not all positive." Kayla placed her mug down and sat behind her desk. "As the saying goes—the Lowcountry will soothe your soul and ruin your hair all in the same day."

"My hair will be fine." I smiled as I sat down in front of her. "How are we going with the expert witnesses for the Holt case?"

"Most of them have responded with their availability. The ones who have responded have confirmed they'll be available for the potential trial dates."

"That sounds promising."

"How did it go in court this morning?"

"Good."

Kayla tilted her head slightly. "What's wrong?"

"Who said anything was wrong?"

"Bless your heart. You might be stoic, but your feelings are written all over your face." Kayla smiled. "I can see when you're hiding something. What is it?"

I smiled back. I could see why Bruce said he couldn't work without her. "I received the original versions of the police files on the murder case. There are some different things in there, some leads that were changed and some notes that were added or taken away, but there's one piece of evidence that stands out." I opened my briefcase and took out the file and showed it to her. "Have you seen this name before?"

"Sam Keenan." Kayla read the name. "I know of the Keenan family, but I don't know Sam. Who is he?"

"The police matched the information from the cell phone provider that Holt used. It has the cell phone number listed for the person who called Holt that night. It also has the name of the person who purchased the cell phone number the week before—Sam Keenan."

"Are we talking a Brady violation?"

"Not likely. The cell phone number was available to Tomlinson and he had a record of receiving the file; but we know how inept he was. They did, however, try to bury it from us."

"Did it match the information you sent to the cell phone provider?"

"They haven't got back to me yet. I expect a response next week."

"How did the police match the record? If it's a burner phone, then he wouldn't have registered it."

"According to the police report, they requested the information from the provider about where the phone was bought, and found it was purchased at the 7-11 near the Walmart off the Robert Smalls Parkway. It was the only pre-paid cell phone purchased on that day, and the police matched it to a credit transaction from Sam Keenan."

"That's good police work," Kayla quipped.

"According to the police file, the call that night was the only one ever recorded from that cell phone number."

"Did the police talk to Sam Keenan?"

"According to the first file, yes. He told them he lost the phone the day he bought it, and someone else must've used it."

"What about Tomlinson? Surely he investigated it?"

"Not once, which is another massive failure on his part. Sam Kennan could've testified about when he lost the phone, and where." I tapped my hand on the file. "We need to find out everything that Tomlinson didn't."

Within the hour, Kayla had compiled a fact file on Sam Keenan—thirty-five years old, had some misdemeanor arrests for drug use, but was now working for a construction company. Had a wife, a young child, and looked to have rebuilt his life after some earlier indiscretions. Going by his social media profile, he used to spend his weekends partying big, having been tagged in posts at nightclubs from Savannah to Charleston, from Atlanta to Miami, but he was now settling into family life, with many photos of his wife and new baby tagged online.

"What are you going to do?" Kayla asked.

"I need to find out what happened to the cell phone," I said. "And I need to go straight to the source."

CHAPTER 25

I drove out to Sam Keenan's home in the neighborhood of Battery Shores.

Tucked away from the main part of Beaufort, Battery Shores was full of suburban charm. Near the Broad River, the streets were wide, the oaks were mature, and most houses didn't have fences. I passed middle-aged men washing their trucks, kids rolling along the road on their bikes, and neighbors chatting in their front yards. Life looked good here. Simple. The type of place where contentment would feel normal.

I parked in the driveway at the address we had for Keenan. It took me a moment to recognize him in the yard. In the older photos we had found online, Keenan appeared skinny and weathered by life, likely the result of heavy drug use, but here, leading a calm, family life, he had put on a healthy amount of weight. His skin looked softer, his clothes cleaner, and his hair, once wild and untamed, was now neat and trimmed. He was tending an abundant vegetable patch at the side of the house. Tomato vines twisted around stained wire, weighty with fruit. Okra pushed tall and thin in the far garden bed. The collard greens looked thick and healthy.

"Sam Keenan," I called out as I crossed the yard.

Keenan eyed me with suspicion. "Who are you?"

"Dean Lincoln. I'm a defense attorney."

"What do you want?"

"To talk about a cell phone you purchased three years ago."

He stood up straighter. He knew what it was about. His wife stepped out of the front door of the clapboard house, nursing a young baby. Keenan told her everything was fine and that I was there about the sedan he was trying to sell. He nodded to me, and I nodded back. When his wife went back inside, Keenan pointed to the rear of the house. I followed him and we stood on the far side of an older red sedan parked in front of a shed.

"Thanks," he said, looking over his shoulder. "My life is good now. Those things I did in the past weren't me. They were the acts of someone in the grip of drugs and trying to do anything to get enough money to buy another hit. I've been sober for two years now, and I couldn't be happier."

"Congratulations," I commended him. "That's a great achievement."

"What I'm saying is that I've left that life behind. I want nothing to do with it now. Whatever you want, I'm not talking."

"We can talk about it here, or we can talk about it in a deposition. But if I need to do it through a deposition, then I'll be digging up lots of information about you, including information about your past life."

"No." He shook his head. "I got clean. Life is good now. I have a wife and young daughter, and they were never a part of that life. I'm working too. A lot. It's a full-time job, and I'm doing lots of overtime. I'm doing everything I can to provide for my family. You can't pull me back to that life."

"And your brother?"

"Leave my brother out of this."

"Just got released, didn't he?"

"He should never have been locked up."

"Drug use. I'd hate for that to be on the public record so his new employer would find out about it. A job that you got him?"

He glared at me. "What do you want?"

"Are you telling the truth about the phone you lost three years ago?"

He put his hands in his pockets. "I'm not testifying about anything."

"You're going to need to, because I'm going to trace that phone you bought. I'll know every cell tower it's been pinged at for every moment it was turned on. And if that doesn't align with what you told the police, then you'll be charged with perjury."

He placed his hand on the sedan and popped the hood. He leaned in and pretended to point at something before he looked to the house and then back at me. "Someone paid me to buy the phone."

"Who?"

He looked around again. "Look, I was down on my luck, and some guy offered me a clean two hundred and fifty bucks to buy the phone and pre-paid SIM card and give it to him. Of course I did it. He said if anyone asked to say I lost it."

"Who was it?"

He didn't answer.

"We can do it here, or we can do it in court."

He sighed. "The man's name was Wayne Cascade."

I spoke to him for another few minutes before I thanked him and walked away, but I could feel it—something had shifted. Wayne Cascade wasn't the end of the trail. He was the start of something much worse.

CHAPTER 26

I drove up a long dirt driveway around fifteen minutes outside of Beaufort.

The chain-link fence that ran alongside the driveway had seen better days. It was rusted and broken in places, with beer cans littering the base, most of them punctured with bullet holes. The driveway opened to a clearing with a small red-brick house sat off to the left. A large shed was to the right. Beside the shed was a cage, barely holding together, with two pit bulls inside. The cage looked weak. The dogs didn't.

Wayne Cascade stepped out of the house as my SUV crunched over the gravel. He was a lean man, not a piece of fat on him, with hollow cheeks, and eyes that were too wide apart. He wore the same dirty camouflage pants and a blue tank top that I'd seen him in last month. I wasn't sure if they'd been washed since.

"What do you want, city lawyer?" he called out as I stepped out of my car.

"Thought you and I could share a sweet tea."

"The last time I shared a sweet tea with a man, I shot him. Is that what you want?"

"You make a habit of shooting people?"

"Ever since I was shipped off to Iraq in '03, I've had a taste for killing. Before Iraq, I was living on the streets and nobody knew who I was, but over there, I was a king. I was a warrior. A man who did what needed to be done. Those were some of the best and worst years of my life. I wouldn't trade those days, but I wouldn't wish them on anyone."

"Thank you for your service."

He looked at me and then stood up straighter. He nodded. I nodded back.

We stood in silence for a few moments, and when the moment of respect had passed, he clenched his jaw, drew several breaths, and then continued. "What do you want?"

"I want to know why Sam Keenan purchased a cell phone number for you."

"Never heard of the guy."

"He gave you the cell phone used to call Malcolm Holt."

Cascade shrugged.

"Holt says he received a call the night Judge Newton was shot. It was an anonymous male voice that informed him there was a girl at Judge Newton's house."

"Is that right?"

"It is."

"What's that got to do with me?"

"The call that was made to Malcolm Holt came from the phone Sam Keenan gave you. It was the only call ever made from that phone. It was a burner. I need to know why someone used a burner phone to call Malcom Holt."

"I can't help you."

I stared at him for a long moment. "I'm going to use a former FBI agent to triangulate all the location data the phone recorded. That means I'll know where it was when it was switched on, when it was used for the call, and when it was switched off."

He scoffed. "Good luck with your theory."

"If I find evidence the phone is connected to you, I'll subpoena you to testify about why you used the phone that night."

"You think you can threaten me? Your court rules don't apply to me." He wiped his hands on his shirt and looked over at his pit bulls. "I'll say whatever I need to say to protect the people I know."

"I know you're involved. And I'm going to prove it."

We eyed each other for a long moment before he walked across to the pit bull cage. It was time for me to go.

CHAPTER 27

"Ken Steward called," Kayla said as I entered the office. "Says he'd love a free steak and beer. Who is he?"

"He's a contact I had in Chicago. That man could never say no to a free meal." I set my briefcase down and headed to the office kitchen. "You want a coffee?"

"Please," she said, and I made two. I handed Kayla her mug and walked toward my office. Kayla followed one step behind.

"Ken moved to Charleston three years ago, retiring to the warmer weather," I explained as I sat down and blew the steam off the coffee. "He worked for the FBI for the Cellular Analysis Survey Team, or CAST team as they were known. They determine the source of a phone call by using cell tower triangulation and geolocation techniques."

"I didn't understand any of your last sentence."

"The records from a cellular provider show which cell tower received the call. The tower logs information about the time of the call and, most importantly, the signal's strength. When analyzing the strength and timing from three to five different towers, the data shows the approximate distance to the caller from each tower. When they analyze the data, they draw circles around each of the towers, and the point where these circles overlap is the likely location of the caller. If the towers are close together, they can pinpoint the call to an exact location, such as a specific address, but when the towers are farther apart, it leaves a larger area."

"Better than GPS data?"

"If the caller's phone has GPS available, it can be better than narrowing the location and time of the call, but often GPS data is turned off on cell phones, especially burner phones."

"And he'll look at the call that was placed to Holt's phone on the night of the murder?"

"This will give us an idea about where they called him from. It could lead us to creating more doubt in the courtroom."

The following night, I made the drive to Charleston with the windows down, the Lowcountry air, thick with salt and humidity, flowing through the car. It was an hour's ride, give or take, and I didn't mind the chance to sing badly to classic rock.

Steward hadn't needed much convincing to meet. As I'd told Kayla, the promise of a free steak and beer was all it took. We met outside a bar off King Street. Nothing fancy. Brick walls, ceiling fans that turned slow, and a waitress who welcomed customers with a large smile. When he spotted me, Steward rose from his chair with a grin. We greeted each other with a solid handshake and a pat on the shoulder.

Steward had left Chicago three years earlier, fed up with the snow, the winters, and the clouds that never seemed to lift. He came South chasing sunshine and silence—and from the looks of it, he'd found both. He'd put on twenty-five pounds, maybe more, and his face looked more relaxed, his eyes brighter. He had a full head of black hair, thicker than I remembered, and I wondered if it was a hair transplant, dyed, or a convincing toupee.

"Retirement got to be too much for you?"

"Life is about balance, my friend." He winked. "I love relaxing, and I love taking it easy, but I still need some spice, you know? I still need to keep this brain and body ticking over."

"I understand."

"And ever since I retired, I've developed the body of a porn star."

"Is that right?" I smiled.

"Yeah. All my clothes say 'XXX.'" He laughed heartily and slapped his hand on the table.

I laughed with him.

"And my wife struggles with having me around all the time, so she nags me to fix things, but I told her, when a man says he'll do something, he'll do it. There's no need to remind him every five weeks." He chuckled and slapped the table again. "But she's good. You know, most women complain their husbands never listen to them, but I'm happy to say I've never heard my wife say that." Again, he slapped the table.

For the next ten minutes, Steward laid out the best jokes he'd been holding on to over the last few years. We ordered medium-rare steaks, a few beers, and a side of comedy.

As we finished our steaks, Steward wiped his mouth and turned the conversation to work. "But enough jokes, Dean. I know you're a man of action, so tell me what you need."

"I need help triangulating a call."

He nodded. "Then I'll need a subpoena."

"I can get you one."

"Alright then. Here's what I can do. I can use historical call detail records from cell carriers to determine approximate locations of cell phones during calls or messages, and with a subpoena, I can get the same data and perform identical triangulation and mapping. I'll conduct a private drive test, where I'll physically measure cell signal strength in an area to verify tower coverage. I'll look at the cell tower logs, GPS data, and ping records for the cell phone to determine the locations it was used at."

"Sounds like you're the right man for the job."

"It's nice to be wanted." He smiled. "And I'd say us private investigators do better than law enforcement at this type of thing because we have less bias toward trying to prove a point. We simply look at the data for what it is, rather than focusing on confirming the law enforcement theory. The CAST team also can only use government-approved software, but there's some new technology that's proving useful."

"Great. How long do you think it'll take?"

"That's the problem. Even with a subpoena, these requests can take months, sometimes years. I can put the squeeze on the companies, but they don't employ enough people to process the information. They have small teams, sometimes only one person, processing all the requests from law enforcement across the country."

"That's a problem," I agreed.

"It is what it is." Steward shrugged. "Nothing we can do about it. I've seen lots of lawyers delay trials until this information is received, but then the data doesn't show them what they want it to show. It's a gamble, and it doesn't always pay off. What's your worst-case scenario?"

"Worst case would be the call came from inside the victim's home. That would suggest the victim invited the defendant into his home before the shooting. That would convict him on the spot."

"Then I wouldn't ask the judge to wait. I've seen it before. If you ask the judge to delay the case, and the data isn't favorable, then they'll still request it to be added to discovery. The prosecution could then use it. So, what's your best-case scenario?"

"Best case is if we can link it to Wayne Cascade, who we know purchased the phone from a man named Sam Keenan. It would then allow us to track Cascade's movements and see if he ever went near Judge Newton's house in the days before the murder."

"Sounds like a risk, either way."

"It is, but I need to know," I confirmed. "The next question is how much?"

"It's around twenty-five hours of work, but for you, Dean, nothing. I owe you for what you did for me in Chicago, and honestly, after my retirement, I don't need the money. Think of it as my way of saying thank you when you helped me out with my son's court case. My son would've been locked up if you didn't defend him. My family owes you, big time."

I brushed his compliments off like it was nothing, and we talked for a while longer about how different life was in Chicago compared to the Lowcountry. After our meal, we shook hands solidly, and I paid the tab.

I left the meeting filled with confidence. We might have a lead.

CHAPTER 28

As I drove back from Charleston, the sun dipped low, stretching long shadows across the two-lane highway.

The road blurred beneath the tires, and my mind was already elsewhere. The call came after I passed the halfway point to Beaufort. Emma's name lit up on the screen, and the moment I heard her voice, I knew something was wrong.

"They took her in an ambulance," she said, not bothering with a greeting. Her voice was tight. "Mom's back in the hospital."

I pulled the car on to the shoulder as she explained.

Despite every precaution, despite all the check-ins and sterile gloves and quiet optimism, Jane had picked up an infection. The kind that moved fast. The kind that didn't listen to plans or protocols. It was already in her blood, already doing damage. Emma repeated what the doctors had told her—half for me, half to hear it out loud: *"Be prepared for the worst."*

They were trying everything. Broad-spectrum antibiotics. IV drips. Isolation procedures. Emma listed off machines they were using—monitors, tubes, whirring pumps—but none of them seemed to be helping. Jane's fever was climbing. She was slipping.

"I don't know what to do," Emma whispered, her voice cracking. "They're not letting me in. I'm just standing here. I can't even see her."

The silence that followed was the worst part.

"You're not alone," I said after a few moments. "She's in one of the best hospitals in the state. These doctors, the whole team, they know what they're doing. They've seen this before. They'll throw everything at it." She didn't respond. I could tell she was fighting back tears. "I'm on my way," I told her. "I'll be there soon."

And I pulled back on to the road, not caring about the speed, not caring about the lights or the line of cars behind me. I drove, chasing down the distance between me and the woman I loved, whose heart was breaking.

All the pressure of the court case, all the emails, the to-do list, all of it fell away, as I raced down the highway.

I arrived back in Beaufort twenty-five minutes later, going straight to the hospital. I spotted Emma sitting outside, holding her stomach with one arm and chewing her fingernails. I parked and jogged across to see her. I held her while she cried.

When she settled, we sat down on an outdoor bench as the evening sun touched the horizon.

"The end is in sight." Emma blinked back tears. "The chemotherapy has made her so weak that her body is completely broken down. This last round was more than she could handle. They think it could be sepsis. They say they're doing the best they can, but her organs are on the edge of failure."

"We knew this was a risk." I held Emma's hand. "She's tough."

"I can't lose her, Dean. Not now. Not with a baby on the way. My mother needs to be able to hold our child. She has to."

"And you know she'll fight to be here. You know she's in the hospital right now fighting as hard as she can."

Emma blinked back more tears and I hugged her again.

We spent the night at the hospital, waiting for word on how she was doing. In the morning, at 5 a.m., the nurse told us Jane had stabilized, but she wasn't out of the woods yet.

It was still touch and go.

CHAPTER 29

Grief has a strange way of making everything feel both loud and quiet at once.

I couldn't sit still—not with everything pressing in. I tried spending the day at the hospital, but Emma told me to go to work. She was surrounded by her aunties and cousins, wrapped in care I couldn't compete with. I'd only get in the way.

After a long night in the waiting room, I returned home, showered, had two cups of coffee, and drove to the office. As I stepped out into the morning humidity, I felt that unmistakable sensation of someone watching me. I scanned my surroundings and spotted a man and a young woman sitting in a beaten-up Toyota on the street outside the entrance to my office building, eyes fixed on me.

One of them got out. She looked like she was in her early twenties, but was small and light, the type of person a strong gust of wind could knock over. Her skin appeared dry, and her blonde hair was loose.

"Mr. Lincoln?" she asked as she walked toward me.

"That's correct. Can I help you?"

"My name is Elizabeth Pennington. I got married a month ago, and my maiden name was Jones. I'm sure you've read my name in the court documents."

I nodded. Elizabeth Jones had been the first woman to accuse Judge Newton of sexual assault. She had worked for him for a year before she filed a police complaint. The file read much the same as Holt's daughter's police complaint—she went to the judge's house to work after hours and awoke several hours later in his bed. She reported there was no consensual sexual activity, but the judge denied any wrongdoing, stating they were both drunk, and that he remembered Elizabeth initiating the physical contact between them. She denied it, but there was no other evidence. It was he said/she said, and when Judge Newton claimed to the police that Elizabeth had approached him for a financial settlement to withdraw the claim, the police declined to pursue the complaint any further.

"Mrs. Pennington, I—"

"I've heard Mr. Malcolm Holt has gotten a new trial and you're defending him. Everyone's talking about it."

"There will be a new trial," I confirmed. "If you don't want your name involved—"

"My name is involved. Every time someone mentions that scumbag of a judge, my heart beats faster, I break out into a sweat, and my anxiety goes through the roof. Every time his name is on the news, people look at me. I feel the pain in my chest every time I hear his name."

"Mrs. Pennington, I—"

"You need to get Mr. Holt out of prison." Her voice was firm. "Mr. Holt did this world a great justice. He did what the police refused to do. He stopped a monster. He should be given a medal, not a prison sentence."

"I understand your anger toward Judge Newton. He did some terrible things and was never brought to justice in our court system."

"I need to testify for Mr. Holt."

"I'm not sure there's anything you can say that will help him."

"Mr. Lincoln, I need this. I need to speak my truth to power. I need to tell the world what he did, and what he got away with. The world deserves to know what a horrible monster he was."

"I understand you want the justice system to right the wrongs of the past, but this case is about Mr. Holt, not Judge Newton's actions. We need to focus on Mr. Holt."

"Mr. Lincoln, if there's any way I can help, I'll be there."

I nodded.

I couldn't imagine what her life must have been like after that—how the years must've dragged on, empty and cruel, the world forgetting while she never could. Elizabeth Pennington had been handed one of the worst fates a young woman could face, and she'd had no choice but to carry the pain all by herself.

"Thank you for listening to her," a voice said behind her. I looked up to see a young man standing nearby. "I'm Dave Pennington, her husband. We both want this to be over."

Elizabeth looked up at me one more time.

"If I can find a way for you to help, then I'll call you," I stated. This was about healing for her. "I'll look into what you can do."

Elizabeth returned to the car, and Dave waited until she had closed the door before he turned back to me.

"Thank you for listening to her," Dave said again. "She's been strong all these years, but this week, after reading all the reports for the new trial, it's stirred everything up again. She wanted to protect the detective who handled her case, she really respected him, and he really tried to help, but she needs to testify. She needs to have her moment in court. She won't sensationalize things, but she needs to have her moment."

"Did she ever get help? Counseling?"

"Lots of counseling. So many sessions."

"I can't imagine that kind of pain."

"She'll be alright. We'll get through it." Dave looked back at his wife, then back to me. "Just . . . make sure you know what you're doing. If this doesn't end the way you hope, I don't know what it'll do to her."

I nodded, but my eyes stayed on Elizabeth Pennington.

This wasn't just another case. This wasn't just another trial. The outcome would impact lives already torn apart. Her anguish was as powerful as my determination—and I knew I had to carry both with me as I pushed forward.

I spent the rest of the day in the office, focused on Julie Steinberg's case, but Elizabeth Pennington lingered in my thoughts. I visited the hospital at lunchtime, and met Emma in the waiting room. She'd been allowed brief visits with her mother in isolation, but there wasn't much anyone could do for her. I stayed for an hour before I returned to the office. I talked to Emma on the phone in the afternoon; she was going to her auntie's for dinner, and then returning to the hospital. I told her she needed to sleep at some point, and she agreed, saying she'd be home later that night.

As the time ticked past 9 p.m., Emma messaged and said she was heading home. I told her I'd meet her there.

When I stepped out of the office, I noticed the truck parked across the road under the beam of the streetlight. There was a man standing outside it. Arms folded, staring at the entrance to my office. Robert Newton. I caught his eye, then turned toward him.

He glared at me for a long moment, and then spat on the ground, before he got back in his truck and drove away.

CHAPTER 30

The following morning, I drove Emma back out to the hospital. She hadn't slept much. She kept checking her phone, looking at the messages, and seeing if the hospital had called. I stayed with her for most of the morning, keeping her company and showing her support. The doctors and nurses didn't have much to tell us. Jane was fighting hard, they said, but the outlook was still uncertain. Around midday, Emma's aunties arrived, and I drove back to the office.

Bruce and Julie Steinberg were waiting for me as I entered the boardroom, chatting about all things Beaufort. Bruce asked about Jane, and I told him it was touch and go. Julie showed her caring side as she said all the right things at the right time. We spoke for a few minutes about the great care at the hospital, about the skilled doctors and nurses, and then when the emotion was becoming too much, I turned my focus to Julie's case.

"Our subpoena for Casper Remington's personal computer was approved, but that's all," I explained. "And you can almost guarantee there will be nothing of value on there. He'll be prepared."

"We didn't get it for the whole house?" Julie asked.

"No." I shook my head. "The prosecution argued for privacy of the father's information, and they got it."

"But we do have good news," Bruce added. "Our investigator, Sean Benning, has run a facial recognition program on Casper over the internet for the month after the incident."

"Any hits?"

"A few. He's active on social media, but there's one great one. The software has identified him in a photo taken at a concert in Savannah one week after the slap. You still slapped him without a legal claim for self-defense, but we can try to convince the prosecution to drop the charges, considering you haven't had any trouble with the law in the last twenty-five years."

"I like that," Julie said. "I don't want to lose everything. I've built the bar from nothing. Twenty years of my life, Bruce. Nights, weekends, holidays. I missed birthdays, missed celebrations, missed funerals. I've poured my heart and soul into the place. The bar's not just a business. It's my name. My reputation. It's the only thing I own." She swallowed, her voice growing steadier.

Bruce said nothing. He didn't need to. As defense lawyers, we'd seen it before—how a small business wasn't just brick and mortar, but blood and memories. Something earned the hard way. A part of a family.

Bruce nodded, letting her words settle. "Then we fight," he said, and looked at me. "How did it go with the potential witnesses?"

"We found twenty-five connections to politicians, high-ranking law enforcement, and large business owners, mostly through Casper's father, and I sent out twenty-five questionnaires last night. I expect they'll all talk to their lawyers before they respond, which is good for us. It buys us some time. What we're doing is ensuring this case gets into the papers. Even if we don't call these witnesses, they'll be associated with the case, and that's all the media needs to create a great story."

"Can you do that?" Julie asked.

"What we're trying to do is pressure the prosecution into acting. The prosecution will appear heavy-handed trying to charge a person with assault for a simple slap in a bar. It'll be an embarrassment for them. Blessington didn't think this would be a media fight, but he's wrong. If they want to play games, then we'll play games."

"I like it," Julie said. "I like it a lot."

"This is high risk and high reward," I said. "It's time to see how much of a risk they want to take."

CHAPTER 31

"A motion to dismiss?" Judge Margaret Connery raised an eyebrow from the bench.

Judge Connery was in her early seventies, and had a strong reputation built on years of hard work, overseeing thousands of cases and sentencing thousands of defendants. She was no frills, no nonsense, and had no time to waste. Her courtroom reflected that—dull colors, consisting of mostly brown and cream, blinds drawn, no distractions.

Angus Blessington stood at the prosecution table, representing the State with a stiff posture and pressed suit. At the defense table, Bruce sat next to me and Julie next to him.

I stood. "Your Honor, the prosecution claims the alleged victim, Mr. Casper Remington, has suffered from severe, ongoing pain since the incident, but we've come into possession of evidence that contradicts their ridiculous narrative." I handed a folder to the clerk, who passed it to the bench. "Mr. Casper Remington attended a heavy-metal concert in Savannah, Georgia, just days after the alleged assault. His photo is posted on social media in the front row, with no apparent signs of a hearing injury. If he was truly in as much pain as the State claims, he wouldn't have been anywhere near the venue."

Blessington's mouth tightened. He rose slowly. "This is the first we're hearing of this, Your Honor."

"The evidence is time-stamped," I said. "Photos, posts, the works."

Blessington recovered quickly. "Even if he attended the concert, there's no proof he wasn't wearing earplugs. Being assaulted doesn't mean you stop living your life. We dispute the context of this evidence and would ask it be left to the jury to decide."

Judge Connery skimmed the folder, then looked up. "Motion denied. I agree with the prosecution—the issues raised are for the jury to determine."

"Thank you, Your Honor," Blessington stated.

"Next we have a Motion *in Limine* to Exclude Prior Bad Acts Evidence," Judge Connery noted. "Mr. Lincoln, please explain your motion further."

"We've submitted a Motion *in Limine* to Exclude Prior Bad Acts Evidence, pursuant to Rule 404(b), South Carolina Rules of Evidence. The defendant was involved in a violent incident twenty-five years ago, where she was charged with the assault of her then husband. However, she was acting in self-defense after years of abuse. She accepted a plea deal with the prosecution and served ten days' jail time for the assault. It's our belief the prosecution will use this to unduly influence the jury."

"It was more than an assault," Blessington argued. "It was a violent attack on an off-duty police officer in which the victim lost several teeth."

"She was acting in self-defense against her abusive husband. Twenty-five years ago, the law looked at incidences of domestic abuse very differently to how they view them today."

"Regardless of the circumstances, past crimes cannot be used to present character evidence against the defendant. Considering the incident was more than twenty-five years ago, and the defendant has not been involved in any violent incidence since, the motion is granted, pursuant to Rule 404(b), South Carolina Rules of Evidence." Judge Connery turned another page. "Next, we have a defense motion to add witness names to the discovery list."

"Thank you, Your Honor." I stood and handed several sheets of paper to the bailiff and a copy to Blessington. "We wish to submit a motion to amend the witness list, pursuant to the South Carolina Rules of Criminal Procedure."

Blessington looked at the list, at me, then back at the list. "Your Honor, this witness list includes a South Carolina Senator, a local mayor, and a circuit solicitor."

"All of whom are associated with this case," I explained. "They've either witnessed violence by the victim, they've witnessed the demeaning sexual comments of the victim, or they've had first-hand experience of the victim's illegal behavior."

Judge Connery squinted as she read the names off the list. "Do you have statements from these witnesses, Mr. Lincoln?"

"Not yet, Your Honor. We've added these names to the witness list in good faith and we've issued questionnaires to each of the potential witnesses and are awaiting their responses. However, we do highlight that they all have connections to the victim."

"This is ridiculous," Blessington whined. "You can't add names to a court case for the sake of it."

"We assure the court that we aren't doing that, Your Honor. In fact, each of the witnesses has their link listed next to their name. For instance, Senator Wainwright witnessed Mr. Remington slap a girl on the behind while he was in a school play. Mr. Casper Remington was suspended from school after that incident. Mrs. Phillips, the Mayor of Ridgeland, was witness to Mr. Remington making comments about girls in school uniforms. Mr. Casper Remington made those comments on Mrs. Phillips' social media account when she posted photos of the local Catholic school."

"But there are potentially hundreds of witnesses to those events, and they're not listed here," Blessington whined again. "Mr. Remington has hundreds of friends on Facebook, but Mr. Lincoln has chosen the most influential ones to add to the discovery list before they've even had the chance to respond to the questions. This is clearly a tactic by the defense to bring media attention to this trial."

"These are legitimate witnesses added to discovery material."

Judge Connery was quiet as she looked over the list. "And have these witnesses agreed to testify?"

"Not yet, Your Honor. We may need to subpoena them to testify in this court."

Judge Connery groaned and tilted her head back. "Mr. Lincoln, you're adding high-profile witnesses without first obtaining statements. Until you have their verified testimonies, I will not rule whether these witnesses are relevant. I will give the defense five weeks to gather the evidence, and if, after that time, you cannot provide a proffer of their testimony, then they will not be allowed to testify."

"Yes, Your Honor," I stated and looked at Blessington.

His face was red, he had a thin line of sweat on his brow, and he was tapping his hand on the table.

Blessington wouldn't say it, but his face said enough. He was cornered, and he knew it.

CHAPTER 32

I sat alone in the office late that night, the hum of the desk lamp the only sound filling the silence. The streets of Beaufort had long since quieted, but my mind hadn't. I stared at the ceiling for a while, wondering what lay ahead of us—not just in the case, but in life.

Emma's mother had pulled through, for now. It was still going to be a hard road ahead. She was surviving, but her body was still weak, and the doctors didn't think she'd make it through another infection. Emma and I knew she was fighting hard to meet our baby.

Emma had started talking about when we might tell people she was pregnant. There was excitement in her eyes, but also hesitation. We were cautious. Apprehensive. We'd decided to wait until after the four-month mark—play it safe, keep the joy close. But this was Beaufort, and secrets didn't last long. As soon as one cousin found out, it would move through the town like a gust through Spanish moss. That was the way things worked here—quiet talk behind church pews, knowing glances at the grocery store, and the unspoken rule that no secret belonged to just one person.

I leaned back and let my thoughts drift. At twenty-one, life had been all about the moment—spontaneity, urgency, living without thinking too far ahead. But life in my late thirties was something else entirely. It was about momentum. About building. Creating something lasting. Proving, somehow, that I mattered. That my days stacked up to something more than just time passed. I'd heard people say that life circles back—that in your fifties, you return to the present moment again. But right now, I was knee-deep in the in-between. In the building years. The weight-bearing years.

And in that moment, I wasn't thinking about legacy in some abstract, grandiose sense. I was thinking about what I'd leave behind for my child. For Emma. For the community I served. I wanted to do something that counted. To leave a mark that wasn't just etched into files or forgotten in court transcripts, but one that lived on in the people I stood up for.

Work, in its own way, was the only thing that calmed me. It was something I could hold on to while the rest of life swirled with uncertainty. It gave me focus, gave me a rhythm, and kept the what-ifs at bay.

My thoughts turned back to Holt's case. To the life Judge Newton had led—and to the shadow he had left behind. I thought about Holt and his choices, and the decisions he had made to protect the people he loved.

And I wondered—if I were in Holt's position, would I have done the same? After pleading with law enforcement to take action, after pleading with the justice system to stop a man who was abusing young women, would I have stepped up and stopped him myself? Would I have shot the judge?

There was a knock at the front door, sharp and deliberate. I glanced at the clock. Five minutes past 7 p.m. Too late for a client. Too early for drunken trouble. The hallway outside had been quiet for hours. I stood, heart beating a little faster. Whoever it was, they weren't expected. I crossed the room slowly, the floor creaking beneath my steps. The knock came again. I opened the door.

"Terry Wallace," I greeted the man at the door, and held out my hand. Wallace, a former high-school classmate and now a Beaufort Police Department investigator, shook my hand. He was aging well. Fit, with a thick head of hair, and not a crease in his clothes. He presented a picture of discipline, holding himself with pride. "It's good to see you."

"Dean." Wallace looked around the porch. "I was doing some rounds, checking the city and I saw your office light on, so I thought I'd drop in. I've been meaning to speak with you."

I stepped out on to the porch. I ran my hand over my head as I leaned against the railing. "What's wrong?"

He was hesitant. "Dean, your case is putting a lot of pressure on a lot of people. Judge Newton might not have been the cleanest of men and some people are fearful of what will come out."

"That seems to be an open secret around here. Seems like everyone in law enforcement knew what he was doing."

"It wasn't like that."

"Really? There were a lot of people making complaints against him, and every single case was brushed under the carpet."

"That's not what happened." Wallace's tone was firm. I let the pause sit between us while Wallace worked through his emotions. He gripped the railing tight and then eased his grip. "There was never any evidence, Dean." His voice was quiet. "I investigated one of the cases, and I believed the young woman who came forward. I believed every word she said."

"But?"

"But that wasn't enough. You're a lawyer. You know that." Wallace took a large breath. "To convict someone of a crime, you need evidence, not just a claim. And the truth is there were two adults in a residence who both claimed to have drunk a lot and woken up with little recollection the next day."

"There was no consent given."

"Where's the evidence of that? None of these girls had any marks on them. There was no evidence of violence, or even forceful behavior. They had alcohol in their system, but nothing else. Sexual assault is so hard to investigate and so hard to convict, because in a lot of cases, there's no evidence that consent wasn't given." Wallace had worked himself up into anger. He looked away for a long moment. "When I investigated the claim of assault, I found Rohypnol in his bathroom."

"The date rape drug?"

"That's right. And by the time the young woman went to hospital after the assault, it was out of her system. It was never going to show up in any blood test."

"It doesn't show up in blood tests, but it shows up in hair follicle tests."

"Alright, Mr. Big City Lawyer. You might've been able to do those tests in Chicago, but we don't have the funds to do them here. We don't have the money or the facilities or the staff required to test every hair follicle in every case." He groaned. "I interviewed Judge Newton, and he said he was drunk, but he said he remembered the young woman consenting to sex. He even took a photo of her sitting on his lap in the living room when she arrived. She wasn't drunk then. She was smiling and happy. I was so angry when I was interviewing him. When it became clear that we didn't have enough to charge him, I told him he was scum, and I was watching him. Judge Newton put in a complaint about me, and after that, the allegations against him were never assigned to me again. He went on to do it another five times, and those are just the women who contacted the police."

"Why are you telling me this?"

"Because the young woman, Elizabeth Pennington, heard about the retrial of Malcolm Holt. She contacted me before the appeal and said she would testify against the judge but didn't want to damage my career. She respected how hard I had fought for the judge to be charged and didn't want to hurt me." He exhaled loudly. "I told her I would be proud for her to testify and speak her truth to power." Wallace reached into his pocket and removed a piece of paper. He looked at it for a long moment and handed it to me. "This is her number."

"She's already spoken to me."

"Of course she has." Wallace smiled. "She's a small woman, but she's very strong. If you need her, she won't hesitate to help."

I nodded my thanks, and Wallace turned and took a step off the front porch.

"I hear you're an AA sponsor," I stated.

Wallace turned back and eyed me. "And?"

"And I hear you're sponsoring Paul Freeman."

"Right." Wallace leaned against the pillar next to the stairs. "Listen, I don't talk about who I sponsor because everyone deserves a second chance. Everyone deserves forgiveness in the eyes of the Lord."

My jaw clenched.

"Dean, I know how much pain the Freeman family caused you. I know what happened with Paul and the car accident and the prison sentence, but he's a different man now. He's moved on from that. It's important for him to make peace with his past—for some, that means asking for forgiveness, and for others, it's admitting the truth, no matter the cost."

"He should still be in prison."

"And if dealing with his past leads to that, he understands that's the cost. He's working hard on himself, on reconciling his past, and asking forgiveness for the mistakes he made. He's worthy of forgiveness, Dean. We all are, but Paul, he never had a chance. He grew up in a corrupt environment, with a prick of a father, and he never learned how to have empathy for others. The church has opened something inside him. He sees the world differently now."

Wallace looked to me for a response, but I didn't answer. He then pulled a cigarette box from his inside coat pocket. He tapped one smoke out and held it between his middle finger and thumb. He lit the smoke, took a long drag, and then shook his head.

"You still smoke?"

"I know. It's disappointing, but I can't give up all the vices. I've given up alcohol for fifteen months now, and I'd go insane without these cancer sticks. My job is mentally hard at times, and it's nice to have something to turn to." He stared at his cigarette and then sighed. "Dean, there's something else you should know."

I waited.

"I wasn't going to tell you this, but you deserve a break." He drew another long drag on the cigarette. "There was a journalist who was investigating Judge Newton's behavior before he died. She was asking me questions a week before he was shot. She wasn't asking about his sexual behaviors, she was asking about his business dealings."

"Why weren't you going to tell me that?"

"I'm a cop, Dean. The people that work for law enforcement around here are my brothers and sisters. We risk our lives every day for the safety of this community. And you, as a defense lawyer, try to pull our work apart to look for the smallest error. Sometimes, we don't like you." He flicked the ash from his cigarette, then looked down the street. "But it's been weighing on my mind. Judge Newton had a lot of enemies. And maybe someone else was involved in his death."

"Who was the journalist?"

"A woman named Marsha Reynolds." Wallace turned and stepped off the porch. "But you didn't hear it from me."

CHAPTER 33

I made my way down the quiet corridor to the courthouse holding rooms. The deputy buzzed me through, and I found Holt waiting in the attorney-client meeting room. He looked tired, with his nerves barely held in check. I sat down, opened the file, and asked him how he was.

"Okay," Holt said, but it wasn't convincing. His leg was bouncing up and down rapidly under the table. "Any other offers?"

"Not yet."

"Why can't they offer me a manslaughter charge?" Holt asked. "Even though I didn't shoot the judge, I'd take it."

"That's up to the prosecution to decide."

"What about the jury? Why can't they decide on a manslaughter charge?"

"That decision is made by the jury during the deliberation phase of the trial. They'll receive instructions from the judge, and when they go to the deliberation room, they'll consider the murder charge first, and if they decide the evidence doesn't support a murder conviction, they consider if the lesser charge of manslaughter should apply. Like murder, manslaughter in South Carolina doesn't come in degrees. It's simply defined as the unlawful killing of another person in the heat of passion upon sufficient legal provocation."

"But that's what they're claiming, right?"

"If we had proof there was another girl in the house, then it's likely the prosecution would put an offer of manslaughter on the table. If we knew who she was, if she was there, then definitely. But right now, there's no evidence there was anyone else in the house. That's why they haven't offered a lower charge."

"This is all too much," Holt said. "I'm more nervous this time than last time. I think it's because I know what's at stake now."

"We're about to go into the final pretrial hearing," I explained. "Our motion to exclude evidence about your daughter is our attempt to derail the prosecution's case. They spent years preparing a case centered around your daughter's assault as a motive, and if we can exclude that information, they won't be able to prove you had a motive. And if there's no motive, then all they have is you being near the scene of the crime at the time of death and your gun, which can't be matched to the crime, found nearby."

"Why didn't we do this earlier?"

"We held off on this motion because if we win, we'll throw the prosecution's case into complete disarray. Timing is important, and by holding off, we have an element of surprise. If we win this motion, they'll need to exclude your police interview. And if that happens, it'll throw their entire case into panic, and they may even settle for a deal that amounts to time served."

"Do they know it's coming?"

"They received the motion on Friday morning. It was late, and they would've been frantically preparing all weekend." I tapped my hand on the table. "And if we don't win, then we've signaled to the prosecution that we've got many plays ready to go. They'll be scared, and they'll offer a better deal." I leaned closer to Holt. "Are you ready for this to happen again?"

"I am."

I nodded and looked at my watch. "Then let's do this."

CHAPTER 34

Sitting behind the defense table, I read over the files in the final pretrial hearing. Bruce sat next to me, with Holt on the other side of him, still nervously tapping his foot on the ground.

At 9:45 a.m., Assistant Solicitor Andrew Harley entered the courtroom, followed by two assistants. Fifteen minutes later, the bailiff read the case number and asked the room to rise for Judge LeBlanc. Judge LeBlanc took her seat, adjusted the folders in front of her, clicked a few buttons on the laptop to her left, and then welcomed the parties to the court.

"A motion to exclude evidence," Judge LeBlanc began. "Please explain, Mr. Lincoln."

"Your Honor, the State has made it clear that they'll be using highly inflammatory evidence to establish the motive of the defendant. They'll be introducing evidence that the defendant's daughter was sexually assaulted by the judge, and after law enforcement failed to charge him, the defendant acted as a vigilante. The State has made it clear they intend to show that the defendant had a personal reason to commit murder. We believe it's not relevant to discuss the defendant's paternity. This information is not relevant to these charges."

"Your Honor—" Harley interrupted, but I ignored him.

"The prejudicial impact of this evidence should not be ignored. This evidence is more prejudicial than probative and could lead the jury to base their decision on irrelevant information rather than on the facts of the case."

"Your Honor, we're very surprised by this motion." Harley stood. "Firstly, we believe the evidence could possibly help the defendant. During the jury deliberation, the jury can use the motive as a possible reason to consider manslaughter charges. Secondly, we believe it's important the jury knows the family connection to the prior assault. It's clear to us that this led to the defendant's retaliation. And the evidence is crucial for establishing a motive for murder."

"And how is the State intending to introduce this evidence?"

"Via the defendant's own police interview. He said it, he talked about it, and he mentioned it. This is nothing more than the defense's attempt to have essential evidence thrown out on the back of a flimsy motion."

Judge LeBlanc adjusted her glasses and looked down at the motion, flipping through the pages without expression. "And the interview, was it voluntary?"

Harley nodded. "Yes, Your Honor. No coercion. He was read his rights. He waived counsel. The recording is clean. He went into the interview on his own, unprompted."

I stood again, keeping my tone even. "Your Honor, the fact the defendant referenced it under emotional distress doesn't make it relevant. He was grieving, angry, overwhelmed. What he said wasn't a confession—it was grief talking. We're not disputing the comments were made. We're disputing their legal value."

Judge LeBlanc leaned back in her chair. "You're saying the motive isn't relevant to this court case?"

"No, Your Honor," I replied, "this kind of motive is personal, emotional, but built on a separate, uncharged crime. The motive the prosecution wants to put forward is so charged with emotion that it risks poisoning the entire trial. We're not trying Judge Newton and his actions. We're not litigating the alleged assault. The risk is the jury sees this as justified vengeance, or worse, as a trial within a trial."

Harley cut in again. "The jury deserves to know the setting, Your Honor. Without this motive, the State's case is a puzzle with missing pieces. We can't show intent without explaining why this happened. We're not putting the victim on trial—we're explaining why the defendant pulled the trigger."

The judge held up a hand, silencing both of us. She stared out into the room for a long moment before speaking. "There's nothing flimsy about considering the probative and prejudicial impact of evidence." Judge LeBlanc's tone was firm. She leaned back, thought over her words for a few moments and then continued. "To consider this evidence, I need to weigh its high probative value against the potential for undue prejudice. The defendant's own statement in the police interview is corroborative evidence of the motive. The defendant waived his right to counsel and discussed it of his own accord. In conclusion, despite its inflammatory nature, the evidence is critical to explaining why the defendant acted the way he did. On the basis of that information, the motion is denied."

Harley nodded once, tight-lipped, but I could tell he was alarmed.

The real fight had begun.

CHAPTER 35

Marsha Reynolds called me back five days after I first reached out, which was long enough for me to wonder if she'd gotten cold feet, or if she'd decided that silence was safer than speaking. Her voice on the phone was crisp, a little guarded, but not unfriendly. She agreed to meet and suggested a quiet spot off Carteret Street—City Latte, one of my favorite coffee spots, and a short walk from my office.

I arrived early. The small café had a warm light and casual charm. The air smelled like cinnamon and dark roast, with a hint of burnt sugar from the pastries in the glass case. Soft jazz played from a speaker tucked into the corner, the kind of music meant to make conversations feel private, even in public. The barista gave me a polite nod as I took a seat in the back corner, where I had a view of the door and enough quiet to think.

Marsha walked in ten minutes later, wearing a fitted black blazer over jeans and boots. She moved with the kind of confidence that didn't ask for attention but got it anyway. Her dark hair was tied back in a high ponytail, and she wore gold hoop earrings. In her late twenties, she looked younger than her years and could've passed for a college freshman.

Originally from Boston, she still carried a trace of the accent in the way she said coffee when she ordered. She had lived in Charleston for several years in her early twenties, working for the local paper. Then came the move west—to Los Angeles, where she was now working for the *Times*. She sat across from me, hands wrapped around her coffee.

"Thank you for coming to meet me," I said.

"My pleasure. I'm visiting my mother in Hilton Head for her birthday. The Lowcountry is such a beautiful part of the world. I love spending time here. I think I'll do what she did—work hard during my earning years, save up enough for a house, then move to the Lowcountry, taking a casual retail job."

"That seems like a great plan." I smiled. "Sounds a lot like my wife and me. We moved back from Chicago about a year ago, and while I miss the buzz of the city, there's something about this place that quietly seeps into your soul."

"Amen to that," she said. "But I guess you want to know about the Southern drama I was investigating?"

"I'd love to know everything you uncovered."

"When I was working around here, I was tasked with uncovering a political drama for the media company I was working for, and I'd heard some rumors about a property developer using his political connections to win contracts and buy into large developments. So, I asked around and started doing a deep dive into the behavior of a property developer named John Remington, and—"

"Remington?"

"Know him?"

"Most people do."

"That's what I heard. I had a source contact me and explain that Remington was convincing people to sell to him because he would threaten them with criminal charges of one type or another. He kept using different crimes so nobody would see the link, but every charge referenced by John Remington came through Judge Newton. And when I dug deeper, I found Judge Newton was heavily invested in Remington's property development business.

Remington would ask law enforcement to lay bogus charges, and that case would always go through Judge Newton."

"Any other names involved?"

She shook her head. "Nothing concrete. There were rumors, but I couldn't find any solid links from Remington to law enforcement. Remington organized drinks and parties, and hunting trips for people in law enforcement, but I couldn't prove they were involved in his business. It was easy to link Judge Newton to the business because he had investments in Remington's development, but I couldn't uncover any others."

"He must've had someone inside law enforcement."

"That's what I thought, but every trail went cold. For each of the crimes I investigated, there was a different arresting officer each time, and a different prosecutor. The only links I could find were between Judge Newton and John Remington. But I did uncover this. A disgruntled employee within Remington Red Rock Inc. passed it to me on the condition of anonymity."

She handed me a folder and I flicked it open. "What is it?"

"It's an internal communication with several high-level investors in Remington Red Rock Inc. A source gave me access to some of the internal communications via the messages they were linked in on, but they've all got stupid code names like 'TLM,' which stood for 'The Liberated Man,' or 'TT' for 'The Tasmanian,' or 'TG' for 'The Gavelstone.' It's like a group of teenage boys made these names up."

"What were they discussing?"

"How to arrest someone and have them charged by the courts. Look at this one here." She reached forward and pointed at the file. "In this piece of communication 'TG,' who was 'The Gavelstone,' says, 'Judicial path is clear. I have the case.'"

"So that's Judge Newton?"

"That's what I thought, but that's also as far as it goes. I didn't have any proof, but I'm sure if I'd dug deeper, I could have found a link. There's also mention of a fishing company named 'Newton Fishing,' and according to these communications, it appears to be a money-laundering front to transfer money offshore. There were very large payments going to the Cayman Islands for 'docking fees,' but I couldn't figure out who the payments were actually going to."

"Why would a local shrimp company need to dock in the Cayman Islands?"

"They put on their website that as part of their expanded offshore operations, they were fishing for yellowfin and bigeye tuna in the Caribbean basin, and the Cayman Islands served as a strategic resupply and docking location for their vessels operating in international waters."

"Clever." I nodded and glanced over some of the details in the file. "So, if Robert Newton, Judge Newton's son, owns the fishing company, he wouldn't like the attention the new trial is bringing to his family name. If he's laundering money offshore, then it explains his reluctance." I stared out the window for a moment to let the revelation sink in. "You didn't investigate it further?"

"I talked to Judge Newton on the phone about this information and he agreed to meet. He seemed to suggest it was more of a date than a meeting, but that didn't worry me. I needed to get the information, and if that was the way to do it, then that's what I was going to do."

"Why would he turn on them?"

"I got the impression that he was about to leave it all behind and retire. On the phone, he talked about how he could take me to Costa Rica, and I would never want for anything in my life. He said he had a place down there, and that we could retire together. He'd seen a picture of me in one of the articles I'd written, and he was very keen to meet up at his house."

"But you never went?"

"He said he would call back to set a time to meet at his house one weeknight after work, but a few days after our conversation, he was dead. I was sad to hear that, but at the time, I didn't think it had anything to do with me." She reached down and took another folder out of her bag. "This is all the information I compiled. There's a lot of theories in there, and not much concrete evidence, but lately, I've wondered whether my contact with him led to his death in some way."

"Thank you. The new trial starts tomorrow morning." I looked at my watch. "Which means I'd better get back to the office to prepare."

I thanked her again and left. As I walked away, I reminded myself that this was the Lowcountry and nothing stayed buried for long.

CHAPTER 36

I stepped out of the office after five as the afternoon sun hung low over Carteret Street, spreading its golden rays across the streets. I spotted Paul Freeman before I even reached the edge of the parking lot. He was leaning against his pickup truck parked on the street outside the lot. Ironed chinos, creaseless polo shirt, sneakers too clean.

I stopped walking and turned toward him. He stood up straighter when he saw me, like it meant something. His hair was shorter than I remembered, cleaner around the edges. He looked lighter too, thinner perhaps. Healthier than I remembered him.

"Mr. Lincoln," he said as I approached.

I didn't answer.

"I've been coming by for the past few days," he continued. "I didn't want to bother you inside your office, because I know you've got a big trial coming up. I figured I'd wait a few days until you were free. But I'm not here to start anything. I just . . . can I talk to you?"

It was almost four years since my sister Heather's death. Years of heartache. Years of pain. Years of anger.

Paul Freeman was sentenced to ten years in prison for drinking, driving, and then slamming into the side of my sister's car when he didn't stop at an intersection. His actions killed her, his decisions ended her life, but all he served was five months behind bars. Five months before his father, former circuit solicitor Stephen Freeman, pulled the strings to enable an early release. The prisons were full, they said. Paul was well behaved, they explained. They didn't have room for him, they said. None of it mattered.

"I don't owe you a second of my time," I answered. My voice surprised me. It was quieter than I meant it to be. Controlled, but fraying around the edges.

"I know," Paul replied, eyes down. "You don't."

He took another step. Only a few feet away. Striking distance. A quick left hook and he'd be out cold.

"I've been clean for fifty-five days now. I haven't touched a drop of alcohol in almost two months," he explained. "I'm in AA."

"With Terry Wallace."

"That's right. He's my sponsor, and he was the one who suggested I come here." Paul bit his bottom lip. "I go every day to the meetings. It's led me to finding God, and the church, but not in a jailhouse sort of way. In a real way that means something."

"And where in the Bible does it say you should park outside the office of the man whose sister you killed?"

He nodded. "No. That's on me. That's guilt, and maybe cowardice. I know what I was. I know what I did. I know how much pain it caused. And I regret it every day since I've become sober."

"You drove drunk, Paul. You ran a stop sign on a suburban street at fifty-five miles an hour and smashed into her driver's side door. You killed her instantly. She had young children. She had a family. She was loved by everyone who met her."

Paul flinched. Good. I wanted it to land. I wanted it to sit in his chest and ache every time he breathed. I wanted him to feel the pain that I felt. I wanted it to break him.

"I live with that," he whispered. "I know that now. I know what I did. Every morning, I see her face. I hear her name. I know what I did."

I stared at him, trying to find even a trace of the entitled little prick who used to use his father's name at every opportunity, but I couldn't see it. It wasn't there. The arrogance had been replaced by something quieter. Shame, maybe. Guilt. I wasn't sure.

"Why the change?" I asked. "Why now?"

"I hit rock bottom." He swallowed and looked away. I didn't interrupt the silence. "Not in a dramatic way, either. I just . . . just woke up in a pool of my own urine after another night of blacking out. It wasn't the first time I'd woken up like that. I did that so many times, and I tried to stop drinking, but nothing worked. Nothing. I couldn't stop it. As soon as I had one beer, it had to be ten. And that happened every night. I fooled myself to think I could just drink one. And then . . . and then I knew something had to change. I had to change. I had to change before I did it again."

"Your change was too late for Heather."

"I know," he croaked, avoiding eye contact. "AA was the only way for me. That was all I could do. I went there thinking I was better than everyone else, that I was somehow special, but I learned about God. For the first time in my life, I felt like I belonged somewhere. These people were like me, and they had my back. I never felt that before. I don't remember my mother before her death, and my father . . . my father was evil to me, and he taught me how to behave. He—"

"I'm not your therapist," I interrupted. My tone was harsh. "I'm not going to listen to your excuses. Get to your point."

"I don't want anything from you, Mr. Lincoln. I'm not asking for peace, and I'm not asking for friendship. But I wanted you to hear these words from me—I'm sorry. Deeply. I'm so sorry for what I did. And now, after learning so much in church, if I could trade places with her, I would."

I didn't speak for a long time. Paul didn't either.

"I don't forgive you," I said after a while. "And I may never forgive you."

"I understand." He looked at me, eyes red but steady. "It's my mistake to own. Thank you for listening to me."

He turned and walked back to his truck, quiet as he came. No dramatics. No parting shot.

I stood there a long while after he left. The wind kicked up off the river. The cicadas hummed loudly. I didn't feel better. I didn't feel healed.

But maybe, just maybe, I felt something shift.

CHAPTER 37

Crime was a pillar of the economy.

In the South, it kept the wheels turning. Courtrooms stayed busy, jails stayed full, and thousands of people drew paychecks off the back of every felony. Law enforcement, prosecutors, public defenders, court clerks, lab technicians, judges, medical examiners—they all had their jobs paid for by crime. Even the companies supplying the tasers, body armor, and patrol cars saw steady profits. It was a big industry, and coming down hard on crime was always a big political win. Take crime out of the equation, and the South wouldn't just lose cases—it would lose payrolls, budgets, and entire departments. Nobody said it out loud, but everyone in the system knew that crime paid—and not in the way most people thought.

I spent the evening reviewing the file from Marsha Reynolds. There were a lot of theories, a lot of possible connections, but not much concrete. I passed the file off to Sean Benning and asked him to dig deeper, but I didn't hold out much hope.

Walking into the foyer of the Beaufort County Courthouse, I spotted Assistant Solicitor Andrew Harley. He seemed to be waiting for me, next to two junior colleagues. His smile was smug, his stance confident, and his tone was incredibly annoying. "Has your client decided to confess to his sins?"

Stopping at the foot of the stairwell, I turned and looked at Harley. "Quite a crowd has gathered to watch you lose."

"Not in this case, Lincoln. This is open, shut, and locked up. As a prosecutor, this case is about as easy as it gets. All I need to deal with is an over-confident defense lawyer."

I didn't respond as I walked up the narrow stairs, taking them two at a time. I walked into the almost empty courtroom and greeted Bruce and Kayla, who were deep in discussion about the jury selection. Harley entered the courtroom five minutes later, followed by his assistants.

The dark wood paneling swallowed the light. My heart thudded in my chest, my jaw was tight, and my fist clenched around the handle of my briefcase. As I sat down, I took five slow breaths, steady and measured, trying to quiet the noise inside my head.

After Malcolm Holt was escorted in, the bailiff called the room to order. There was no crowd for the jury selection process, and the bailiff's deep voice reverberated off the walls.

I read over my notes as Judge LeBlanc entered. She greeted those present, confirmed there were no further pretrial motions, and then asked the bailiff to bring in the first group of potential jurors.

The bailiff led in a large group, their footsteps echoing across the polished floor. Some looked uncertain, some eager, some already looked bored.

Judge LeBlanc started the questioning. Her tone was brisk and efficient. A few were dismissed outright—childcare issues, work conflicts, important medical appointments. Others were excused for failing to grasp even the simplest legal concepts, and it was clear some were relieved to be cut loose.

As soon as Bruce got the list, he dove into their digital footprints. It was routine now—part of the modern defense playbook. He scoured whatever scraps they'd left behind on Facebook, Instagram, LinkedIn. Public posts, photos, liked articles. Nothing private.

Nothing that would trigger an ethics complaint. The American Bar Association had set clear guidelines. Lawyers were allowed to look, not touch. No fake profiles. No messages. No backdoor snooping. Just what the internet offered to any stranger on the outside.

Kayla handled the broader sweep. She flagged anyone who had commented on Judge Newton's case, shared headlines, or clicked the heart button on anything remotely emotional. A few had called it an execution. One had posted a prayer chain for Judge Newton's family. Another had tagged the local sheriff and demanded justice. Bruce scratched their names off the list without a second thought.

We moved through panel after panel, burning through the day in the dull rhythm of *voir dire*. It was slow work, calculated and exhausting, but by the time the clock in the courtroom pushed past 4 p.m., one seat remained. The final juror came from the last batch of the day. I hadn't expected much from that group, but sometimes that's when the right one surfaces.

The twelve who made the cut came from a broad cross-section of life. There was a paramedic who worked night shifts in the local hospital, a delivery driver, and a divorced librarian with a quiet voice and sharp eyes. A mechanic from Port Royal. A former Army chaplain. A part-time Uber driver who coached Little League in the summer. One woman ran a floral shop near the highway, another cleaned offices downtown after hours. A welder. A widowed piano teacher. A retired school principal. A second-grade assistant who brought a notebook and didn't stop writing. Seven men. Five women. Ages ranging from twenty-five to seventy-five.

Four alternates were also seated—there if someone dropped out, got sick, or cracked under pressure before the verdict was in.

Juror Five stood out from the start. He was a soft-spoken welder, barrel-chested, with a quiet authority. People turned toward him when he spoke, even the ones who didn't seem to like what he said. Juror Ten appeared just as commanding—petite and sharply dressed, she didn't blink when pressed with tough questions. Her lipstick didn't smudge, nor did her certainty. They were the ones I knew I'd need to reach. If I could convince them, the rest might follow.

By the time we'd finished, Judge LeBlanc looked ready to call it. She adjusted her glasses, glanced at the time, and dismissed the room. Opening statements would need to wait.

CHAPTER 38

INDICTMENT

STATE OF SOUTH CAROLINA COUNTY OF BEAUFORT

IN THE COURT OF GENERAL SESSIONS INDICTMENT NO.: 2026-AB-05-275

STATE OF SOUTH CAROLINA, V. MALCOLM BENJAMIN HOLT, DEFENDANT

At a Court of General Sessions, the Grand Jurors of Beaufort County present upon their oath:

Murder.

S.C. CODE SECTION 16-3-10. MURDER

That on or about 5th of May, the defendant, MALCOLM BENJAMIN HOLT, in Beaufort County, did murder with malice afore-thought. To wit: MALCOLM BENJAMIN HOLT did murder STANLEY OSCAR NEWTON per violation of Section 16-3-10 South Carolina Code of Laws (1976) as amended.

Against the peace and dignity of the State, and contrary to the statute in such case made and provided.

By the time I arrived at court, the circus had already pitched its tents.

The street outside the Beaufort County Courthouse was lined with news vans, camera tripods, and reporters shouting over each other. Satellite dishes pointed skyward. Producers barked into headsets while interns ran coffee and cables. The courthouse loomed over the chaos like a watchtower.

I kept my head down as I approached and didn't stop moving. I didn't take questions, and I didn't make eye contact. I had one job—get through the noise and get to the courtroom. Everything else was a distraction.

Inside, the foyer was crowded but quiet. Conversations were murmured and clipped. All eyes turned when I entered. After years of headlines, speculation, and outrage, the town wanted justice—or something that looked like it.

The tension was thick as I passed the Newton brothers. They glared at me as I strode past. When I reached the bottom of the stairs, five men blocked the path—broad-shouldered, dressed in jeans and checkered shirts, all scowls and grunts. Friends of the Newton brothers, no doubt. I met the gaze of the one in the center, the tallest, and didn't blink.

"How's the city car?" he grunted.

I stared at him but didn't engage. I didn't have time to deal with him now. He stepped to the side slightly, and I pushed through, bumping my shoulder firmly into his.

Upstairs, the courtroom was still settling. I greeted Bruce and Kayla, took my seat at the defense table, and opened the folder containing all my notes. Harley and his two assistants arrived. They greeted us quietly. The Newton brothers arrived next, followed by Stephen Freeman. They sat in the row behind the prosecutor's table.

Reporters followed, with their notebooks and phones, then came the rest of the crowd, filling the seats until there were none spare.

Holt was escorted in through the side door. He looked confident, firm, but not arrogant. He sat, shoulders squared and hands resting in front of him.

When the bailiff called the courtroom to order, the crowd stood. A hush fell over the room as Judge LeBlanc entered the courtroom without ceremony, her eyes cast down as she moved toward the bench. She didn't acknowledge the crowd until she was seated. She smoothed her hair with one hand, cleared her throat, and looked up to see the packed room.

Judge LeBlanc opened with the standard procedure—an outline of how the trial would unfold, a reminder to both sides of courtroom decorum, and a short word on the seriousness of the charge. She then turned to the bailiff, who gave a curt nod and moved to the side door.

A moment later, the jury entered in single file, most of them quiet, a few visibly unsure. Twelve citizens pulled from grocery stores, offices, school drop-off lines—now seated in judgment over a murder.

Judge LeBlanc spoke to them carefully, her voice low but firm. She explained their responsibility, emphasized fairness, and reminded them that what they thought they knew didn't matter, they could only consider what they would hear from the witness stand. Once she was satisfied with their nods and silence, she turned to the prosecution.

"Mr. Harley," she said, "you may begin."

Assistant Solicitor Andrew Harley rose from his chair. He adjusted his tie with one hand, gave a polite nod to the bench, and stepped toward the lectern.

"May it please the court, ladies and gentlemen of the jury.

My name is Andrew Harley and I'm a circuit solicitor with the Ninth Judicial Circuit. I represent the great state of South Carolina in bringing the charges of murder against the defendant, Mr. Malcolm Holt.

We're here today because the evidence shows Mr. Holt murdered Judge Stanley Newton.

That's what we need to focus on—the evidence. The facts. The undisputed truth.

Over the course of this trial, you'll hear from witnesses who will present the evidence to you, as nothing I say in this opening statement can be considered evidence. The opening statement is to provide you with a roadmap of what these witnesses will show.

You'll hear from the investigating officer from the Beaufort Police Department, and he'll tell you about the crime scene, where the judge was shot, and the steps they took that led to the arrest of Mr. Holt.

You'll hear from the deputy coroner, and she will explain what caused Judge Newton's death, the angle he was shot at, and whether the judge had any defensive wounds.

You'll hear from witnesses who saw Mr. Holt around the scene of the crime as gunshots rang out around their neighborhood. You'll hear from witnesses who will testify that Mr. Holt made very public and direct death threats against Judge Newton in the days before the shooting.

You'll hear from a witness who will testify she saw Mr. Holt throw a gun into the Beaufort River. You'll hear from forensic experts who recovered a gun from the Beaufort River and traced the serial number to match a firearm purchased by Mr. Holt a year before the shooting. You'll hear from a psychologist who interviewed Mr. Holt in the weeks after his arrest. She'll tell you Mr. Holt said he was feeling massive amounts of white-hot rage, and that, in his own words, he was happy the judge was dead.

You'll hear from a person who was close to Mr. Holt for a period of time, and how Mr. Holt confessed to him, in fine detail, to shooting Judge Newton.

And best of all, you'll hear from the defendant himself via the police interview he provided the day after the arrest. You'll see the recording of that interview, and you'll hear Mr. Holt admit he went to the judge's residence that night. Mr. Holt admitted to the police he was at the scene of the crime, and that he went to 'stop' Judge Newton.

All this evidence will point to one thing—Mr. Holt murdered Judge Newton.

The defense team will try to spin a story of doubt. They'll suggest this happened or that happened. But it'll only be that—a story. They can't dispute the evidence, they can't dispute the truth, and they can't dispute the facts.

At the end of this trial, after you have heard all the testimony and evidence available, I will stand before you again and ask you to provide the only reasonable outcome—guilty.

Thank you for your time."

Trials weren't just about facts.

They were tournaments of tactics, nerve, and persuasion. Every word counted, every pause a test of resolve. Some lawyers lived for this part—the performance, the pressure, the showpiece.

Harley was one of them. He seemed to have a different presence in court, as if he put on a mask and cape and became someone else. Here, to a new audience, he could be strong, he could be confident, and he could be powerful.

Harley returned to his seat. He'd delivered the prosecution's case with the confidence of a man who knew he had the weight of evidence behind him.

Across the jury box, the signs weren't hard to read.

Juror Five—the welder—had nodded almost reflexively during Harley's final points. Every reference to motive, every mention of opportunity, every appeal to justice. He didn't blink, didn't question, just followed along like the script had already been written.

Juror Ten wasn't much better. She sat rigid, lips pressed together, her expression carefully neutral but her eyes tracking Harley like he'd just handed her the answer key. She'd been that way since she stepped into the courtroom—reserved, polite, but quietly aligned with the prosecution. Body language didn't lie.

Others were harder to read. Juror Eight leaned back, arms crossed, skeptical. Juror Two hadn't moved at all, except to glance occasionally toward the defense table. Maybe she was still open. Maybe not.

I adjusted my tie, rose from my chair, and walked toward the lectern. My footsteps echoed against the wood floor. No rustle in the gallery, no murmurs. This was it. My chance to change the narrative, to reframe everything they thought they understood. The prosecution had given them the bones of a story—motive, anger, opportunity. But they hadn't given them certainty. They hadn't proven what they needed to prove.

Now it was my job to show them why.

I placed both hands on the lectern, glanced at the jury box, and paused, not too long, just enough to let the silence work, and then began.

"Thank you for your time. My name is Dean Lincoln, and with the support of my team, I act as the defense attorney for Mr. Holt.

Assistant Solicitor Andrew Harley was right about this trial—it is about the facts. It is about the evidence. And it is about the truth.

What he hasn't told you is that they have none of it.

They don't have an eyewitness to the crime. They don't have the murder weapon. They don't even have a reliable confession. So, let me be clear from the start—there's nothing that shows beyond reasonable doubt that Mr. Holt committed this crime.

There's no physical evidence that links Mr. Holt to this crime. None.

There's no witness that ties Mr. Holt to this crime. None.

And there's no forensic evidence that ties Mr. Holt to this crime.

This case is about the reasonable doubt in the story the prosecution will present to you. What is reasonable doubt? It's the doubt a reasonable person would have. And like any reasonable person, you will have reasonable doubt at the end of this trial.

What the prosecution wishes to make you do is believe a story that Mr. Holt was angry. Yes, he was angry with Judge Newton. He readily admitted that in his police interview. Is being angry a crime? No. Does being angry mean you committed murder? I hope not, or there would be thousands of suspects out there today. They want you to believe that anger is enough to prove motive. It's not.

The prosecution will ask you to ignore all the holes in this case. They'll ask you to forget about the errors. They'll ask you to substitute suspicion for proof.

But suspicion is not enough. Not in this courtroom, not in any courtroom in this state, and not in any courtroom in our great country. Suspicion is not enough.

The prosecutor has painted a picture full of drama, full of assumptions, and speculation. But when you look at what they will present, you'll find yourself asking—where is the proof?

There's no DNA evidence that links Mr. Holt to the crime. There's no blood, no tissue, and no fingerprints that link Mr. Holt to the crime.

There's no forensic evidence. None. Even after the police searched his house, his car, and his shed, they found nothing that links him to the crime. There was no blood on his clothes. No murder weapon. What they have is a weapon that belonged to Mr. Holt that shows no forensic connection to the crime.

They can't place Mr. Holt inside Judge Newton's home. There's no evidence, none, that shows Mr. Holt was ever inside the judge's home.

You'll hear from witnesses who will testify they saw two other people closer to the scene of the crime when the gunshots rang out around the neighborhood.

You'll hear from forensic witnesses who will testify there's nothing that connects Mr. Holt, or his weapon, to this crime.

In Mr. Holt's police interview, he states he received a call from a man who claims that another woman was going to be at Judge Newton's house that night. Did the police department investigate that lead? No. Did they follow that link and see how it connected to the murder? No. Instead, they let their biases and their assumptions rule this case. They ignored the leads, they ignored the links, and they focused on Mr. Holt.

Listen for the lack of evidence in this case. Listen for the lack of facts. Listen for the lack of truth.

At the end of this case, you'll only have one choice, because the prosecution will not be able to prove this case beyond reasonable doubt. That choice will be not guilty.

Thank you for your time."

CHAPTER 39

At five minutes past eleven, with opening statements completed, Judge LeBlanc asked the State to call their first witness.

Every seat in the gallery was taken, elbows brushing, knees pressed close. People shifted in their chairs, whispered behind hands, eyes fixed on the front like something might erupt at any moment. A woman near the back clutched her purse tighter. A man in the second row kept checking his watch, his foot tapping out an anxious rhythm on the floor. No one smiled.

A good first witness is essential to any murder trial, and Investigator Thomas Gray, as one of the most experienced employees in the Beaufort Police Department, was the right person for the job. A compact figure full of strength, his features were sharp. Short-cropped brown hair, clean shaven, spotless clothes. He spoke in a considered manner, with a confident tone.

"Thank you for taking the time to talk with us today," Harley opened, standing behind the lectern at the side of the room. "Can you please begin by stating your full name and current position for the court record?"

"My name is Thomas Gray, and I've been employed as an investigator by the Beaufort Police Department for over fifteen years. Prior to that, I was employed as a detective within the Boston Police Department, but Massachusetts was too cold for me. I didn't like investigating cases when it was snowing." He looked to the jury and smiled. They politely smiled back. "I much prefer the warmer weather. Give me blue skies over a snow storm any day."

"I agree with you there." Harley smiled, and the jury warmed to both of them. "Investigator Gray, can you please describe your connection to this case?"

"I was the lead investigator assigned to the homicide that occurred on May 5th three years ago at the residence of Judge Stanley Newton on Spanish Point Drive."

"Did you attend the scene of the crime?"

"I did. I attended the residence around fifteen minutes after the first officers arrived at the scene. I got the call that there was a deceased male in his living room, with apparent bullet wounds to his chest."

"And what were your initial observations when you arrived at the scene?"

"Shock. I knew the owner of the residence, Judge Newton, and I'd been to the judge's home previously, so I knew my way around. I walked up the steps to the front porch, where the first officer to attend the scene provided a debrief. He led me inside to where the judge was still in his recliner, with several bullet wounds in his chest. His head was slumped to the side, and his eyes were still open."

"Would you call the scene disturbing?"

"Objection," I stated. "Leading the witness."

"Withdrawn," Harley was quick to respond. "Investigator Gray, how would you describe the scene in your own words?"

"In my own words, I would describe it as disturbing." Gray looked at me and shrugged. "It's the vacant eyes that stick with you, especially when it's someone you've met before. It's something you never get used to. I've seen lots of blood, lots of shootings over the years, but it's the eyes that stick with me. Seeing a dead body is one thing, but that look is something else."

"Was there anyone else at the scene at that time?"

"The two officers, Officer Jones and Officer Pena, were the first to respond after a 911 call from several concerned neighbors to report the gunshots in the area. The officers arrived at the scene and after knocking on the door, they looked through the window and saw a body. They could also see blood on the person's chest, and the person wasn't responding to their calls. They entered the residence through an unlocked side door and, upon inspection, it became apparent the person was deceased. They secured the area, ensuring there were no other threats, before they called it in to their supervisor. The supervisor alerted me, and I arrived around ten minutes later. The EMTs, the Emergency Medical Technicians, arrived a minute or so after I arrived, but it was clear to all of us that the person was deceased."

"What were your next steps?"

"After the EMTs stated that due to the traumatic injuries of the gunshot wounds to the chest, the person was beyond resuscitation, we took photos, and began the search for evidence or witnesses."

"Why did the paramedics declare Judge Newton 'beyond resuscitation' and not deceased?"

"In Beaufort County, the EMTs aren't legally allowed to declare someone deceased, although they can determine they're beyond resuscitation. The deputy coroner needs to make that call. Deputy Coroner Dr. Joan Goulds arrived twenty-five minutes after the EMTs and officially made that determination at that time."

"Thank you. Was there anyone else in the home?"

"Not that we could see. We checked the residence and surrounding yard and couldn't find anyone else present. Officers Jones and Pena conducted a sweep of the grounds and the nearby buildings, but apart from the neighbors themselves, nobody else was around."

"Who were the gunshots reported by?"

"We received several calls from concerned residents along Spanish Point Drive. The first call came from Mrs. Gladys Jonty, Judge Newton's next-door neighbor. She called to say she had heard several gunshots near her home, and she was frightened. She told the operator that she was sure the gunshots came from next door. The two officers went out to investigate and that's when they saw the body through the window at the front of the house."

"How long did the officers take to respond?"

"The first officers arrived at Spanish Point Drive around five minutes after the first 911 call was received."

"Were there any other witnesses near the scene?"

"There were several people around the area near the time of the shooting, but we didn't speak to them all that night. Several witnesses later came forward after we put out a call for anyone who saw anything, but on the night, we only spoke to the direct neighbors of Judge Newton."

Harley turned a page in his file. "And when you arrived at the scene, were you able to tell how the victim died?"

"It was clear that it was the gunshot wounds to his chest that caused the death. His white T-shirt was covered in blood and there was also blood spattered all over the room."

"Were photos taken of the scene?"

"Yes. One of our investigators took photos of the scene."

"And are these the photos here?"

Harley pointed to his assistant, who typed several lines into her laptop. The screen at the side of the room came to life, and Gray confirmed they were the photos of the scene. When one particularly gruesome photo of Judge Newton appeared, several jury members looked away. A person in the gallery gasped.

After scrolling through ten photos of the scene in the living room, Harley continued. "At what point did Mr. Malcolm Holt become a suspect in your investigation?"

"Very early on. Mr. Holt had made very public threats against the judge in the days before the murder, and Judge Newton had reported his concerns to the police. Mr. Holt also called the police department earlier that night to claim Judge Newton was about to assault a young woman, so he was one of the first people we talked to. We went to his home at 8 a.m. the next morning and asked his whereabouts for the previous night. When he couldn't give us an alibi, we asked if he would come to the station to answer some further questions. He agreed to come with us."

"Was he arrested at this point?"

"No, and we made that clear to him. He voluntarily came to the station to answer our questions and was free to leave at any time. When we first questioned him, we hadn't told him what it was about. When we arrived at the station, we provided him coffee and a bagel and asked several questions about his relationship with Judge Newton."

"Did he ask for a lawyer during the interview?"

"Not for the first twenty-five minutes."

"And was the interview recorded?"

"It was."

Harley turned to his assistant again, and she typed more lines into her laptop. The recording of the police interview came on to the screen. Harley explained to the jury what they were about to watch, and then played the interview in full. It was convincing. Holt began by saying he was home the previous night, but ten minutes into the interview, he conceded he was lying. He stated he had gone to Spanish Point Drive the night before, and was intending to go to the judge's house, but panicked and fled when he heard gunshots. When the officers asked why Holt had gone to the judge's house, he avoided answering the question.

Fifteen minutes into the interview, the officers reminded Holt that he had called the police department earlier in the night to claim the judge was about to abuse another woman. Holt admitted he had gone to the judge's home to protect a girl who was under threat. He stated he had received an anonymous call that Judge Newton was going to assault another girl. He explained why he was furious with law enforcement, the justice system, and the judicial process. He talked about his daughter, and how the justice system had failed her.

Twenty minutes into the interview, Holt said he didn't own a gun.

Twenty-five minutes into the interview, when the police asked Holt why he shot the judge in the chest, he asked for a lawyer.

It was twenty-five minutes too late.

The interview recording was skipped forward an hour, and when defense attorney Chris Tomlinson arrived in the interview room, the investigators advised Holt they were placing him under arrest for the murder of Judge Newton.

When the recording concluded, Harley allowed the silence to hang in the courtroom for a while. The jury members shifted uncomfortably in their seats, there were murmurs from the gallery, and Holt didn't move, staring at the table in front of him.

When he was sure the moment had lasted long enough, Harley tapped his hand on the lectern and continued. "Investigator Gray, how did Mr. Holt seem when you first talked with him at his home?"

"Objection to the word 'seem,'" I called out. "It calls for speculation."

"Sustained," Judge LeBlanc agreed.

Harley nodded. "Can you please tell the court about his demeanor?"

"Objection. Again, the question calls for speculation. It asks for a subjective conclusion, rather than a factual observation."

"Agreed." Judge LeBlanc's tone was firm. "The objection is sustained."

Harley took a long breath to calm himself and moved on. "During your investigation, did you find the weapon that Mr. Holt owned?"

"Eventually, but not straight away. We received a witness report from a neighbor who stated she had seen someone throw something in the river moments after the shooting, and we thought this might be the murder weapon. We conducted a search of the river in the days after the homicide. However, the Beaufort River was quite swollen after a few days of heavy rain, and we didn't find anything. A week later, after a high tide, a lady was walking her dog when her dog brought the weapon back to her."

"And where was the weapon found?"

"Around two hundred and fifty yards from the residence of Judge Newton. Initially, we weren't sure if it had been used in the shooting. However, a member of the forensic team at the South Carolina Law Enforcement Division traced the serial number, looking at the purchase history of the registered firearm. On the record, the weapon was originally purchased by Mr. Holt a year prior to the shooting."

Harley nodded for a few moments, read his notes, and then continued. "You mentioned that the reason you first went to talk with Mr. Holt was that he had made death threats against the judge in the days before the homicide. What were these threats?"

"Mr. Holt waited outside Judge Newton's office after work and told Judge Newton that he was scum and said he would kill him, if given the chance. In his statement, Judge Newton reported the words as, 'If I ever have the chance, I'll kill you.'"

"Did Mr. Holt tell you why he wanted to murder Judge Newton?"

"Yes." Gray moved in his seat and adjusted his tie. "Mr. Holt's twenty-one-year-old daughter, Tennille Holt, claimed she was sexually assaulted by Judge Newton. She was doing work experience for the judge and claimed that he invited her to his home to do work after hours. While there, she stated she was drugged and sexually assaulted. The claims were investigated by the Beaufort Police Department; however, there was no evidence that what she claimed was true. Miss Tennille Holt later asked the judge for money to keep quiet about the claims."

"Were there any charges laid against Judge Newton?"

"No. There were no charges laid because there was no evidence the claims were true."

"Thank you, Investigator Gray." Harley turned back to his notes. "And what were the next steps in your investigation?"

For the next two hours and forty-five minutes, Harley walked the court through the investigation. One step at a time, one building block of evidence after the next. He didn't raise his voice. He didn't dramatize his questions. He didn't try to bend the truth. He presented cold, hard facts, one after the other, all pointing to the guilt of Malcolm Holt.

When the questioning was finished, Judge LeBlanc called for an end to the day. The jurors filed out in silence, and it was clear the prosecution had won day one.

CHAPTER 40

The following morning, the courtroom was wrapped in an expectant silence. I rose from my seat, papers in hand, and walked to the lectern. The air was cool, but my palms were warm. Every eye in the room followed me, some with curiosity, others with caution. I adjusted the microphone, cleared my throat, and met the witness's gaze.

"Investigator Gray, you made an arrest very early in your investigation. Did you consider any alternative explanations for what happened to Judge Newton?"

"We move quickly in the Beaufort Police Department, so I'll take that statement as a compliment. And yes, we considered other theories about what happened. You need to be open and flexible in a murder investigation, and once we heard what Mr. Holt told us in the interview, we made the arrest. Mr. Holt admitted he had wanted to murder Judge Newton, he admitted he had made death threats against the judge, and he admitted he had attended the scene of the crime at the time gunshots were heard."

"Did you ask him if he shot the judge?"

"Yes. You can see that in the interview."

"Please refresh our memory. What was his answer?"

"He said no."

"Did you find it strange he admitted to attending Spanish Point Drive, but denied shooting the judge?"

"No. People do all sorts of strange things under pressure."

I tapped my hand on the file in front of me. "Did you ask Mr. Holt what clothes he was wearing the night before the incident?"

"We did," Investigator Gray answered, shifting in the witness chair. "He told us he was wearing a black hooded sweatshirt and black jeans."

"And did you locate those clothes?"

"During the search of his home, we found a black hooded sweatshirt and black jeans in his bedroom closet. They matched the description he gave."

I paused for a moment. "And did you test those clothes for blood spatter?"

"We did," Gray said, then cleared his throat. "Yes, they were submitted for analysis."

"And what were the results?"

Gray hesitated. He shifted again in his seat, eyes flicking toward the prosecution table before returning to me. "There was no blood. At least not on those clothes."

I tilted my head. "No blood at all?"

He nodded once. "Correct. The report came back negative."

"So, the clothes the defendant himself admitted to wearing on the night in question were completely clean?"

"Well," Gray said, holding up a hand, "we can't say for sure those were the exact clothes he wore. Just because he said he was wearing black clothes doesn't mean it was those black clothes. He might have multiple sets of the same clothes. We didn't catalog his entire wardrobe."

"Investigator Gray, is there any forensic evidence, any at all, that ties those clothes, or any clothes in Mr. Holt's possession, to the scene of the murder?"

"No."

"No blood, no fibers, no DNA?"

"No."

I let the silence speak for itself. Two jurors exchanged quiet glances. Gray shifted again.

"Interesting," I noted. "Investigator Gray, what were your other theories about what happened to Judge Newton?"

The witness sat up straighter. "At first look at the scene, we considered if it was a burglary gone wrong, but we concluded that it appeared nothing was stolen from the home and nothing was out of place. We were still considering that line of enquiry when we began to interview people who might've had a grudge against Judge Newton."

"And Mr. Holt was the first person you interviewed?"

"He made a very credible death threat against the judge two days earlier. That was a good place to start."

"Were there many death threats against the judge?"

"It's part of being in law enforcement and the justice system. The judge had several death threats made against him over the years."

"Did you talk to the other people who had a grudge against Judge Newton?"

"Yes."

"Did you talk to them before you arrested Mr. Holt?"

"No. We talked to them after the arrest was made."

"But you interviewed them after you had made the arrest?"

"Yes."

"How long after?"

"One year, as we prepared for the trial."

I squinted. "That seems like you were trying to close the gate after the horse had bolted."

"Not at all. We knew we had the right person, but we needed to ensure he hadn't been working with anyone else."

"'*We knew we had the right person*,'" I repeated. "Do you think that sort of attitude might have caused bias in your investigation?"

"No."

"During your police interview with Mr. Holt, where he talked openly and freely, he mentioned that a call came to his cell phone that night. Mr. Holt stated"—I flicked open a file and read off it—"'*An anonymous caller called my cell and said Judge Newton was going to sexually assault another young girl in his home.*'" I left a long pause before I continued. "Did you investigate where the call came from?"

"We did."

I waited for him to continue, but he didn't. I pressed further. "And what did you find?"

"Nothing concrete."

"But something?"

"Yes."

"What does that mean?"

"It means we searched for the location of the caller, and where the number came from, and we found nothing. We sent out a subpoena to Mr. Holt's cell phone company and saw that he received a call that night. That call lasted fifty-five seconds."

"So, you were able to verify from Mr. Holt's cell phone records that a call was received that night?"

"Yes."

"But you didn't investigate further?"

"No. We didn't see how it could've been connected to the case. Mr. Holt received many calls from many people about his work as a mechanic, sometimes at all hours. We didn't see anything unusual for that pattern."

"Did you believe Mr. Holt's statement that the call was in regard to a potential sexual assault?"

"We didn't have anything that verified the caller or their information."

"But nothing to doubt it?"

"I suppose."

"In the interview played to the court, Mr. Holt said the caller claimed there was going to be a young woman at Judge Newton's house. Did you find the girl who was supposed to be there that night?"

"No."

"At any point during the investigation, did you attempt to locate the woman who was supposed to be there that night?"

"No."

"Why not?"

Gray's voice tightened. "We didn't find any evidence for the call suggesting that was said. We believed Mr. Holt fabricated those details to justify his actions."

"But you had evidence there was an anonymous call to his cell phone that night?"

"That's right."

I nodded, making my movements clear to the jury. "How many complaints of sexual assault were made against Judge Newton?"

"Objection. Relevance." Harley stood. "The victim isn't on trial here, and none of the complaints led to actual convictions."

"The State has tried to establish the motive of the defendant in their opening statement, and we believe the number of complaints against Judge Newton establishes a clear pattern of behavior. Under Rule 404(a)(2) of the South Carolina Rules of Evidence, evidence of a pertinent character trait of the victim is admissible."

"Agreed," Judge LeBlanc stated. "The objection is overruled."

"How many allegations were there against Judge Newton for sexually assaulting younger women?"

"None of the allegations led to a conviction."

"How many allegations?"

"I need to say that an allegation doesn't mean it happened. Anyone can make an allegation, but that doesn't mean it happened."

"How many allegations?"

He groaned. "Five."

"Were the situations the same in each one?"

"I didn't take the reports."

"But you've read them, yes? If you haven't read them, I would imagine it was quite an incomplete investigation into his death."

Gray sighed. "I've read the reports about the claims of sexual assault."

I paused, letting the silence stretch long enough to draw every eye. Then I turned toward the jury box. Their attention was fixed. I looked back at the witness. "During the search of Judge Newton's residence, did your team find the drug Rohypnol?"

Harley leaped to his feet. "Objection, Your Honor. Relevance."

I stepped in before the judge could respond. "The prosecution introduced this as part of their motive theory during opening statements and initial witness testimony. We are merely building on their foundation."

"Agreed." Judge LeBlanc nodded. "The objection is overruled. The witness may answer."

The investigator cleared his throat. "Yes. We did find Rohypnol in the residence."

"Did Judge Newton have a prescription for it?"

"No, he did not."

"Are you familiar with the common uses of Rohypnol?"

"Yes."

"Then, for the benefit of the court, could you please explain what that drug is typically used for?"

"Rohypnol is a sedative," he said. "It's not legally prescribed in the United States, but it's available on the black market. It's known for its ability to induce deep sedation, impair memory, and render someone incapacitated. Because of those effects, it's commonly associated with drug-facilitated illegal activity."

A murmur moved through the courtroom. I let it hang for a moment before continuing. "And how is it used illegally?"

"It's commonly referred to as a date rape drug."

"A date rape drug." I looked to the jury. Several were shaking their heads. "Do you have an explanation why he had this drug in his house?"

"He wasn't alive to ask."

"Did you find any other drugs without a prescription present in his home?"

"No."

"What about prescription drugs?"

"Judge Newton had a prescription for Alprazolam, sold under the brand name Xanax, and Sildenafil."

"Sildenafil. Is there a common name for that?"

"Viagra."

"Viagra?"

"That's correct. It's used to treat erectile dysfunction."

I looked to the jury again and nodded. When several nodded in return, I continued. "Five claims of sexual assault, five claims that young women were drugged at Judge Newton's home, five claims that were lodged with your police department over a period of several years, and not one claim led to a conviction. Do you think if those investigations found the presence of Rohypnol in Judge Newton's residence, the outcome would've been different?"

"Objection. Now we're getting well off the path. Is Mr. Lincoln claiming a defense of third-party here?"

"Mr. Lincoln?" Judge LeBlanc questioned.

"No, Your Honor."

"Then the objection is sustained."

It didn't matter. You can't un-ring a bell. The jury were all thinking the same thing—Judge Newton had it coming.

CHAPTER 41

Beaufort County Deputy Coroner Dr. Joan Goulds entered the courtroom with an indifferent look. Dressed in a black skirt with a black blazer, she showed no emotion as she swore her oath. She didn't look at the jury, and she didn't look at Holt. She waited for Harley to begin his questions, not moving once as he organized his files.

"Thank you for your time, Dr. Goulds," Harley began. "Can you please begin by telling the court your name, occupation, and what your office does?"

"My name is Dr. Joan Goulds, and for the last five years, my employment has been as a deputy coroner with the Beaufort County Coroner's Office. I've previously served as a military medical doctor, and I'm a member of the South Carolina Coroners' Association. The Beaufort County Coroner's Office investigates deaths in Beaufort County where the cause is unnatural, sudden, or unexpected, involving suspicion, or a death in custody."

"Dr. Goulds, did you examine the body of Judge Stanley Newton?"

"Yes, along with the assistance of consulting physician Dr. Marie Colston."

"And based on your examination of Judge Newton, can you please confirm the cause of death?"

"The cause of death was homicide due to multiple gunshot wounds to the torso. I examined the body, and my forensic findings were that the five gunshot wounds were consistent with close-range discharge, which caused damage to the internal organs of his torso and catastrophic hemorrhage."

"Did you examine the trajectory of the bullets?"

"I did."

"And what did that evidence tell you about the position of the shooter?"

"Given the location of the entry and exit wounds, all five gunshot trajectories traveled from the upper chest toward the lower chest, suggesting the victim was below the shooter at the time he was shot. This supports a conclusion that the shooter was standing in front of the seated victim when the shots were fired."

"Were there any defensive wounds on the judge's hands?"

"No, and there was no evidence the judge tried to defend himself at all."

"Would that suggest that he knew the victim?"

"I can't answer that, but I can tell you there was no evidence that he acted in defense when the shooter was in front of him. Given the blood spatter patterns, the evidence suggests his hands were by his side when he was first shot."

"Would he have been alive after he was shot?"

"Given the massive injuries, it's unlikely he would've survived more than a few seconds, if at all."

Harley read over the lines of the report like it was the first time he was seeing it. It wasn't. He knew the report off by heart. "Was there anything unusual about the death?"

"Unusual? No. Considering the wounds he obtained, I wouldn't say it was an unusual death. Given the shooting, I would expect that he would pass away from those wounds."

"And what time of death did you record?"

"My autopsy confirmed the findings in the paramedic report. Both the cause and the timing were consistent."

"Is there any evidence that Judge Newton could've done this to himself?"

"Absolutely not. There were five bullet wounds in his chest. There was no possibility that he did this himself. He would've died after the first two."

"In your experience, as a trained professional with more than five hundred autopsies performed, do you think these bullet wounds were an act of rage or a calculated targeting of the victim?"

"I can't speak about the shooter's state of mind, but I can tell you there was no doubt that the shooter aimed to kill the victim."

"No doubt the shooter aimed to kill the victim," Harley repeated. "Thank you, Dr. Goulds. No further questions."

I had expected more from Harley. More questions, more theatrics, more of the drawn-out fencing he was known for. It caught me off guard. He didn't even glance at the jury. Just sat back down, calm and unreadable. For a moment, I stayed seated, flipping through my notes. I stood, smoothed the front of my jacket, and made my way to the lectern. The room was hushed. Some members of the jury leaned forward, sensing the change in tempo.

"Dr. Goulds, in your examination of Judge Newton, did you conduct a toxicology report?"

"Yes. His toxicology report showed his blood alcohol reading was above 0.09, which is generally associated with higher levels of intoxication."

"Were there any other substances in his system?"

"Yes."

"And what were they?"

"There were traces of Sildenafil, which has a half-life of around four hours."

"Sildenafil. Is there a common name for that?"

"Viagra. It's used to treat erectile dysfunction."

"Was Judge Newton planning on doing something with that Viagra?"

"I can't talk about his state of mind, because I don't know. All I can tell you about is his toxicology report."

"Interesting." I let the pause sit in the room long enough for the jury to process that fact. "Dr. Goulds, was there any Rohypnol in his system?"

"No. There were no other foreign drugs found in his system other than alcohol and Viagra."

"How long is the half-life of Rohypnol?"

"Objection. The defense is trying to suggest that there is some link that isn't there. There's no relevance to the question."

"Not at all, Your Honor," I argued. "We're trying to establish the victim's state of mind before he was shot. The police found Rohypnol in his bathroom, and I would like to explore if there's any possibility that it was in his system."

"Overruled. You may answer the question."

"Eighteen to twenty-five hours."

"And would that indicate, despite the presence of the drug in his bathroom, that he hadn't used the drug in the last day. However, he had a dose of Viagra?"

"That's correct."

I tapped my hand on the folder several times. When I saw a few heads nodding, it was clear that several members of the jury knew what I was alluding to. "In your professional opinion, what do you think he was going to do with that combination of drugs?"

"Objection. This question is asking the witness to speculate. Dr. Goulds can't comment on the deceased's intentions."

"Sustained."

"Dr. Goulds, does anything you found in the autopsy indicate who shot Judge Newton?"

"No, but that's not the purpose of the report. The purpose of the report is to determine how he died."

"Does anything in your report indicate who else was in his residence at the time?"

"No, but again, that's not the purpose of the report."

"Does anything in the report indicate Mr. Holt pulled the trigger?"

"No."

"And is there anything in the report, anything at all, that points to Mr. Holt as the guilty party?"

"No."

"Thank you, Doctor." I nodded and sat down. "No further questions."

CHAPTER 42

I couldn't sleep.

No matter how hard I tried, Andrew Harley's smug smile kept reappearing in my mind. By 5 a.m. of the next morning of the trial, I had given up trying to sleep. After two cups of coffee, two Advils, and an apple, I was back at the office, reviewing file after file, line after line. At 8 a.m., I traveled to the courthouse, fueled by another cup of coffee and another two Advils.

The media pack were waiting. They swarmed around me as soon as I stepped out of the car. I had no time for them. I kept my eyes forward, and my walk steady, not saying a word to their many questions. After security checks, I entered the courtroom and continued reviewing the files.

Over the next hour, the prosecutors came in, followed by the crowd of interested parties sitting in the gallery. Holt was escorted in via a side door. He looked stressed. His shoulders were slumped, and his walk lacked energy.

Judge LeBlanc entered a few moments later, and the bailiff opened the door for the jury members.

"The State calls Kane Newton." Harley stood to begin the next day.

Kane Newton came to the court in his best suit, complete with a red tie perfectly tied into a Windsor knot, and along with his Breitling watch, he oozed a sense of wealth. He walked to the stand with his shoulders back and his head held high.

"Mr. Newton, thank you for coming to court today," Harley opened with as he stood and moved toward the lectern. "Can you please state your full name and occupation?"

"My name is Mr. Kane David Newton, and I've been employed as a day trader for the past twenty years. Originally, I was based in Manhattan, but I grew up in Beaufort, and wanted to do everything I could to get back here. Five years ago, I was able to get to a position where I could do most of my work remotely and move back to the Lowcountry. I still fly to New York once a month, but most of my work is here now."

"Did you know the deceased, Judge Newton?"

"He was my father."

"And what were you doing on the night of May 5th, three years ago?"

"I had been out to dinner at Bay Street Barbeque and was returning home at around 11 p.m. I live up the road from my father's house, and I drive past his home on the way back from Bay Street. When I was driving toward his house at 11:05 p.m., I saw Mr. Holt walking down the street, away from my father's residence."

"And how did you know it was Mr. Holt?"

"Because I saw his face. I know what the man looks like, and he looked straight at me as I drove past. My headlights shined straight at him as I approached. He was wearing a hooded sweatshirt, and he turned away from the lights, as if he was trying to hide his face."

"What were the weather conditions like that night?"

"It was a clear night. Warm. No clouds or fog."

"Are you sure it was 11:05 p.m. that you saw Mr. Holt?"

"I am, because I sent a message to my wife via voice to text to tell her that I had seen Mr. Holt walking around down my street. I asked her if she was okay, and that message was sent at 11:05 p.m."

"Was she okay?"

"She was. She responded that she was in bed, and there hadn't been any disturbances on the security footage around our home."

"What did you do next?"

"As I continued to drive back to my house, I passed my father's house. I sent a text to my father at 11:06 p.m. but didn't receive a response. He wasn't great with answering text messages, so I figured he had gone to bed. He was also struggling with some health issues, and I didn't want to wake him with a phone call. I figured I would message him in the morning and check in."

"And why would you be worried about him?"

"Because Mr. Holt had threatened him numerous times, and I was worried he would go after my family. If I'd known what had happened, I would've stopped Mr. Holt—"

"Objection. The witness is speculating what he would've done under different circumstances."

"Sustained. Let's stick to the facts, Mr. Newton."

Newton nodded to the judge and Harley continued. "What sort of threats were made against your father?"

"Death threats. Holt confronted my father several times, and I witnessed the last confrontation on the Monday before his death. I was with my father at lunch in Beaufort when Mr. Holt pointed his finger in my father's face and said, 'You're a dead man.' And then Mr. Holt ran his thumb along his own neck, indicating a slicing motion."

"What did you do?"

"I did what anybody would do. I stepped in front of my father and told that piece of dirt to get out of there. Mr. Holt then said, 'I'll kill you and your family as well.' I pushed him and he stumbled back. I'm a lot bigger and stronger than Mr. Holt, so he didn't come back at me, but I could see he was angry. He looked like he was scheming, like he was planning something."

"Did you report those threats to the police?"

"We did. It wasn't the first time Mr. Holt had made threats against my father, so the police said they'd add this new threat to his file and talk to him. But they spoke to him too late."

"Thank you, Mr. Newton. I understand this is hard for you." Harley let the silence sit in the room for a while and then continued, "Did Mr. Holt appear nervous as you drove past?"

"Objection. Speculation."

"Withdrawn," Harley responded. "Let me rephrase. Was Mr. Holt walking fast?"

"Objection. Again, this is speculation. Fast or slow is relative to his normal walking speed."

"Overruled," Judge LeBlanc stated. "You may answer the question."

"Yes. Uncomfortably fast. That's why I thought it was important to check in with my family. Mr. Holt had his head down but looked up at the headlights as I turned the corner. That's how I got a good look at his face. My headlights were shining straight at him."

"Can you confirm you saw Mr. Holt at the end of the street, only fifty yards from Judge Newton's home, on the night of the murder at 11:05 p.m., and he was walking fast with his head down?"

"That's correct."

"Thank you for your time, Mr. Newton. No further questions."

I stood to begin my questioning. "Firstly, my condolences for your father," I stated, but Kane Newton didn't respond. He looked away and waited for me to continue. "Mr. Newton, how far away was Mr. Holt as you drove past?"

"I was on the road, and Mr. Holt was on the shoulder, so I guess no more than ten feet."

"And what speed were you going at?"

"Slow. I always drive slow at night."

"Do you drive slow when you're drinking?"

"I drive slow when going down that street."

"I'll be more direct—were you drinking that night?"

"Ah, come on." He groaned. "I saw Mr. Holt walking down the street while I drove past."

"How many drinks did you have?" I pressed.

"It was him." Newton pointed his finger at Holt. "There's no doubt about it."

"Mr. Newton." My tone was firm. "How many drinks did you have that night?"

"A few."

"A few? What is that? Five, ten, fifteen? Tell me when I'm getting close."

"I don't know."

"You don't know? Is that because you had so many you could not possibly remember?"

"I can handle my drink and I know what I saw."

"There are staff members at the bar you frequent who say you regularly pass out in their bar. Is that handling your alcohol?"

"I wasn't drunk that night."

"Then tell us how many drinks you had?"

"I can't recall."

He had been prepared by the prosecution to roll out that statement whenever the question came up. It was hard to prove how much he had. He had a tab at the bar, but they only kept records for a year. His credit card total was paid at the end of every month, and there was no footage inside the bar.

"Given the amount of alcohol you drank that night, so much that you can't remember, can you be completely certain you saw the defendant on the other side of the street?"

"He looked straight at my headlights as I turned the corner."

I tapped my hand on the folder again. Thinking they were above the law seemed to run in the family. "Mr. Newton, did you know Mr. Holt personally?"

"Like I said earlier, yes."

"Were you angry with him?"

"He threatened to kill my father and threatened to kill me and my family, so yeah. I know who I saw and it was him."

"Would it be convenient for you to point the finger at Mr. Holt, even if you were drunk and it was late at night?"

"Not convenient, but truthful. That man killed my father, and my family deserves justice."

"Judge Newton deserves no justice!" A voice exploded from the back of the courtroom. Gasps rippled through the gallery. Heads turned. "He was scum!" the man continued. "And I want to shake the hand of the man who killed him!"

Judge LeBlanc slammed her gavel, the crack echoing through the room. "Silence!" she roared. "Bailiffs, remove him!"

But the man wasn't finished. "He was a rapist! And no cop was going to stop him!"

I turned to get a better look. I recognized the man from a file photo. He was one of the fathers of the young women who had suffered at the hands of Judge Newton.

"His son is no better!" he shouted as the bailiffs reached him. "Another Newton thinking the rules don't apply to him!"

The gallery was frozen. No one moved. The bailiffs dragged the man out, still yelling, his voice trailing down the hallway as the doors slammed shut.

Judge LeBlanc leaned forward, eyes blazing. "This court will have order," she said. "One more outburst like that, and we clear the room."

When the court doors slammed shut, the stunned silence hung in the room for a long moment. Judge LeBlanc composed herself and then turned to the jury. She instructed them to disregard the outburst and told them that it was to have no bearing on the evidence, or their deliberations. She confirmed their understanding, excused the witness when I confirmed I had no further questions, and called for a recess.

Her gavel dropped. The tension didn't.

CHAPTER 43

"The State calls Dr. Belinda Lyon."

Dr. Lyon walked with confidence. She swore her oath and sat in the witness box with the calm stillness of someone who believes in themselves. Her auburn hair was pulled back, her suit was tailored but serious, and her glasses were modern enough to suggest relevance without being flashy.

She presented herself as measured, neutral, and a person whose knowledge of their chosen subject was unquestionable.

"Thank you for taking the time to talk with us today, Dr. Lyon," Harley began, still sitting behind his desk, with his laptop open in front of him, but to the side. Harley opened by reviewing Dr. Lyon's extensive background, a necessary step to demonstrate her authority to testify in a professional capacity. Unlike a lay witness, who can only recount personal observations or actions, a specialist is permitted to interpret scientific findings and offer conclusions based on their field of expertise. "Can you please tell the court your occupation and experience?"

"My name is Dr. Lyon, and I'm a licensed clinical and forensic psychologist. I have a doctorate in clinical psychology from Clemson University, and I completed a postdoctoral fellowship in forensic psychology from the University of Denver. I have been practicing for fifteen years, and over the last five years, my area of focus has been the evaluation of persons involved in the criminal justice system. I make assessments related to criminal responsibility, risk of violence, and trauma-related disorders."

"Did you interview Mr. Holt following his arrest?"

"I did. Multiple times. We met five times during the first month after he was taken into custody."

"And you documented those sessions?"

"Yes. I compiled a detailed report based on my clinical impressions and Mr. Holt's emotional responses during those meetings."

"And what was your impression of his emotional state?"

Dr. Lyon sat up a little straighter. "He expressed satisfaction. He was glad Judge Newton was dead."

"Objection," I said, rising from my seat. "Speculation."

"Your Honor," Harley interjected, "Dr. Lyon is a qualified expert and may testify to her observations and interpretations during clinical interviews."

"Overruled," Judge LeBlanc said. "She may continue."

"I'm not guessing," Dr. Lyon added. "Mr. Holt told me, in his own words, that he was happy Judge Newton was dead. He said more than once that he was relieved Judge Newton could no longer hurt anyone."

Harley stepped forward, and his tone sharpened. "Dr. Lyon, in your experience, is that a typical emotional response from someone who claims to be innocent?"

"No," she replied. "Innocent individuals usually express remorse, grief, or anger—sometimes confusion or frustration. Rarely do they display relief or happiness over the death of another person."

Harley lifted the report in his hand. "This is the document you prepared?"

"It is."

"And in the report, your findings remained consistent?"

"They did."

"And in your professional opinion, Dr. Lyon, was Mr. Holt competent to stand trial?"

"Yes. He demonstrated a full understanding of his legal situation, the charges he was facing, and the nature of the proceedings."

"Did he express any regret at any point during your sessions?"

"No. None at all."

"Can you describe the defendant's emotional state at the times you interviewed him?"

"Objection," I said. "This is conjecture. The question is asking the witness to guess or assume an emotional state of which she cannot be sure."

"We've established she's an expert, Your Honor," Harley argued. "Dr. Lyon can comment on her findings."

Harley didn't need to explain any further as Judge LeBlanc waved for him to stop. "Overruled. You may answer the question, Dr. Lyon."

"He was filled with rage toward the judge. His face would twitch every time I said the judge's name, and he refused to say the judge's name. He called him, 'that man.'"

"Did you ask him to call the judge by his name?"

"I did. And he refused to give the man a name."

"Did he describe the night to you?"

"He did. He said he received a call on his cell phone saying that the judge was going to abuse another young woman in his home. Mr. Holt stated that he called the police about this, and they said they weren't going to do anything about it. Mr. Holt then explained that he worked himself into a rage, unable to think straight. Under this 'haze of rage,' as he called it, he drove to the judge's house. He drove past the house twice before stopping farther down the street.

He said he stopped farther down the street so nobody would see him. He then exited the car. He said he got out of his car with the intention to stop Judge Newton abusing another woman. He said he walked toward the judge's house, and that's when he heard five gunshots. He said he didn't know where the gunshots came from, so he ran back to his car and left before the gunman turned on him."

"Seems like a reasonable reaction to the situation, would you agree?"

"If that's what happened, yes, but I must add that I'm only relying on what he told me. And, as noted in my report, it's possible the rage he was feeling made him disassociate when he approached the judge's house. It's a very real possibility that he doesn't remember going into the judge's home, because his mental state was altered."

"Interesting," Harley noted, highlighting the fact for the jury. "Did Mr. Holt describe any physical or verbal clues that are associated with someone in the grip of rage?"

"He did. Mr. Holt described going white and blanking out before arriving at the judge's house. He said he was 'under some sort of spell.'"

"In your professional opinion, did the defendant's response align with someone who was experiencing intense and uncontrollable rage?"

"Yes."

Harley asked several more questions over the next fifteen minutes, but it all amounted to the same thing—Holt was angry at the judge and was not at all saddened by his death.

When Harley finished, I rose from my chair, straightened my jacket, and stepped away from the defense table. This was my moment to challenge and reveal what the prosecution had missed. I took a breath, steadied my voice, and locked eyes with the witness. "Dr. Lyon, thank you for talking to us. Is it true that assessing someone's personal state in hindsight, especially an emotion as complex as rage, is highly subjective?"

"That's true. Although, in this case, I was assessing what Mr. Holt told me."

"Could nerves, anxiety, or anger be mistaken for rage?"

"At times, yes."

"Did the defendant state he was experiencing rage, or was that the conclusion you drew from the interview?"

"It was both. He said it, but I also drew the same conclusion from the interviews."

"Would significant stress also explain the behaviors you observed?"

"Possibly, yes."

"Dr. Lyon," I said as I approached the lectern, "do you use social media?"

"Yes," she replied, sitting up a little straighter.

"Did you use it in 2005?"

She squinted slightly, confused. "I used a website called Myspace when I was in college, but I'm not sure where this is going."

"Let me clarify. Did you post, in 2005, the following statement on Myspace: 'Criminals will say anything to stay out of prison.'?"

Harley was on his feet in an instant. "Objection—relevance. That comment is over two decades old and has nothing to do with her testimony today."

"She's been qualified as an expert witness," I countered. "Her impartiality and credibility are open to scrutiny."

Judge LeBlanc nodded. "Overruled. She may answer."

Dr. Lyon hesitated. "I . . . I'm not sure. That was a long time ago. I have no idea what I posted over twenty years ago."

I held up the printed post for the record. "Is this your account?"

She leaned forward, reading the paper. Her lips pressed into a line. "Yes, but that quote is taken out of context. I was a student back then, and I hardly think it reflects my current professional judgment."

"It speaks to bias," I said, keeping my tone level. "Please answer the question. Did you write it?"

She exhaled. "Yes. I wrote it. But again, I was in college. I've grown a great deal professionally since then."

"And yet you're here testifying about the mindset of a man whose freedom hangs in the balance."

"And I stand by the contents of my report," she snapped. "Every exchange between Mr. Holt and myself is fully documented. I do what's right—for the court, for the process."

I nodded. "Even though, by your own admission, you once believed all criminals will say anything to avoid prison."

She stiffened. The courtroom was quiet. Her breathing had quickened. Her reputation hung in the stillness.

I shook my head lightly, appearing more disappointed than angry. "No further questions."

CHAPTER 44

"Please state your name and occupation." Harley tapped his pen on the open file in front of him, fixing his eyes on the witness.

"My name is Dr. Matthew Jones, and I'm a forensic analyst for the South Carolina Law Enforcement Division, or SLED as we are often referred to." Dr. Jones was a large man, large enough for the bailiff to change the chair in the witness box during the break. Standing over six foot five and at least 300 pounds, he trudged past with heavy feet and heavy breathing. "Throughout South Carolina, forensic evidence in homicide cases is often analyzed by us at our central laboratory in Columbia, the state capital."

"And what were you asked to analyze?"

"A handgun that was found near the scene of the crime a week after the incident. We were asked by the Beaufort Police Department to forensically analyze the weapon."

"What did you find when you examined the firearm that was recovered from the river?"

"It was a Glock 19. Using federal records, we traced the serial number and were able to trace the purchase history of the firearm. It was originally purchased by Mr. Holt."

"And in what condition was the weapon when it was recovered?"

"It had been submerged in water for several days and had been exposed to high humidity, sun, salt, and river water. The prolonged submersion in a damp environment impacted our ability to examine the forensic evidence."

"In what way?"

"We couldn't test the weapon to match the bullet. It's common for exposure to the elements to degrade the microscopic markings used for a conclusive bullet match. When analyzing forensic ballistics, there's the potential to match a bullet to a specific firearm. When we study the microscopic striations, which are the unique marks left on a bullet when it's fired through a gun's barrel, we can match a bullet to a gun. However, when the gun is exposed to adverse conditions, such as being submerged in water, or exposed to high humidity, the markings can be obscured or eroded."

"But you could match the bullet to a gun type?"

"Yes. We could match it to a Glock."

"Thank you, Dr. Jones."

Harley closed the file on his desk and I stood. "Dr. Jones, was there any evidence at all that this weapon had been fired recently?"

"No, but there wasn't any way to check this due to the condition of the weapon."

"And given that you cannot match the bullet, nor prove whether it had been fired recently, how can you be confident it was used in the murder?"

"We can't. What we know is—"

"Thank you, Dr. Jones. How do you account for the possibility that similar firearms, which are widely available, might share these same physical characteristics?"

"It was found near the scene of the crime."

"And?"

"That's it."

"That's it?" I scoffed. "So the link is less than certain?"

The witness shrugged.

"Please answer the question verbally."

"Maybe."

My voice rose. "Maybe? Is it true that there's nothing, nothing at all, that links this weapon to the murder?"

"There's the location."

"The location?! Are you suggesting that every gun within a mile's distance could've been used in the shooting?"

"No."

"Is it true that there's nothing, nothing at all, that links them together?"

"The make and location link them to the crime."

"And I'll ask again—are you suggesting that every Glock within a mile's distance from the scene could've been used in the shooting?"

"No."

"In your analysis, and your analysis alone, what else links them?"

He sucked in a deep breath. "Nothing."

"Nothing," I repeated. "Nothing." I shook my head several times and sat down. "We have no further questions for this witness."

CHAPTER 45

Harley called Mrs. Stacey Curtis next.

She was quiet as she made her way to the stand, eyes lowered, avoiding eye contact with anyone in the gallery. Her blue dress was modest, paired with a fitted black blazer and understated gold earrings that caught the light as she moved. Harley asked the preliminary questions about her name and occupation, then stood and walked to the lectern. "Mrs. Curtis, where were you at 11 p.m. on May 5th three years ago?"

"At the time, I lived five doors down from Judge Newton's residence. My husband and I have since moved from that address, not long after the shooting, but we lived on Spanish Point Drive for around five years. We moved out of the family home because my daughter moved to LA, and the house seemed too big without her in it. She's an actress. She won several beauty pageants when she was little and always knew she was going to be successful. She's had two roles now on two different sitcoms. I'm so proud of her."

"Well, congratulations," Harley quipped, but it sounded patronizing. "And on the night in question, did you notice anyone entering or lingering around the street?"

"I did. I noticed a man parked in his car down the road from me. I thought it was suspicious that he was sitting in his car, and I thought he might've been there to rob a house. He was sitting in a dark blue Chevy sedan. I called my husband, who was at work at the hospital, and he told me to lock the doors and call the police if he got out of the car."

"Did you see the man exit the car?"

"No. I was going around the house, locking the doors and all the windows, when I heard several gunshots. After I heard the gunshots, I looked out the window at the car and saw it was empty. I looked in the other direction and that's when I saw Mr. Holt. And I know it was Mr. Holt because he fixed my car several times when there were some faults with it. He was a good mechanic, and he treated us well. He even came out to change a flat tire for me one day when I hit a curb. I trust him, and whatever he did, I would say he had a good reason for doing it."

Harley squinted and shook his head. This was not going the way he rehearsed. "When Mr. Holt was walking back to his car, did you observe him doing anything else?"

"Yes."

"And what was that?"

She sighed and looked at Holt like she was sorry she had to tell the truth. "Two cars passed him in the street, and that's when he turned toward my house. I thought about going down to see him, to see if he was alright, but I was scared by the gunshots. He walked past my house, and then to the river. I saw him go to the edge of the river and throw something in there. From where I was, it looked like a gun."

"And how far away were you?"

"About twenty-five yards. He took the gun out of his pocket and looked at it for a while, like he was thinking about what to do next. Then he tossed it as hard as he could into the river, and it landed in the water."

"And what did he do next?"

"He jogged back to the car and looked like he was trying to stay in the shadows. When he got back in his car, he sped off and I didn't see him again. The police sirens came about a minute or two later, and for the rest of the night, the street was filled with swirling lights."

"Did you notice the defendant interacting with anyone else, or was he alone?"

"No, he was alone."

"And what was Mr. Holt wearing?"

"A black hooded sweatshirt and black jeans. When he went into the shadows, he was hard to see."

"And which window of the house were you watching this out of?"

"The bedroom window on the upper floor. It's where my husband keeps his gun, so I thought that's where I would be safest. Spanish Point Drive is usually a quiet area, and except for that night, we didn't get any trouble. That's why I was so stunned to hear gunshots. I didn't expect it, and I was curious to know what had happened. I like to know what happens in my neighborhood."

"Thank you, Mrs. Curtis. No further questions."

As soon as Harley sat down, I stood. "Mrs. Curtis, is it true you didn't see Mr. Holt engage in any criminal activity?"

"I saw him throw something in the river, and from where I was, it looked like a gun. I don't know what make it was, but the way he looked at it, seemed like he was contemplating something."

"Did you see him fire the gun?"

"No."

I waited a few moments, tapping my hand on the file I had compiled about her, and then began my next line of questioning. "Mrs. Curtis, were you drinking that night?"

"Maybe. I don't mind a glass of wine now and again."

"Now and again? Mrs. Curtis, did you enter a rehabilitation program for alcohol abuse only five weeks after that night?"

"Ah." She sat up straighter. "Yes."

"So, it is likely you were drinking alcohol that night?"

She nodded. "Yes. I was probably drinking a lot of alcohol at that time. My daughter had moved out, and I was dealing with empty nest syndrome. It was lonely without her in the house, and alcohol was an easy fix for that."

"And had you been using drugs that day?"

She stared at me. Her mouth was firmly shut.

"Mrs. Curtis? Were you using drugs that day?"

"I had a prescription for Valium."

"Valium?"

"Yes. It was for my nerves. I get overwhelmed at times and really anxious."

"And how does this interact with alcohol?"

"Objection," Harley said. "There's no relevance to this line of questioning. The witness is not on trial."

"Your Honor," I argued. "The witness is claiming to have seen something on the day in question, and we are merely establishing her mental state at that time."

"Overruled." Judge LeBlanc didn't take long to consider the objection. "You may answer the question, Mrs. Curtis."

"Uh." Curtis stumbled over her answer. "It makes you drowsy."

"Drowsy," I repeated. "And Mrs. Curtis, when the police came door-knocking later that night, did you answer the door?"

"Yes."

"Were they able to take a statement from you?"

"No, they said they would come back in the morning to talk to me again."

"Why is that?"

"Because . . ." she sighed. "Because I wasn't very coherent when they were talking to me. I guess the alcohol and Valium did that."

"Incoherent. That's what the police officers noted in their report when they door-knocked your house that night. Do you think, in your incoherent state, that you might have mistaken what you saw in Mr. Holt's hands?"

"I don't know." She shrugged. "Maybe."

"Maybe. In your incoherent state, you claimed to have seen the defendant throw something in the river, but you were high on alcohol and Valium." I looked to the jury, and several were shaking their heads in disappointment. "Your Honor, we have no further questions for this witness."

CHAPTER 46

The following days of the trial moved with a slow, methodical rhythm that only seasoned courtroom veterans could endure. It was a week where the truth didn't arrive with a bang but with a series of dull thuds—one witness at a time, one report after another, one more detail added to the pile.

Sharon Kelley, an administrative employee of the court, testified. She was calm on the stand, dressed in a navy pantsuit, her voice clear and certain. She testified that two weeks before the murder, she had overheard a confrontation outside Judge Newton's office. Holt had confronted the judge, and while she couldn't quote it word for word, she was sure of the tone—and the threat.

"He said the judge was going to get what he deserved," she told the jury. "Said he wasn't finished with him."

Harley guided her through her statement, then stepped aside. I asked a few questions in cross-examination, but it didn't matter. There wasn't much to argue. What was said was said.

The next two days were consumed by forensic testimony—painstaking and precise. Blood spatter analysts, a crime scene technician, and a forensic pathologist took turns explaining, with diagrams and photographs and reports, how the crime had unfolded.

The blood on the judge's floor told a story, they said. A short-range shot to the chest. Close enough that the blood mist had hit the bookcase behind him. Consistent with the angle Holt would've fired from, given his height, the room layout, and the entry wound. The crime scene technician stated there was no sign of forced entry.

Then came Trevor McMillan, a former colleague of Holt's. He didn't want to be there, and it showed. He shifted in the witness chair, trying to find a comfortable position. His eyes scanned the courtroom like a man looking for an escape.

"He hated the judge," McMillan said, after being pressed. "I'm not proud to say it, but he talked about him all the time. Said he was corrupt. Said he ruined people. I heard him say more than once that he wished the guy would disappear."

"Disappear?" Harley asked.

"Yes, sir."

"Did he ever mention harming him?"

Trevor hesitated. "Not directly. But you didn't need a dictionary to figure out what he meant."

No witness landed a knockout punch—but together, they pushed the needle. Motive. Intent. Threats. Harley was playing the long game, stitching a narrative of subdued anger that grew louder and darker over time.

Holt sat through it all without flinching, his hands folded on the table. Bruce took notes like a machine. I listened, knowing our turn would come—but also knowing the damage was starting to show.

The week ended on a Friday afternoon with another expert from SLED—the South Carolina Law Enforcement Division—who testified that digital traces of Holt's movements near the judge's home couldn't be ruled out. Cell tower pings. Weak signals, but signals, nonetheless.

By the time the court recessed for the weekend, the jurors looked tired. So did the judge. But Harley looked calm, composed, and confident.

He had drawn the outline. He had set up the finish. And next, he would hammer it home with the jailhouse snitch.

CHAPTER 47

On the second weekend of the trial, I received a call from Julie Steinberg. She sounded nervous and asked me to meet with an old friend of hers for coffee. We met beneath the awning of the Wisteria Café on Carteret Street. It was a gorgeous little café, full of Southern charm and welcoming smiles. The smell of local coffee roasted strong, competing against the smell of freshly baked breads.

Bill Randall, a senior manager with the South Carolina Department of Revenue, was sitting with Julie, sipping a mug of coffee. He greeted me with a firm handshake and a solemn nod. A solid man with a stern face, he was an old friend of Julie's, and also a veteran. As was the way of the South, we didn't move straight on to business. We chatted about our common connections for five minutes before I moved the conversation on.

"What have you found out, Bill?" I asked.

Bill drew a breath and sighed. "A few weeks ago, I called Julie to tell her that her license within my department had been flagged. I had no idea who flagged it, but the information was there." He looked at Julie and sighed. "But now her account has been marked."

"What does that mean?"

"Flagging the account means it's being watched, but once the account is marked, it means the department will take Julie's liquor license if she's found guilty of any further charges."

"Even for a misdemeanor?" I questioned.

"I'm afraid so. When an account is marked like this, there's no going back. You can try to fight it, but you won't win. The rules clearly state that, if found guilty, she has violated the terms of the liquor license." Bill looked around the café. Nobody was listening. "I hadn't seen a file marked before a conviction. I've only ever seen them marked afterward, and even then, it can take months before the license is suspended."

I sat back in shock while Julie nodded her head.

"There must be a hundred people with liquor licenses and previous misdemeanors. Why is Julie being targeted?"

"Someone accessed her file. I work in a related office, but liquor licenses aren't one of my responsibilities. Someone made the effort to find her file and mark it down for suspension."

"You're saying there are other influences here?"

"I'm saying I'm surprised Julie's file was marked *before* a conviction." He leaned forward and lowered his voice. "Anything beyond that and you're going to have to draw your own conclusions. I don't have information on who marked the file or when, but it's being monitored closely."

I sat back and let the thoughts settle. We were fighting an uphill battle, fighting against powerful enemies, and I wasn't sure if we could win.

CHAPTER 48

I didn't have time for a game of golf, but Bruce insisted we hit balls at the driving range. It was good to let off steam, he said. I relented and joined him for an hour at lunchtime on Saturday.

"I'm worried about Stephen Freeman, Dean."

"I'm sure he can handle the trial."

"Not like that." Bruce shook his head. "He's going off the deep end. He came to my house yesterday and started talking about all sorts of crazy things. He didn't even make sense. He started talking about the river and the building zones approved by the council in the nineties. It had nothing to do with me, or the conversation. He wasn't just talking; he's losing his grip on reality. The court case, and Paul finding religion, have sent him into a spin."

"Needs medication?"

"Probably needs the whole pharmacy," Bruce quipped. "But I'm serious, Dean. Watch where you step. If Stephen Freeman is losing it, he might explode before then. And you've been the one so determined to antagonize him. You might become his target."

His words lingered in my head as we took out our frustration on the driving range, launching one ball after another into the distance. It wasn't about aim, it wasn't about the distance, it was about the release of anger.

Later, after a few hours at the office, I still couldn't shake the tension. That evening, I drove Emma down to Tybee Island—a quiet stretch of coast around ninety minutes south of Beaufort. It was the type of place that softened your breathing the moment you arrived. Salt in the air, waves licking the shore, no cell signal worth chasing. For a while, it almost worked. The case faded into the background. Almost.

Emma and I found a quiet seafood place off the main road—low lighting, white tablecloths, a small menu. We talked about everything but the case. We talked about our hopes for the future, discussed potential names for our unborn baby, and laughed at their potential career choices. Astronaut, I suggested. More likely a lawyer in the making, Emma retorted. She was sure the baby would have more of my genes than hers. I hoped they didn't.

After dinner, we walked the shoreline as the sun dropped, and the shadows grew long, stretching toward the dunes. The sky turned a pale orange pink, and the ocean, dark as the evening set in, seemed to move slower, gentler, as if it was winding down for the night. The air smelled of salt and something earthy, seaweed maybe, or driftwood baked in the sun. There was a soft wind, just enough to keep the sand shifting in waves across the beach. Everything was quiet. No traffic. No voices. Nothing to distract us from Mother Nature's beauty.

For a while, I forgot about the trial. About the Freeman family. About all the danger and chaos waiting for me back in Beaufort.

"I love coming down here." Emma snuggled into my arm. "It's where my mother and father used to come when I was little. Dad grew up around here, and had family nearby, so we were always down this way. Mom loved it too. I had cousins that lived near the beach, and we would spend hours walking along these dunes. Mom would have to call us in every night we were here, and sometimes, when the days were long, we'd rush in, fill our faces with food, and then run back out to the dunes."

"How is your mother?"

"Recovering. She's determined to beat the infection and the doctors think she will. She's fighting hard so she can meet bub." Emma rubbed her stomach and looked out to the horizon. "Time moves so much slower here. Maybe we should all move down here and stretch out the time we have together."

"Time moves slower because we're closer to the equator."

"What does that matter?"

"According to Einstein's theory of relativity, the faster you move, the slower time passes for you. The Earth rotates faster at the equator than at the poles. While gravity is weaker at the equator, which would cause time to pass more quickly, overall, time moves slower near the equator than at the poles due to the higher rotational speed of the planet."

"How much slower?"

"Nanoseconds per year."

"Thanks, Mr. Science." Emma laughed and punched my arm gently. "Here I am talking about the magic of the world, and you want to prove it's not magic, it's science."

I offered her a small smile.

"You're still stressed, aren't you?" she asked.

"The jailhouse snitch takes the stand Monday," I said, exhaling hard. "I can't stop thinking about it. Everything's moving fast now. We're getting close to the edge."

Emma stopped walking and placed her hand gently over her stomach. Her protective instincts kicked in. "Do you think the baby's safe?"

"Safe?"

Her voice dropped. "Things are escalating, Dean. Freeman . . . he's unraveling. Rumors around town are that he's descending into madness."

I nodded. "Maybe you should leave Beaufort for a few weeks."

She shook her head. "I can't. My mother's still recovering. She needs me right now. I need to be here."

I pulled her close, lowering my voice. "It's okay. The threat level's low. We'll be fine."

Emma didn't answer right away. She bit her lip, hesitated. That hesitation said more than her silence.

"What is it?" I asked.

"I've seen someone on our street," she said. "The last two nights. Walking up and down the street and watching the house."

My pulse ticked up. "What did he look like?"

"Thin. Maybe in his thirties. Jeans, boots, black T-shirt. Has a scar on his face. Wanders up and down the street a few times, looking around at the houses. I've never seen him in the neighborhood before."

"Could be a gardener," I said, though even as the words left my mouth, I didn't believe them.

She didn't either.

"There's not much time left in the case," she said. "We need to hold on for a little while longer."

I gripped Emma's hand tighter. The pressure was building, and the risk was already too high.

CHAPTER 49

On Sunday morning, I parked my SUV at the edge of the dockyard. As I stepped out, I was hit by the strong smell of seafood, salt, and pluff mud. Incredibly strong. Almost overpowering. The wooden deck was aged, sitting at the edge of the marsh on St. Helena Island, with two shrimp trawlers clinking in the wind. Seagulls squawked overhead, a constant in this part of the world. I noticed the beaten-up pickup that had run me off the road weeks earlier parked on the far side of the lot near the shrimping boats. It only increased my anger.

I strode across the parking lot and pushed open the glass door to the Newton Fishing offices. The single-story red-brick building appeared modern and clean, a stark contrast to the boats and the dock only yards away.

The secretary looked up from her computer as I strode inside.

"Where's Robert Newton?" I asked firmly.

"He's in his office." She smiled and pointed toward the end of the hallway. "He doesn't usually have appointments on a Sunday. Is he expecting you?"

I didn't offer a response as I marched toward his office. I didn't knock. I threw the door open.

Robert Newton looked up from a stack of paper files, startled.

"Well, well. Dean Lincoln," he said. He closed the file in front of him and his jaw clenched tight. "You here to get a job? I could do with someone your size out on the shrimp boats."

I stepped inside his office and leaned my hands on his wooden desk. "You've been by my house."

"Beaufort's a free town, last I checked. Maybe I enjoy long walks by the water. Maybe I like that old historic neighborhood you live in."

My hands clenched, and I narrowed my eyes. "My wife has seen you twice in the last week. Lingering. Outside the azaleas. You think that's some kind of game?"

Robert laughed. A dry, brittle sound. "Women are jumpy, aren't they? You can never trust them. That's why I always make sure I have a mistress. Keeps everyone happy."

"What were you doing at my house?"

"Who said I was there? Maybe your wife saw a shadow. Maybe she saw a ghost."

I leaned forward and lowered my tone. "You come near my house again, I'll file a court injunction so fast your boats won't leave the dock for ten years. And if I catch you within fifty yards of my wife, I won't need a courtroom."

Robert's grin faded.

"I got nothing to hide," he muttered.

"You do." I held his gaze. "You're worried about what's going to come out in Holt's court case. You're worried about what I already know. You're worried that I know about the Cayman Islands and the exorbitant amount you pay for docking fees."

"That's for tuna fishing," he said, but his voice wavered.

"You're sloppy, Robert."

Robert's jaw twitched and he stood. "You think you're some kind of big-shot lawyer—"

"I am the lawyer that can tear you apart," I cut in. "And I'll never be threatened by a fishing-boat thug who can't keep his books clean. This is your only warning. Stay away from my wife, stay away from my house, or next time I'm not coming with words."

Robert didn't answer. He stared at me as he sat back down, avoiding eye contact. I turned and left the building. My threats had been received.

CHAPTER 50

By 8:55 a.m. on Monday morning, the courthouse was humming.

Media clustered outside like vultures. The victim's family talked to the media, and the family's supporters hovered in the background. Sheriffs stayed around the court, ensuring order was maintained. Interested onlookers, of which there were many, lined up to pass through security. Inside the courthouse, the tension remained.

At 10 a.m., the bailiff called the court to order, and Judge LeBlanc entered. She welcomed the lawyers, commented on the size of the gallery, and then asked the bailiff to bring the jurors in. When they were settled, she instructed Harley to start week two.

The doors opened, and the witness was escorted in by a deputy. No handcuffs, no shackles, just a plain gray blazer over an open-collared shirt. Despite his casual appearance, everyone knew what he was—the type of witness who didn't get called unless the prosecution was out of better options. A hush fell over the courtroom as he took the stand. The jurors watched closely, but their faces were unreadable. A jailhouse informant always carried baggage, no matter how neatly he was dressed.

Dalwick was a small man, with pale, patchy skin. His head looked too big for his body, his eyes were shifty, and he flinched at any loud sound. Despite his meek appearance, his long list of convictions showed an anger problem. It was often said that the cruelest bullies were the ones who had endured the worst bullying and judging by Dalwick's stepfather's long list of domestic violence offenses, Dalwick had endured violence most of his life. He didn't know any other way.

Again, I objected to the witness, but again, Judge LeBlanc overruled my objection.

"Please state your full name for the record." Harley's tone was cold as he sat behind his desk.

"Jonathon James Dalwick."

"What facility are you currently incarcerated in, and how long is your sentence?"

"Broad River. And it's ten more years before I get out. I got done for robbing a gas station and injuring the attendant. I didn't mean to. I was messed up on drugs and that took over. I regret that every day of my life, but I'm clean now. I've given all that away."

"Have you been promised anything in exchange for your testimony today?"

"Yes."

"And what is that?"

"The solicitor agreed to recommend a one-year sentence reduction if I testified truthfully."

"So you're receiving a benefit for cooperating?"

"Yes, sir, but it's no easy thing. Telling the truth in a case like this puts a target on your back. Snitches don't do well in prison. But I had to come here and say what I heard. Because what he told me . . . it stuck."

"Thank you, Mr. Dalwick. Were you in contact with the defendant during your stay in Broad River?"

"Yeah. We shared a cell. Broad River has two people to a cell, and Malcolm and I were together for a few weeks."

"Did you talk with the defendant?"

"Many times. You don't have much choice in prison. There's not much else to do. So, we talked about all sorts of things. Like, what we would do when we got out, the girls we'd known throughout our lives, the guards, and the best way to survive back there."

"Did you talk about the crimes you committed?"

"You've got to pass the time somehow. After a while, you run out of things to say to each other, so you start talking about what put you behind bars. All prisoners talk about it, but most people say they were set up. Some guys, well, they can't help but tell the truth because they're proud of what they did."

"Did Mr. Holt talk about what crimes he had committed in the past?"

"He did. Like I said, some guys are proud of what put them there. So, yeah, Holt talked about what he did. He talked a lot about Judge Newton."

"And what did he tell you happened that night?"

"He said he got a call that Judge Newton was going to abuse another girl, so he called the police. They didn't do anything about it, but he knew he had to stop it. So, he drove to Judge Newton's place and went there to kill Judge Newton. He said he walked up to the front door, saw it was locked, and then went through the side door. That's when he saw Judge Newton was waiting for a girl, so he went in and shot him five times in the chest."

"Was there anything else he told you?"

"He said he picked up three of the bullet shells, but two rolled away and he couldn't spend much time looking for them. He said he then went to the river and threw his gun into the water so nobody could match it to the bullets."

"Any other details?"

"Yeah. He said that when he went into the house, the lights were off, but there was a candle burning in the living room."

"A candle in the living room," Harley repeated. "Are you aware that information was never made public?"

"I didn't know that until the detectives told me."

"Did Mr. Holt talk about his mental state while he was shooting the judge?"

"He did. He said he was so consumed with rage that he could barely remember what happened. He remembered walking into the judge's home, and then shooting him, but blacking out after that. He said it felt like a white-hot rage of anger."

"Did Mr. Holt mention the word 'revenge?'"

"Not really. He was more interested in stopping the judge from abusing someone else. I don't think it was about revenge for him. It was about stopping the judge because the police couldn't. And I get it. I would do the same if the judge assaulted my daughter."

"Thank you, Mr. Dalwick." Harley paused. "Were you the only person he discussed it with?"

"Yeah. I think so. He felt comfortable with me because we went to the same high school, even though he graduated a decade before me. We had the same upbringing and could relate to the same sort of life."

"When he was talking about shooting the judge, did Mr. Holt express regret?"

"Nope. He was happy about it. He even said he was happy the judge was dead."

"Thank you, Mr. Dalwick. No further questions."

Harley sat down and I stood. It was time to tear this prisoner apart.

CHAPTER 51

Dalwick shifted in the witness chair, his hands restless in his lap, his eyes darting between the jury and the floor. He wasn't used to this kind of attention—the glaring spotlight on him, a dozen strangers judging every word, and a defense lawyer eager to drag every uncomfortable truth into the open. Dalwick had told his story. He'd told his lies. Now he had to hold it together while I tried to break him down.

"Mr. Dalwick, do you understand that you're under oath, and that your testimony will be scrutinized?" I raised my voice as I walked to the lectern.

"Yeah."

"Were you offered certain benefits or leniency in exchange for your cooperation with the prosecution?"

"Yeah. I said that."

"Were you ever coached or given instructions by law enforcement on what details to report about your conversation with the defendant?"

"I wasn't coached about anything. I told the truth about what Holt said to me."

"Were you alone with Mr. Holt when he made this confession?"

"Yeah. That's what happens in cells, pal. Two to a cell. That's it."

I paused. I was getting under his skin. That was good. "How clearly do you remember that conversation?"

"Clear as day."

"Can you provide the exact words the defendant allegedly used?"

"Well, not the exact words, but I know what he said. I know everything he told me."

"So, not as clear as day?"

"I remember the conversation, man. What more do you want? I couldn't write it down because I didn't have a pen and paper."

"Considering the stressful conditions of incarceration, is it possible your memory of that conversation is unreliable?"

"Nah. What I said was real. I said that."

"And when did you come forward with this information about his so-called confession?"

"After he told me. I couldn't do it before he told me, because, he hadn't told me. Are you stupid, man?"

He was quick to anger and that was working in our favor. "And Mr. Dalwick, how could you be sure he was telling the truth?"

"You can see it in their eyes, man. You spend enough time in prison, and you learn a thing or two about a man's behavior. He was telling the truth about every word of it. I have a sense of these things, man."

I tapped my hand on a file on the lectern. "Mr. Dalwick, are you aware that every meeting you have is recorded in the prison record?"

"Yeah. So what?"

"Did you have a meeting with Investigator Gray before you were transferred to a cell with Mr. Holt?"

"Yeah."

"And what was that about?"

"He knew I was good at getting people to talk. I'd done it before. People open up to me, man. That's the type of guy I am. So, Gray asks me to share a cell with Holt, and get him talking."

"Did Investigator Gray tell you what he needed from Holt?"

"Yeah. He told me Holt shot the judge and I needed to get all the details from Holt."

One of the jury members groaned, unconvinced by the coincidences. I pushed on. "And in that first meeting, were you offered a possible reduction in your sentence?"

"That's how it works, man."

"So, it would be beneficial to you to make up a confession, even if those words weren't said to you?"

"Nah, man. I didn't do that. I got him talking. I asked him about it, yeah. A few times. And when he was comfortable with me, he opened up and started telling me the truth."

"And you received a reduction in your sentence because of it," I stated firmly. I looked at the jury. I could see several of them shaking their heads, showing they were doubting the whole scenario. "Is it possible you made up the confession so you could benefit from the offer of reduced prison time?"

"No. He told me!" He looked at the judge. "I've told the truth. I need those fifteen months off my sentence. I have a little girl I need to get home to."

I paused, waited, and then went for the big questions.

"Have you ever served time under a different name?"

"Yeah. In North Carolina."

I turned and looked at Harley. He was searching through his notes, but the shock was written on his face. "And in North Carolina, did you testify in a case against a man named Justin Duffey?"

"Yeah."

"And did you receive a reduced sentence for that testimony?"

"Look, man. People open up to me. I have a friendly face. That's all it is."

"You didn't answer my question."

"Yeah. Okay. Sure. I received a reduced sentence for the testimony."

"And is it true that that confession has since been proved false by other evidence that exonerated Justin Duffey?"

"I don't know what happens out here. I only know what happens in there and what people tell me. If they lie to me, then that's on them. I'm saying what I know. That's it, man."

"Even if it's lies?"

"It's not lies, man!" He slammed his fist on the edge of the witness box and the bailiffs' hands went to their weapons. Dalwick instantly eased back, raising his hands in surrender. "Listen, I just know what I'm told. If the other person is lying, then that's got nothing to do with me."

"You testified that Justin Duffey told you he committed a violent assault. However, none of it was true. Mr. Duffey was later shown to be in another city when the assault occurred. Is that correct?"

"Whatever, man. I know what Duffey told me. I can't help it if he was lying."

"And do you think your history of telling lies in court should lead the jury to question your credibility?"

"Nah, man. Holt told me he did it, and I believe him."

"Like in North Carolina?"

Dalwick looked away and didn't answer.

I looked at the jury and raised my eyebrows. Several jurors shook their heads. I looked back at Dalwick and did the same. "No further questions."

Harley declined to redirect. He didn't want to make a bad situation worse.

CHAPTER 52

"A motion for a mistrial." Judge LeBlanc stared at the piece of paper in front of her.

The walls of the judge's chambers were lined with old law books, their spines cracked and faded, and covered in dust. A dark leather couch, worn and well used, rested near the door. The judge's hefty mahogany desk sat near the rear of the room, in front of a large burgundy Persian rug.

Harley stood behind one chair, and I stood behind the other.

"This case needs to be declared a mistrial," I stated. "We argue that testimony from a lying jailhouse snitch taints the proceedings and makes it impossible for the jury to remain impartial. The witness had incentive to testify and admitted to previously lying on the stand. This is a fundamental issue that prevents fairness or impartiality from the jurors. Their opinion will be biased by that testimony."

Judge LeBlanc stared at the piece of paper in front of her for a long moment before she placed it down and leaned back in her chair. "Mr. Harley?"

"We believe that while the testimony could be considered prejudicial, the error is not so irreparable as to require restarting the trial. I think we all understand Mr. Dalwick had incentive to lie to the court."

"And what would you have me do?"

"We believe that with the right instructions to the jury members, the case can continue. With the right instructions, the jury can weigh the informant's statements appropriately without rendering the trial biased and unfair."

"This is a man with a history of lying to the court. He's flaunted the rule of law, and he's disrespected this court. The trial is prejudiced against the defendant."

"It's unbelievable that you would present this witness to the court, Mr. Harley," Judge LeBlanc said.

"In our defense, he served time under a different name in North Carolina, and we weren't privy to those records."

"But the defense was?"

Harley nodded.

Judge LeBlanc drew another long breath. "My courtroom will not be intimidated by people who flaunt the rule of law. I will issue instructions to the jurors to not consider Mr. Dalwick's testimony as part of their decision."

"Your Honor—" Harley tried to argue.

"My decision is final," Judge LeBlanc said, her voice low but unmistakably firm. "The motion is denied. Now I don't want to see either of you again unless it's at the counsel tables, and even then, only if you're useful."

Her tone didn't rise, but the message was loud and clear. The bailiff opened the door. We didn't argue. We didn't look back.

Fifteen minutes later, we were in the courtroom. The gallery was packed, the jurors stone-faced, and the media row fully occupied.

Judge LeBlanc took her seat, adjusted her robe, and gave a glance toward the prosecution's table. "Mr. Harley," she said, "you may call your next witness."

Harley leaned over, whispered something to one of his assistants, then stood and buttoned his jacket. "The prosecution rests, Your Honor."

CHAPTER 53

I lodged a motion for a directed verdict at the end of the prosecution's case.

The motion requested that the judge dismiss the case as there wasn't enough evidence presented by the prosecution for a reasonable jury to convict the client. This was a routine motion, lodged by most defense attorneys without confidence. Judge LeBlanc wasted little time in rejecting it and asked me to begin the defense case.

I opened with Alannah Drew.

Alannah Drew exuded care. She had been employed as a certified nurse and midwife for the past twenty years, and it showed in her caring eyes and soft smile. She was a short woman, carrying some extra weight, and well dressed.

"Please state your full name for the record," I said, sitting behind the defense table.

"Mrs. Alannah May Drew."

"Mrs. Drew, can you tell us where you were on the night of May 5th three years ago?"

"I was at home. I lived around two hundred yards from the judge's home with my husband and two teenage children."

"What did you observe in that area on the night in question?"

"I was outside sitting in the dark. If I'm honest, I was having a cigarette. I don't smoke any more, but sometimes, after a stressful day as a nurse, I sneak outside and have one or two. My husband is a doctor, and he doesn't want any smoke in the house, so I have a chair near the end of the yard, which looks down the street. That evening, I saw a white pickup truck drive up the street very slowly. It did two laps of the block before it came to a stop outside my house. That was around 8 p.m."

"How did you know it was the same pickup that drove past twice?"

"Because it was a new white pickup. My brother is a mechanic and owns a Ford like that one."

"How many people were in this vehicle?"

"At that time, one."

"And how long was the vehicle there?"

"I kept checking on it because I thought it was unusual. It parked off the road and in the bushes, and the driver never got out. It left at around 10:30 p.m., but then I saw it return just before 11 p.m., when I went back out to check the street again."

"And when it returned, was there anyone in the passenger seat?"

"Yes. This time it was two people. They parked and got out and walked toward the judge's house."

"Did you see both people moving in the direction of the judge's residence?"

"Yes. Two people got out of the pickup and walked down the street. They were both men, around five ten and six foot. Slim build. Both were wearing black jeans and black jackets."

"And do you live close to Mrs. Curtis?"

"No, I live at the other end of the street. I know Mrs. Curtis, everyone knows everyone in that street, and she wouldn't be able to see my house from her place. The road turns, and there's lots of trees."

"So, this was a different vehicle to the one that Mrs. Curtis saw?"

"It must've been. Our place is around three hundred yards from her place, so yes, it must've been a different vehicle."

"Did you hear the two men say anything after they exited the pickup?"

"I heard them talking to each other as they moved along, but I couldn't hear what they said. I can be nosy sometimes, so I tried to listen, but I couldn't make it out."

"And were these figures moving together or separately?"

"Together. I thought they might be going to rob one of the houses, so I kept my eye on them, and they went down the street. One guy stopped near the bushes across the road and waited, while the other guy jogged further down the street."

"What happened next?"

"About a minute later, I heard gunshots. They echoed around the neighborhood. My husband heard them as well and ran downstairs to grab me. He had his handgun and waved me toward the front door. Once we were inside, he locked all the doors in the house and told me to keep low. We had children upstairs, and he wanted to keep them safe."

"Did you hear any other noises?"

"Yes. My husband was by the door, looking up and down the street, and I was behind him. We heard two male voices come past around a minute after the shooting. And then we heard an engine start up and drive away. We watched them through our front window, and they started driving without their headlights on. There are not many streetlights in our street, so it looked like they were trying to disguise themselves. And our street is very quiet, and we don't get a lot of noise around there."

"Did you call the police?"

"I did. As soon as I got my cell phone, I called 911."

"And did you go back outside?"

"Once we heard the cop cars arriving in the neighborhood, we went out to see what was happening. My husband checked the property to make sure there was nobody around, and then we went outside."

"And when did you talk to the police?"

"An officer came past that night to take our statements. I told them about the pickup and the two men, and the officers took down all the information."

"Thank you, Mrs. Drew."

Harley stood. He wasted no time asking the first question. "Mrs. Drew, was there anything that indicated these men were involved in the gunshots?"

"Other than the timing? No, but I should add that we have a very quiet street. I know all the cars that come and go. This wasn't a pickup I knew, and they weren't people that I recognized."

"Do you think the two men could've been running away from the gunshots?"

"That's possible."

"And do you think they left their lights off in their pickup so the shooter wouldn't follow them?"

"Again, that's possible."

"That's what I thought," Harley said in a condescending tone. "No further questions."

CHAPTER 54

Dr. Harry Ling came to the stand next.

He was thin and pale, with a slight forward lean, having spent most of his life in crime labs, leaning over evidence, reports, and tests. His salt-and-pepper hair was well trimmed, and he wore a brown jacket over a blue shirt, which was tucked into his black trousers. Well spoken, well educated, he never seemed hurried.

"Dr. Ling, can you please describe the process by which a bullet is typically matched to a firearm using rifling marks?"

"Certainly. When a bullet is fired, it moves through the barrel. The barrel has spiral grooves known as rifling. These grooves have a legitimate purpose, which is to spin the bullet for stability. In the process of spinning, the grooves also leave unique microscopic scratches on the bullet's exterior, which are called striations. This is unique to each weapon, like a fingerprint, and if they line up, we can say the bullet was fired from that specific weapon."

"And in this particular case, were you able to match the bullet to the weapon recovered from the river?"

"No."

"There was no match?"

"That's right. There was no forensic match from the bullets used to shoot Judge Newton to the weapon recovered from the river."

"Were your conclusions reached after a thorough analysis of all the available evidence?"

"Yes."

"And Dr. Ling, based on this analysis, could you claim in any way that the recovered weapon was used to fire those bullets?"

"No. There's no forensic evidence that matches the bullets used in the homicide to the weapon recovered from the Beaufort River."

"Is it possible the forensic evidence merely indicates that a firearm of that type was used in the crime, rather than identifying a specific shooter?"

"From the bullets, we know a Glock was used, but that's it. That's all that can be established by the forensics."

"And is there any forensic evidence that matches that weapon to the bullets?"

"I don't know how many ways we can say this, but no, there is zero forensic evidence that matches that weapon to the bullets used in the homicide."

When I was sure the point was clear, I sat down. "Thank you, Dr. Ling. No further questions."

Harley was quick to stand and begin his cross-examination. "Dr. Ling, are you aware that the firearm was recovered from the Beaufort River in the days following the homicide?"

"Yes, I'm aware of that fact."

"Isn't it standard forensic practice to account for some environmental degradation when analyzing evidence from a submerged scene?"

"Yes, that's correct."

"So even with exposure to water and sediment, can you confirm that critical features—such as the pattern of rifling marks—can remain sufficiently intact for analysis?"

"Sometimes, but there were none there in this instance."

"Dr. Ling, can you please explain to the court how prolonged submersion in water might damage the microscopic markings in the weapon?"

"The markings become almost non-existent when exposed to those conditions."

"In your extensive experience, how often does a handgun show these signs of degradation after being exposed to such conditions?"

"In my experience, always."

"Given the clear patterns you observed—even if partially degraded—would you say the most plausible interpretation is that this is the same type of firearm used in the crime?"

"The same type, but I cannot say it's that weapon."

"But can you rule that weapon out?"

"No."

"No," Harley repeated. "That's the question here, isn't it? The weapon recovered from the Beaufort River cannot be ruled out." He looked at the jury and then sat down. "No further questions."

CHAPTER 55

"The defense calls Mrs. Elizabeth Pennington."

Elizabeth looked younger than she was—small, slender, almost fragile, with features that hadn't yet hardened with life. Her skin was soft, her hair pulled back in a loose knot, and she wore a simple blouse and cardigan. There was no doubt she would be asked for identification every time she purchased alcohol.

"Objection." Harley stood when he saw the witness. She stopped at the gate, standing awkwardly as Harley raised his objection. "May we approach, Your Honor?"

"Approach." Judge LeBlanc waved Harley and I forward.

"Your Honor, we believe this witness will talk about her alleged attack by Judge Newton and provide no other relevant details." Harley spoke in a hushed tone. "The victim is not on trial here."

"Your Honor, the State presented information about the judge's misconduct. They're the ones who have introduced the evidence. This additional, corroborative testimony is relevant to the case. It helps establish a pattern of misconduct, which only builds upon the information the State has introduced."

"This should've been dealt with in pretrials, Mr. Harley." Judge LeBlanc's voice was quiet but firm, and she kept her hand over the microphone next to her. "Why was an objection not raised then?"

"Because Mrs. Pennington was known as Miss Elizabeth Jones in the files we have. We didn't see her name on the updated witness list."

"She's married, Your Honor," I explained. "She has changed her last name in the last few months."

"Considering the State introduced the evidence, I believe the probative value of this testimony outweighs any potential for prejudice. The objection is overruled. However, Mr. Lincoln, don't stray too far into hearsay."

"Yes, Your Honor."

I returned to the defense table and took a breath. Judge LeBlanc waved Elizabeth forward to swear her oath. Her hands were shaky as she sat in the witness box.

I treaded softly, used a measured tone, and easy cadence. "Mrs. Pennington, can you please tell the court how you knew Judge Newton?"

She sat upright in the witness chair, hands clasped in her lap. "I worked as his assistant for around a year."

"And why did you leave that position?"

She hesitated, but then spoke clearly. "Because he sexually assaulted me."

A murmur rippled through the gallery. Harley was on his feet. He didn't raise his voice. "We wish to object again, Your Honor. This is prejudicial and irrelevant."

"Your Honor, we're establishing a pattern of conduct directly related to the prosecution's theory. It speaks to motive and credibility. We'll tie it in."

Judge LeBlanc paused, her eyes locked on me for a long moment. Then she turned to Harley. "Overruled. Proceed."

I turned back to the witness. "Mrs. Pennington, how did Judge Newton assault you?"

"In the office, he used to grope my breasts and bottom whenever I was close enough. I really needed the job, and the pay was great, so I didn't make a complaint. Then one night, he said I needed to work from his home. I went there, and I had one drink, and then I passed out. I woke up hours later in a bed at his house. When I asked what had happened, he said I had drunk too much and passed out, but I know that didn't happen. I was so confused."

"Did Judge Newton say you had sex with him?"

"He did. He said I had initiated it, and he was also drunk. He said I had started it, but I know I didn't."

The jury was silent, eyes fixed on her. Even Harley had stopped shuffling his papers.

"Did you make a police report?"

"That time, yes."

"And did you conduct a rape kit?"

"Yes."

"And what did the rape kit show?"

"That I had had sex the night before, but I don't remember anything after the first drink."

"In your mind, was the sex consensual?"

"No."

"Your Honor," Harley interjected. Again, his tone was hushed. "I must put in another objection here. There's no relevance to the murder of Judge Newton."

"Your Honor." My tone was firm. "We're establishing the reason Mr. Holt attended the residence that night. The prosecution put forward their theory in the opening statement and in their case, and we're putting forward an alternative theory."

"Agreed. Overruled."

"Where and when did this incident take place?"

"A year before his death at his home on Spanish Point Drive."

"And what happened to your report to law enforcement?"

"The officers were great, but after two months, they told me there was not enough evidence that anything non-consensual happened. It was my word against his, and he told the police that I was out for money."

"Were you?"

"No. I never asked for money. He lied to the police about that. And that's not what this was about. This was about an old man taking advantage of me. I was sure I was drugged that night. I know he spiked my drink. I had one drink, and then I blacked out. That's never happened to me before, and it's never happened to me since."

"Did you remain working for Judge Newton?"

"No. I quit the job the night after the assault. I couldn't bear to look at him again."

"How did he react when you quit?"

"I sent him an email after calling out sick for the week. He called me right away. He was outraged, and told me if I ever told anyone, he would destroy me."

"Did you feel rage at the time of the incident?"

"Yes."

"And if you had a gun, would you have defended yourself?"

"Absolutely. I would've shot him if I'd known what he was going to do to me."

"Objection." Harley stood. "This is pure speculation."

"This time I agree. The objection is sustained," Judge LeBlanc agreed.

I nodded at the jury members. "No further questions."

Harley took a moment and then stood behind his desk. "Mrs. Pennington, do you think it's reasonable for a person to shoot someone after they've had consensual relations?"

"It wasn't consensual. He thought he was above the law," she snapped. "He said nobody could touch him."

Harley scoffed and waved her comment away. "No further questions."

CHAPTER 56

The rest of the week was spent in expert testimonies.

We were building a case, brick by brick, casting doubt on Holt's guilt. We brought forward a blood spatter expert to prove there were no blood spatters on Holt's clothes. More ballistics experts to prove there was no match between the gun and the bullet. More forensic investigators to prove there was no evidence that placed Holt inside the judge's house. Every question was calculated. Every answer pre-planned. Little emotion, no opinions—just facts. The week was full of procedure, full of polish, and so incredibly dull.

Stephen Freeman showed up to court every morning. He sat in the back row, watching the day's proceedings before disappearing at lunchtime. His presence was unsettling, but it mattered little to the case.

One evening, after proceedings had finished for the day, Bruce asked to meet at the ice-cream store off Bay Street. It was a classic sweets and ice-cream store, full of character, charm, and great service. Bruce stood outside the shop, licking his double ice-cream cone, as I approached. He looked as happy as a ten year old.

"Vanilla?" I asked.

"With choc chips."

I couldn't help but smile at the childish grin on his face. He suggested I should have one as well, but I passed on the offer, and we started walking toward the waterfront, catching a fresh breeze as it blew off the river. Bruce talked about the case, about the previous witness, and how he was watching the jury members react to the witness testimonies.

"I hate to say it"—Bruce crunched into the cone after he'd eaten all the ice cream—"but I think we're losing. They see Holt's presence at Spanish Point Drive as more than a coincidence. And even though you pulled apart Stacey Curtis's testimony, they still believed that she saw Holt throw a gun into the river."

"Well, I have good news," I said. "We might have a break."

"Go on."

"I just got off the phone with Ken Steward, the former CAST team member who I asked to triangulate the call from the phone that called Holt that night."

Bruce looked at his watch. "Wow, that's cutting it tight. You asked for that weeks ago."

"And he told me then that even with a subpoena, it would take weeks, sometimes months to receive the data from the cell phone companies. We couldn't request to delay the trial, because we had no idea what the information would show. It could've been bad for Holt. If it showed the call came from Judge Newton's house, it could've convicted him on the spot. The jury would've assumed that Judge Newton invited Holt to the house."

"And if we received it after the trial, and it was favorable, then it could've formed the basis of a post-conviction relief motion."

"Exactly," I agreed. "Once Steward received the data late yesterday, he was able to work his magic within hours and call me today. The evidence shows the cell phone was at Cascade's house before it traveled to another location."

"We know Cascade had the phone. The question is—what happened next?"

I took a folded-up piece of paper from my pocket and handed it to Bruce. He put the rest of the ice-cream cone in his mouth, crunching on it loudly, and then unfolded the piece of paper. He looked at it, and then looked at me. "Are you sure this is right?"

"That's the summary. Steward will email the full report tonight."

"Will Steward testify?"

"I'm not sure he needs to."

"You're going to call Cascade to the stand?"

I nodded. "I sent him a subpoena five weeks ago. He's on the witness list already, but I need to establish his connection first, so I'll use Sam Keenan to create the link. I can't submit this report into discovery yet, or we'll lose the element of surprise."

"That's a big risk, Dean. Cascade could get on the stand and say anything. He could lie up there."

"That's not the biggest risk," I said. "The biggest risk is what will come after Cascade's testimony."

CHAPTER 57

"The defense calls Sam Keenan."

Sam Keenan walked to the stand with his head down, wearing jeans and a plaid button-up shirt. The jeans looked too tight, and the shirt had a stain on the arm. He didn't look at the jury. It wasn't his first trip to a courtroom, but it was his first trip to the witness box.

He didn't want to be there, and it showed. His shoulders were tight, his oath was mumbled, and his eyes avoided mine. But I hadn't given him a choice. A man's life was on the line, and whatever Keenan had been trying to forget, it was time he faced it in the light.

Once he had settled, I stood and walked to the lectern. "Mr. Keenan," I began, "can you please tell the court what you were doing on May 1st three years ago?"

He shifted in the witness chair, his fingers drumming nervously on his knee. "I bought a new cell phone and a new number."

"A number?"

"A prepaid SIM card, along with a cheap handset."

"And why did you do that?"

His voice was flat. "I was paid to."

"How much were you paid to buy the cell phone and phone number?"

"Two hundred and fifty dollars to buy the phone handset and register the new number."

I paused, let the number hang in the air. "That seems like a lot, just to buy a phone. Who paid you the money?"

He looked down, then back at me. "Wayne Cascade."

I pressed forward. "Did Mr. Cascade tell you what the number was going to be used for?"

"No. Just that he needed it. Wanted it clean."

"Did you ask him what it was going to be used for?"

"No. You don't ask Wayne Cascade questions if you want to stay on his good side."

"And once you bought the number—did you activate it yourself?"

"No."

"Did you ever use the cell phone associated with that number?"

"No."

"What did you do with it?"

"I handed it over. To Wayne Cascade."

"And when did that exchange take place?"

"Same day. May 1st. Around five in the afternoon."

I nodded slowly, letting the timeline sink in. "Thank you, Mr. Keenan."

He exhaled, and his relief was clear.

"No further questions."

CHAPTER 58

Wayne Cascade stepped through the gallery doors when the clerk called his name.

He wore a gray sport coat over a white shirt buttoned to the collar, black tie. His dark slacks were ironed but dusty at the cuffs. His boots were polished and shiny. He kept his eyes down as he approached the stand, jaw tight.

"Please state your full name for the record," I began.

"Wayne Cascade," he replied, his voice grumbling above a whisper.

"Mr. Cascade, on May 5th three years ago, did you place a call to the defendant, Mr. Holt?"

Cascade shifted in the chair. "I don't recall."

I turned back, eyes locked on Cascade. "On May 1st of that same year, did you receive a cell phone from Sam Keenan?"

"I don't recall."

"You don't recall being handed a prepaid SIM and phone?"

"That's what I said."

"Your Honor." I looked to Judge LeBlanc. "The defense requests permission to treat the witness as hostile."

Judge LeBlanc didn't blink. She'd been watching Cascade since he took the stand, tracking every flicker of hesitation, and every dodge wrapped in vague language. She didn't need convincing. "The request is granted."

"Using call triangulation techniques, we've been able to trace the movements of that cell phone. It was traced to your residence during the dates of May 1st, when it was first switched on, and May 5th, before it left your house, and went to another house, after which it was switched off. Is that correct?"

Cascade didn't move. He hadn't expected that question.

"Mr. Cascade?"

"I don't recall," he whispered.

"It pinged off several cell phone towers less than half a mile from your house, which enabled our forensic technician to geolocate the cell phone location to your property." The courtroom was silent. The jury was listening. And Wayne Cascade was already starting to sweat. He knew what was coming next. "Do you recall using that phone?"

"No." He tried to compose himself. "Like I said, I don't recall."

"We can confirm the phone was at your house before it went to another residence. We've triangulated the data to show where the phone went next. Can you please tell the court whose house the cell phone went to after it left your property on the early evening of May 5th?"

Cascade's mouth hung open for a few moments before he closed it again. "I don't recall."

"Your Honor, the defense moves to introduce this report, compiled by a certified mobile forensics expert, which tracks the cell phone in question from the purchase date, May 1st, to when it was switched off on the evening of May 5th." I picked up a file and handed one copy to Harley and another copy to the bailiff. "The phone was at your property, then it traveled to the residence of the Freeman family on Morgan River Drive in the Ashdale neighborhood, ten minutes from Beaufort."

I turned and saw the shock on Stephen Freeman's face.

"Objection!" Harley said, already on his feet. "We haven't been given time to verify the authenticity of this analysis. This is all new information to us."

Judge LeBlanc didn't hesitate. "Granted. The prosecution will have twenty-four hours to examine the data. We'll reconvene tomorrow at noon."

Within moments, the entire courtroom had emptied. Harley had pushed through the crowd, desperate to catch Stephen Freeman. I had no doubt Harley would spend much of the next twenty-four hours trying to discredit the findings, while Stephen Freeman would be looking for a way to distance himself from the mess.

When we all returned the next morning, the courtroom felt heavier.

The jurors sat straighter than they had all week. No crossed arms, no bored glances. This was different. They sensed it—not from anything that had been said, but from the way everyone in the room was holding their breath a little tighter.

Harley stood, adjusted his jacket, and gave a single, silent nod toward the judge. He'd reviewed the cell phone data, and their experts couldn't find a fault with it. He knew what it meant. There was no use objecting, no procedural trick left to play. The numbers didn't lie, and he wasn't going to waste credibility pretending otherwise.

When invited by Judge LeBlanc, I stood and continued questioning Wayne Cascade. "Mr. Cascade, we can confirm the phone was at your house before it went to the Freeman family residence on Morgan River Drive in the Ashdale neighborhood. Did you drive the phone there?"

"I don't recall." His answer was firm. He had been prepared by Harley.

"And why don't you recall, Mr. Cascade?" Judge LeBlanc questioned.

Cascade moved in his seat. "You're asking about a random night more than three years ago. That's why I don't recall."

It was clearly a lie, but it was an effective one.

I picked up the questioning again. "What prompted you to use that cell phone and call the defendant at 8 p.m. on May 5th?"

"Like I said, I don't remember."

"You admit you made the call?"

"I don't recall."

"During the call, did you provide the defendant with any information regarding Judge Newton?"

"I don't recall."

"Can you recall exactly what you told him about the judge's actions?"

"I don't recall anything from that night."

It was a blatant untruth, and it opened the floor for me to ask all the right questions to plant the thoughts into the jurors' minds. Cascade was saving himself, but he was also saving our case.

"Did you mention the judge was sexually abusing another girl that night?"

"I don't recall."

"Did you feel the information you relayed was accurate and important for the defendant to know?"

"I don't recall."

"Were you certain, at the time of your call, that the details you provided about the judge were true?"

"I don't recall."

"Did you experience any hesitation before making the call to Mr. Holt, and if so, can you explain why?"

"I don't recall anything about that night."

"After your call, did you ever follow up or discuss the information further with anyone?"

"I don't recall anything about that night."

"Can you describe the tone of the conversation—did you sense urgency in your message to the defendant?"

Cascade's jaw clenched. His frustration was clear. "I don't recall anything about that night."

"When the defendant later told the police that the caller did not identify themselves, does that align with your recollection?"

"I don't recall."

"In your own words, would you agree that your call was intended solely to alert the defendant about what you believed was a critical matter involving the judge?"

"I don't recall."

I nodded for a few moments, and then looked to the jury. The questions were written all over their faces. There was more to the story, more to why the call had been made to Holt that night, but they had no information to build upon.

"No further questions."

Harley stood before I had even sat down. "Mr. Cascade, is your inability to recall anything proof that you were involved in any illegal activity that night?"

"No."

"Thank you." Harley sat back down. "Nothing further."

CHAPTER 59

Harley requested a recess, which Judge LeBlanc granted, due to the new information presented.

She recessed the case for Friday and told him to return on Monday, and that he'd better be prepared for the trial.

As we stepped out of court, I made a call to an old friend. He listened to my request, and then reluctantly said he would see what he could do.

At 7:15 a.m. on Friday morning, Harley called my cell. His voice was croaky, and his speech pattern was slow. He needed to meet. I called Bruce and Kayla, and we met at the courthouse at 8:45 a.m. Harley was waiting for us.

He looked like he hadn't slept a wink. He led us to the large conference room and said he was as shocked as anyone by the names involved in the case. He presented an offer of ten years for manslaughter, but I said that Holt wouldn't take it. Give him time served, I said, and he'd take it. Harley stared off into the distance for a long moment, and then advised he couldn't do it. He didn't like where the case was heading, he didn't like the people that were being brought into it, but his superiors wouldn't let him go lower than ten years for the death of a judge, even if it was manslaughter. They had to protect the court, he said, which I found laughable.

Who was protecting the innocent girls Judge Newton abused? I asked. Harley said nothing.

We met with Holt at 10 a.m. in the detention center. He thought about the offer of ten years for manslaughter, about how he could be out in seven, about how he could see the outside world again. Seven more was better than thirty more, he said. He looked to Bruce and I for advice, and we told him it was his decision, and his decision alone, but we thought the jury had doubts.

"I need to testify," Holt said at one point. "I'm the only one who can tell the court what that call was about. I'm the only one who can say that Cascade called me and told me a girl was going to be abused at Judge Newton's home. There's no other way we can say it."

"But then what?" Bruce said. "What happens next? The jury will believe you went there to defend a girl. You went to Judge Newton's house to stop him. If you testify, you'll look guilty, even if it's manslaughter."

"It's clear that they're involved!" Holt complained. "Cascade wanted me there! He set me up. Can't you see that? He baited me. He has to be involved."

My phone buzzed in my pocket. I ignored it.

"I need to testify," Holt continued. "I need to tell the court the truth. What else are we going to do?"

"We can either rest the case here, where the jury is confused, and has lots of doubt," Bruce said, "or we could call Stephen Freeman and ask him why Cascade was at his house on the night that Cascade called you."

I stared at the wall. It was a risk. "Freeman could say anything."

My phone buzzed again.

I looked at the number. It was my old friend. I stepped out of the attorney-client meeting room, while Bruce and Holt argued about the next steps.

When the call ended, I went back into the room and looked at Holt. "You don't need to testify. We have one last play to make."

CHAPTER 60

"The defense calls Mr. Paul Freeman as a clarifying witness."

There was silence in the court that Monday morning before Harley leaped to his feet. "Objection! The witness is not on any defense witness list."

"That's true, Your Honor. However, in light of the testimony of Mr. Cascade and the information confirmed by the cellular phone analysis, we request to call Mr. Paul Freeman to clarify and corroborate details regarding the phone call made from his residence at 8 p.m. on May 5th."

"This is nothing more than a strategic surprise, Your Honor. The defense is playing games with the court's time."

"This is not a strategic move, Your Honor. Due to lack of investigation by the law enforcement involved, this trial has become more of a fact-finding mission than it should've been. This information should've been uncovered by law enforcement; however, it wasn't. The defense is acting in good faith. The witness's testimony will be both relevant and necessary to ensure a fair trial."

"This witness was not disclosed during discovery!" Harley argued. "Allowing his testimony now would unfairly prejudice the State. We haven't had the chance to prepare, to review statements, or to investigate potential inaccuracies in the witness's statement."

"Which seems to be your own doing, Mr. Harley." Judge LeBlanc's tone was flat. "Mr. Lincoln, do you have a statement that summarizes what the testimony is intended to show?"

"We do, Your Honor." I handed a piece of paper to Harley and to the bailiff, who handed it to the judge.

Harley's eyebrows rose and his mouth dropped. "Your Honor, this cannot be serious."

Judge LeBlanc squinted. "Mr. Harley, did you or law enforcement question this witness at any time?"

"Not to my knowledge, Your Honor. But—"

"That's enough, Mr. Harley." She held up her hand as a stop sign. "Mr. Lincoln, is there evidence that corroborates this testimony?"

"There is, Your Honor. It's listed at the end of the witness summary."

Judge LeBlanc sighed heavily and sat back in her chair, staring at the summary. "Given the relevance, and the supporting evidence, I have no choice but to allow this testimony."

"Your Honor—"

"That's enough, Mr. Harley. It's a failure of the State not to have interviewed this witness. Given the probative value of this testimony, I have no option but to allow it."

"Then, Your Honor, we respectfully request a continuance of thirty days."

"You don't have that time, Mr. Harley." Judge LeBlanc stared at him. "You can have one day, because I deem it sufficient time to address the new evidence while safeguarding the defendant's rights and ensuring a timely trial."

"Yes, Your Honor," Harley said, like a good little schoolboy.

"Your Honor, given the continuance, we have safety concerns for the witness."

"Noted and agreed, Mr. Lincoln. The Court shares your concerns." She looked at the bailiff. "The Court instructs the Sheriff's Office to coordinate appropriate protective measures, including, if necessary, overnight accommodations in a secure location and supervision to ensure no outside influence." When the bailiff nodded, she turned back to the court. "We reconvene tomorrow at 10 a.m. I expect Mr. Paul Freeman to be present and prepared to testify. Court is adjourned."

CHAPTER 61

The Sheriff's Office had kept Paul in protective custody overnight. He showed up the next morning wearing the same clothes as the day before, eyes bloodshot, slightly unshaven. If he'd slept at all, it didn't show. He looked like a man who'd spent the night staring at the ceiling, thinking about everything he was going to say, and what might happen once he said it.

"Please state your full name for the record," I began, standing behind the lectern. Every time I looked at him, I thought about my sister. I did my best to avoid eye contact.

"My name is Paul Joshua Freeman."

"What is your current address and occupation?"

"I live with my father, Stephen Freeman, on Morgan River Drive in the Ashdale neighborhood, ten minutes from Beaufort. Currently, I'm studying Business Administration at USCB."

"And why have you made the decision to testify today?"

"Because I want to tell the truth."

"And why haven't you told the truth previously?"

"Because over the last few months, I've been on a journey of self-discovery and healing. I've found religion, or God found me. I don't know which way it happened, but I'm glad it did. I know my life has been a mess up until a few months ago, but I want to do the right thing. I want to right the wrongs of my past. I've been going to AA meetings, and part of that process is making peace with the hurt you've caused. That's what I'm doing here. I'm making peace with what I've done before the court, but most importantly, before the Lord."

"And what's your intention for today's testimony?"

"I want the truth to come out. I've hidden so many secrets and so many lies, and it's time to undo all that."

"And on May 5th, three years ago, where were you and what were you doing?" My tone was flat. I had no interest in his redemption story. The only thing I wanted from him was the truth.

Paul Freeman looked at the crowd and caught his father's eyes. His father was seated in the front row of the gallery, arms folded across his chest. A thin layer of sweat appeared on Paul Freeman's brow. "That night, I was at home, before I drove out to Spanish Point Drive and parked near Judge Newton's house."

"Why?"

"Because I was told to keep an eye out for anyone going toward Judge Newton's house."

"Who asked you to keep an eye out?"

"My father, Stephen Freeman."

"Did you know why?"

"No. I often did things for him without knowing the reason. He paid my bills, gave me money, and helped me out when I got in trouble with the law, so I owed him a lot. When he asked me to go to Spanish Point Drive and watch the house, I didn't question it. I just did it."

"And what time did you arrive?"

"8 p.m."

"And did you see anyone coming or going from the judge's residence that night?"

"No."

"What time did you leave?"

"My father called me, and I left at 10:30 p.m. I drove to pick up Wayne Cascade from a dive bar off Boundary Street at 10:45 p.m. and returned to Spanish Point Drive before 11 p.m."

"Why?"

"Because my father told me to."

"Were you the one driving your vehicle that night?"

"I was."

"What did the passenger, Wayne Cascade, tell you about his intended destination?"

"He said I needed to park in the bushes on Spanish Point Drive, near where it turns into Stuart Town Court. I told him that's where I was parked earlier anyway."

"Did Mr. Cascade mention any specific reason for going to that destination?"

"He said he had a job to do. He didn't tell me who it was for, or what he was going to do. All I knew was that he had a job to do."

"As you were driving, what conversation did you have with the passenger regarding his plans?"

"We didn't have a conversation. Wayne isn't much of a talker."

"And upon arriving, did Mr. Cascade exit your vehicle?"

"He stepped out and we walked a few yards before he told me to stay at the pickup. He told me to wait in the truck while he went and talked to someone."

"Do you know who he went to talk to?"

"No."

"What happened next?"

"About two minutes later, when I was sitting in the driver's seat of my pickup, I heard five gunshots and a few seconds after that, Wayne came jogging around through the bushes. He said it was time to go. I turned the pickup around and we drove out of there."

I let the pause sit in the room. "Did you notice any blood stains on Mr. Cascade?"

"It appeared he had blood spatter on his jacket, but I didn't look closely."

"And did Mr. Cascade say anything to you when you were driving out of there?"

"No."

"Where did you go next?"

"I took him back to the bar on Boundary Street, where his truck was parked."

"Why did Mr. Cascade need you to drive your vehicle and not his own vehicle?"

"Some jobs require a driver. That's what my father said to me."

"At any point, did you know what the job was?"

"No."

"Is there any evidence that backs this story up?"

"There was a dashcam on my pickup truck, and the pickup also has GPS location data. I guess my phone does as well. They will all prove I was there that night."

I turned and faced Harley. The tension in his face was clear. He looked like he was about to explode. I turned back to Judge LeBlanc. "No further questions."

CHAPTER 62

Harley didn't waste a second before standing.

He was straight to his feet before I'd even reached the defense table, and once asked by Judge LeBlanc to begin questioning, he turned and took a long look at Stephen Freeman behind him. When Freeman provided a subtle nod, Harley turned back to the witness stand, eyes narrowing on Paul.

"Mr. Paul Freeman." Harley said the name with a level of distain. "Did you see Mr. Cascade shoot anyone that night?"

"No. I was in the truck when I heard the gunshots."

"Did you see him enter Judge Newton's residence?"

"No."

"Did you see a firearm in his possession at any point that night?"

"No," Paul said. "But I assumed—"

"Assumed? Let's stop right there." Harley took a step closer to the jury, letting the pause do the work. "We're not here to deal in assumptions, Mr. Freeman. This is a court of law. We deal in facts. And the fact is—you were sitting next to a man in your pickup, and at no point did you see a weapon. Is that correct?"

Paul hesitated, then nodded. "That's correct."

"Did Mr. Cascade tell you where he was going when he got out of the pickup?"

"No. He didn't say much at all that night."

"Did he say he went to the judge's house?"

"No, but again, he didn't say much at all."

"So, you don't actually know if he went there at all?"

"I guess so."

"Guess so?" Harley leaned in. "Is it possible Mr. Cascade wasn't running from the crime scene but running to avoid it? Away from the sound of gunfire, like anyone else might do?"

Paul looked uneasy. "It's possible. All I know is that we were in the area at that time."

"In the area, at that time," Harley repeated, glancing at the jury. "But not on the property."

"No," Paul admitted. "Not on the property."

"Could the gunshots fired by Mr. Holt have—"

"Objection!" I stopped Harley's attempt to trick the jury. "Assumes facts not in the evidence."

"Withdrawn," Harley was quick to state. "Could the gunshots have frightened Mr. Cascade, and that's why he was running from the scene?"

"Yeah. That's one possibility."

"Did you ever discuss the details of that ride with anyone else before coming forward with your testimony today?"

"No."

Harley returned to his table and flicked open a file. He tapped his finger on it several times. "And have you provided a consistent account of your recollection since the night of the incident?"

"Nobody asked me about it, so I haven't lied about it."

Harley looked back at Stephen. Stephen nodded again. "Mr. Freeman, have you used drugs in the past?"

Paul sat up straighter. "Yes."

"What type of drugs?"

"Many."

"Name some."

"Heroin, cocaine, meth, fentanyl, ketamine, MDMA, and lots and lots of alcohol. I used to take it all, but I've been sober for months. I've found religion, and that's set me on the right path. I know my true calling now. I've—"

"When you were driving Mr. Cascade that night, were you under the influence of drugs?"

"It was likely that I had been drinking, and I was probably using some coke around that time as well."

"Coke as in cocaine?"

"That's right."

"You have quite the past." Harley glanced at me. "Mr. Freeman, is it true you crashed a car while drunk and killed—"

"Objection!" I stood. "Relevance. The witness is not on trial, and that incident has nothing to do with this case."

"Mr. Harley?" Judge LeBlanc questioned Harley for a response.

"We withdraw the question." Harley looked at me with a slight smirk. I wanted nothing more than to break his jaw for daring to bring my deceased sister into the trial. Harley turned back to his notes. "Mr. Freeman, in the past, have you spent time in prison?"

"I have."

"And do you have a history of mental health issues?"

Paul sat back. "I've had issues in the past."

"Have you ever lied in court?"

Paul nodded. "I've told lies in court, but I was a different man then. I need to do what's right now. I need to follow my religion and that means following the truth. I want to tell the truth. I'm not getting anything out of this."

Harley scoffed. "Do you expect this court, this respected institution, to believe that someone who was constantly under the influence of drugs and alcohol, with a history of lying to the court, someone who kept their evidence suppressed for years, is now coming clean?"

"I'm telling the truth."

"The truth? You were so high that you didn't know the truth," Harley scoffed. "We have nothing further for this witness."

CHAPTER 63

I rested the case on the back of Paul's testimony.

Judge LeBlanc called for a fifteen-minute recess, then extended it another fifteen without explanation. The extra time did nothing but deepen the pressure sitting in my chest.

When we returned to court, Holt looked stressed. His leg bounced under the table. He held his arm across his stomach. Had we done enough? I didn't know the answer to that question. Only twelve people in the room could answer that.

Across the aisle, Andrew Harley shifted in his chair. He looked confident, but not comfortable. His fingers tapped the table, restless and rehearsed. Every few seconds, he leaned toward one of his junior assistants and whispered something. He hadn't expected Paul's testimony to land the way it did. It had cut through the prosecution's clean narrative and left a mark. Harley was scrambling to stitch the story back together before the jury carried it into the deliberation room.

There were two competing stories. Two competing theories.

When Judge LeBlanc returned, Harley snapped to attention. He adjusted his tie and straightened his posture.

Before calling for closing arguments, Judge LeBlanc turned to the jury, reminding them of their oath, their role, and the burden that belonged not to the defense, but to the State. She walked them through the legal standards, what constituted reasonable doubt, what didn't, and what the law required before a man's freedom could be taken.

Then, without further pause, she nodded toward the prosecution table.

"Mr. Harley," she said. "You may begin your closing."

"Ladies and gentlemen of the jury, thank you. You've listened patiently. You've taken notes. You've paid attention, not just to the words spoken but to how they were spoken. And now, the burden falls to you—to weigh the truth from the noise.

Let's start with what we know.

The defendant had a motive—a personal, powerful motive. His daughter suffered an alleged assault at the hands of Judge Newton. Not just her, but others too. You heard that. You saw the emotion in the witnesses. The defendant didn't just talk about the trauma in his police interview—he lived it. And during the police interview, he made no effort to hide how he felt. He didn't say he regretted what happened. He said he was glad Judge Newton couldn't hurt anyone else.

Now, is that motive alone? Maybe not. But when a man admits satisfaction in someone's death, it's not just motive—it's mindset. And that matters.

Then there's the jailhouse informant. I know what the defense wants you to think—that this man had something to gain. That he's lying to help himself. But consider this: he didn't make vague claims. He gave you details, things only the killer would know. Things that were never released to the public. That's not luck. That's not a coincidence. That's a confession.

There are multiple witnesses who identified Mr. Holt in the area at the time of the murder. Even Mr. Holt himself admitted in the police interview that he was there. Another witness testified she saw Mr. Holt, a person she knew, throw a weapon into the river near her home.

That weapon was later recovered downstream. Yes, the weapon was degraded. It had been in water. But our forensic experts didn't give you a guess—they gave you a match in type, consistent with the weapon recovered. That gun didn't appear out of thin air. It was connected to the defendant. The chain of custody was clean. And as the forensic expert told you—a partial match doesn't mean an unreliable one. It means we consider it with everything else.

And when you do—when you put it next to the fact the defendant was placed near the scene by multiple witnesses, when you add in his own words—this case becomes clear.

The defense wants to distract you. They want to make this about assumptions. About 'what ifs' and 'maybes.' They brought you a witness who said he drove the killer to the scene, but not that he saw the killing. Not that he saw the gun. Just that someone was there. It muddies the waters, but it doesn't change what we already know.

This is not about whether the judge was a good man. This is not about whether you understand the defendant's pain. This is about whether that pain justifies murder, and the law says it does not.

You're not being asked to decide if the system failed Mr. Holt's daughter. You're being asked to decide if the defendant took justice into his own hands and committed murder.

This case isn't built on a single piece of evidence. It's built on layers—testimony, motive, forensic science, and the defendant's own words.

Is there reasonable doubt? That's your standard. And I submit to you, when you look at this case in its entirety, when you measure the evidence with clear eyes and calm minds, the answer is no.

The defendant killed Judge Newton. He did it with motive. He did it knowingly. And he confessed—not just with his words, but with his actions.

We ask you to return a verdict of guilty. Thank you."

Harley returned to his seat with a bit too much swagger, the courtroom version of a victory lap.

As he passed the defense table, he tilted his head just enough to catch my eye and offered a wink—smug, calculated, and meant to rattle. I didn't react. I'd seen that act before. Instead, I kept my eyes on the page in front of me, scribbling notes across the margins of the closing—tightening the structure, sharpening the words, trimming the fat. There was no room for theatrics now.

"Ladies and gentlemen, the prosecution has asked you to see the full picture. I'm asking you to do the same, but to see it for what it really is—incomplete, unclear, and filled with doubt.

You've been told this case is built on layers. Let's talk about those layers.

Start with the forensic evidence. The supposed firearm pulled from the river was degraded, badly. Submerged in water, exposed to the elements. The analyst said the markings were partial at best. And yet we're supposed to accept that as definitive proof? Even the State's own expert admitted it wasn't a conclusive match—just a possibility. The forensic analyst admitted there was nothing that linked the weapon to the crime. That's not certainty. That's reasonable doubt.

The witness who claims to have seen a gun being thrown in the river was high on alcohol and Valium.

The prosecution's expert psychologist admitted she was driven by bias against criminals.

And let's consider the so-called confession, given to a man serving time, who magically remembers details after being promised a deal. He got something in return. You heard it. A reduced sentence. And we all know what that's worth inside prison walls. What he gave you wasn't truth—it was theater.

Then there's the motive. The prosecution leaned heavily on it, saying the defendant had a reason to want the judge dead. But motive is not proof. Pain is not proof. Grief is not guilt. Did he say he was glad Judge Newton couldn't hurt anyone else? Yes. But being relieved that a predator is gone does not mean he pulled the trigger. Emotion is not the same as evidence.

And let's not forget the prosecution tried to bury the witness who came forward and said he drove the shooter to the scene. That's not a throwaway detail. That's an entirely different narrative. And the prosecution's response? Shrug it off. Push it aside. Because it doesn't fit their version of the story.

But your job as jury members, your duty to this court, is not to pick the story that feels most satisfying. It's to weigh the evidence and determine whether the State has proven its case beyond reasonable doubt. That's the standard. That's the law.

And when you sit back and look at all of this—the shaky ballistics, the incentivized testimony, the missing connections, the alternative explanations—what you have is reasonable doubt. You have questions. Too many questions to convict a man.

This isn't about sympathy. It's about fairness. If there's even one unanswered question in your mind—about the weapon, about who really pulled the trigger, about what actually happened that night—then you cannot find Mr. Holt guilty. Because that's what reasonable doubt is. And in this case, it's everywhere.

You're not here to deliver justice for the judge, or for the defendant's daughter, or for anyone else. You're here to decide whether the prosecution has met its burden.

And they haven't.

So we ask you to return the only verdict the law allows under these circumstances—not guilty.

Thank you for your service to the justice system."

Judge LeBlanc adjusted her glasses, glanced down at the typed pages before her, then looked at the jury.

"You've heard the charge of murder in the first degree," she began. "Under South Carolina law, murder is defined as the unlawful killing of another with malice aforethought. If you find the State has proven all elements of that charge beyond reasonable doubt, then your verdict shall be guilty of murder." She paused, letting the words settle. "However, if you do not find the killing was committed with malice, or if the evidence leaves you with reasonable doubt as to the defendant's mental state at the time of the killing, you may consider the lesser-included offense of voluntary manslaughter."

I didn't move. Neither did the jury.

"Voluntary manslaughter," Judge LeBlanc continued, "is the unlawful killing of another in sudden heat of passion, upon sufficient legal provocation. It's still a serious offense, but one that recognizes the possibility of an emotional or impulsive act rather than one born of premeditated intent." She looked up again. "If you find the defendant not guilty of murder, you must next consider whether he is guilty of voluntary manslaughter. If you find him not guilty of either, then your verdict shall be not guilty."

The courtroom remained still. Twelve jurors sat in readiness, some scribbling notes, others just listening. The arguments had finished.

It was now time for judgment.

CHAPTER 64

The wind was shifting over the marshland, rolling in low across the Beaufort County coastline, stirring the tall grass around the weathered picnic tables. Storms loomed in the distance—thick gray clouds pressing low against the horizon, occasionally lit by flashes of lightning, the thunder too far off to hear.

The Sands at the tip of Port Royal comprised of a long boardwalk stretching out over the marshes toward the water, and tidal flats that were a mix of wetland grasses, sand, and dark, shifting mud.

"No word yet?" Emma asked as we walked along the sand toward the boardwalk. "It's been two days."

I turned to face her. "Not yet."

Emma stepped toward the edge of the sand and stopped at the faded sign, glancing at the faraway glint of town. "I remember coming here as a kid," she said. "Back when they tried to make it a tourist thing. Doesn't look like much now."

"No," I said. "But it's quiet. I needed that today."

"Well, I'm glad I came along. I figured you'd be pacing holes in your office floor by now."

"I was. This was the much better option."

Emma turned her eyes toward the sky, squinting against the light. "At least the heatwave broke."

"Yeah," I said. "But it brought company." I nodded toward the storm line, growing darker by the minute.

We went quiet for a moment as we studied the storm.

"What's your read?" Emma asked. "Two days feels . . . long."

I nodded. "It means there's someone in there holding the line. It means someone isn't convinced. The longer they go, the more pressure builds. We need one juror to look at the lack of evidence. That's all. They've come back and asked the judge a dozen questions, but they haven't given anything away." I shrugged. "It's a waiting game now. Everything we could do has been done."

Emma looked out over the far fields. "What happens to Paul Freeman and Wayne Cascade if the decision comes back not guilty?"

"Paul Freeman is staying with friends from his church. He hasn't gone home since the testimony. His father was furious that Paul sold his family out like that. If what he said was true, it creates a lot of trouble. Stephen still has a lot of connections, but Paul might go down."

"And Cascade?"

I shook my head. I didn't know the answer to that.

Another moment of silence passed, broken only by a strong gust of wind pushing against the old signs.

Jury deliberations had always felt like suspended animation to me. No control. No pacing. No argument left to make. Just waiting and wondering and wishing. Thinking about if the words I'd chosen were the right ones. If the timing of my objections had mattered. If that one witness could've been handled differently.

Another gust of wind came through, and with it, the first hint of rain in the air.

My phone buzzed in my pocket. I pulled it out, glanced at the screen, then answered. "Dean Lincoln."

I listened. A few seconds passed. Then I lowered the phone and looked at Emma.

"The jury's back," I said. "Judge LeBlanc wants everyone in court right away."

We didn't speak as we climbed into our SUV.

The storm was coming. And so was the verdict.

CHAPTER 65

I walked into the courtroom with Bruce and Kayla behind me.

My steps were measured. Harley was already at the defense table, prepared as usual, his case file arranged meticulously, every document in its place, ready for whatever came next.

The gallery was full. Reporters sat forward in their seats, pens poised, their attention as sharp as the quiet in the room. Supporters whispered behind folded programs. The onlookers, some of whom hadn't missed a single moment of the trial, were all there for the final chapter. The low hum of anticipation filled the room.

I scanned the gallery. My eyes fell on Wayne Cascade, sitting near the aisle in the second row. His posture was tense and rigid. Closer to the front, Stephen Freeman waited. His eyes locked on to me as I stepped toward the bar. He adjusted his jacket, leaned in, and spoke in a voice quiet enough to keep it private.

"Nice of you to show up," Freeman said. "This should be quite the day."

I didn't respond.

He leaned in closer. "If the verdict's not guilty, you, your client, and that pretty wife of yours, need to get in your car and keep driving. Don't stop. There are folks in this town who don't wait on court decisions."

I turned slightly, keeping my voice calm. "Don't ever talk about my wife."

"I'm just giving advice," Freeman said. "And it's the last time I give it."

I didn't bother answering. I turned away, jaw clenched.

The side door opened. Holt stepped in with a deputy by his side, no handcuffs, but the stiffness in his movement said they were still there in spirit. He was thinner than when this trial had started, worn down by the weight of the days, and the nights that had passed without sleep. He moved toward the defense table, sinking into the chair.

Behind him, his family sat close—his mother, wife, uncles, cousins, and his daughter. It was the first time she had come to the trial. His wife's eyes were glassy, her lips trembling as she clutched a crumpled tissue.

Holt turned to me, his voice barely above a whisper. "This is it?"

I nodded. "It is."

He swallowed hard, looking more vulnerable than I had ever seen him. "You think I've got a shot?"

"We made our case," I said. "That's all we can do. If the worst happens, we appeal. We've got solid grounds."

His voice cracked. "I don't think I'll make it long enough to see an appeal."

I didn't have an answer for him.

Before I could say anything else, I felt a hand on my arm. I turned to see Emma, calm on the outside, but her eyes full of everything she didn't say. She leaned close, her voice low. "Whatever happens, I'm proud of you."

I nodded, a lump forming in my throat. "Thanks for being here."

"I wouldn't be anywhere else."

She walked to the end of the gallery and took a seat next to Granddad Lincoln. He nodded to me.

The door behind the bench opened, and the bailiff emerged.

"All rise. Court is now in session. The Honorable Judge LeBlanc presiding."

Judge LeBlanc entered, her face unreadable, her presence commanding. She eased into the chair with her gaze sweeping over the room. She nodded once. "Bring in the jury."

The door creaked open.

The jurors entered, moving slowly. Most of them avoided looking toward the defense table. One brushed a chair as he passed, nearly tripped, and muttered an apology.

My hands curled into fists at my sides.

Judge LeBlanc's gaze fell on the foreman. "Mr. Foreman, has the jury reached a verdict in the case of the State versus Malcolm Holt?"

Juror Ten stood. He'd been a statue throughout the trial, eyes stone-cold, face impassive.

"We have, Your Honor."

The paper was passed from the bailiff to the judge. She read it, expression unchanged, then passed it back.

"Please read the verdict."

The room was still. Silent.

"In the matter of the State of South Carolina versus Malcolm Holt, on the charge of murder . . ."

I could feel every muscle in my body tense, every nerve alert, every fiber of my being straining toward what came next.

". . . we, the jury, find the defendant . . ."

A breath.

". . . not guilty."

Relief.

"And on the charge of voluntary manslaughter . . ."

Another pause.

". . . not guilty."

The silence that followed was deep and full. It felt like time had stopped. The air didn't move, and the room didn't breathe.

Then, the dam broke.

Holt's wife stood, moved towards him and crumpled, sobbing against her husband's shoulder. A low murmur rose from the gallery. Bruce let out a breath.

I stood still. I didn't smile. This moment wasn't mine to own.

Holt turned to his wife and dropped his face into his hands, his shoulders shaking, not with tears, not yet, but with disbelief. She leaned forward and hugged him. He was free. Their nightmare was over.

Judge LeBlanc banged the gavel once, loud enough to bring the room back into focus.

"This court thanks the jury for its service. You're dismissed with the gratitude of the court."

The jury began to file out, but the gallery stayed frozen in place.

I leaned in, placed a hand on Holt's shoulder.

"It's over," I said. "It's time to go home."

CHAPTER 66

The late-afternoon light slanted across the Beaufort County Courthouse steps, long and golden, as the crowd poured into the parking lot. The verdict had left a lot of tension in the air.

Reporters fanned out like vultures, snapping photos and shoving microphones toward anyone willing to speak. Some people wore relief like armor. Others kept their heads down, walking straight to their cars.

I stood at the base of the steps, tie loosened, top button undone. I was tired, but it was the kind of tired that comes from a win that was earned. I couldn't help but let the moment linger, just for a second, before moving on.

Emma was there, waiting in the parking lot, next to the car with Granddad Lincoln. One hand rested above the small swell of her stomach, and I couldn't help but notice how radiant she looked, even amidst all the chaos—calm and grounded.

She met my eyes and smiled as I made my way toward her.

"I still don't know how you do it," she said, her voice quiet but full of wonder as I leaned in to kiss her goodbye.

"Do what?" I asked, brushing a strand of hair from her face.

"Carry all that weight in there." She nodded toward the courthouse. "And then walk out looking like you just returned a book to the library."

"Habit." I smiled. "And a little bit of self-delusion."

Granddad Lincoln, standing behind her, let out a low chuckle. "Don't forget good genes. He gets it from me."

Emma grinned. "We'll meet you at home?"

I nodded, adjusting my jacket. "I shouldn't be long. Just need to wrap up a few things with Malcolm and the court."

She reached out and squeezed my hand, her touch warm. "Be safe."

I watched her turn, walking toward the car with Granddad, my heart still light in the warmth of her presence. But then, just as they reached the car, a voice called out.

"Wayne!"

I turned and saw Terry Wallace, moving fast across the lot, hand brushing the butt of his weapon. He was headed toward someone near the end of the parking lot. Someone I didn't need to see to know.

Wayne Cascade.

My stomach dropped.

Cascade stood half-shaded by an old oak, wearing a tired denim jacket and dark sunglasses. His body was stiff—too still. And when he turned and saw Wallace coming toward him, something in him snapped.

I saw it first in his posture. A twitch of the neck. A shift of the shoulder. Then—

Cascade spun and ran into the parking lot. He grabbed the nearest person.

Emma.

My heart stopped.

"Get back!" Cascade yelled, his voice harsh, full of panic and desperation. "Everybody back!"

Emma let out a short scream as Cascade wrenched her sideways, pressing the barrel of a pistol into her ribs.

Granddad Lincoln took a step toward him, but Cascade waved the gun. Granddad Lincoln stopped and raised both hands in surrender.

"Wayne, put the gun down," Terry called, his voice firm but controlled. His weapon was drawn.

"Stop!" Cascade screamed. "Don't take another step."

Emma's hands were frozen in mid-air, her breath coming fast and panicked, her eyes wide and darting toward me.

I didn't hesitate.

I ran toward my car, heart hammering in my chest. I yanked open the passenger side door, reaching into the glove box. My fingers closed around the grip of my Glock.

I came around the hood, holding the gun low.

Cascade was backing toward the far side of the lot, dragging Emma with him, his grip on her arm tight. "You think I'm going to prison? I'm not going to rot in a cage. I've got a life to live."

"Then don't make it shorter," Wallace shouted. His gun was drawn. "Let her go."

I edged closer. Moved behind a large pickup truck. I had a clear shot.

Cascade's eyes flicked around the lot but never landed on me. "You're too late, Wallace. I'm not going down for this." He shoved the gun harder into Emma. "She's leverage. You want to keep her safe, then everybody backs off."

Wallace was circling, slow and careful, trying to keep himself between Cascade and everyone else. Other officers drew their weapons. "Wayne, no one wants this to end in blood. Put the gun down."

"Don't tell me what to do!" Cascade barked. He stepped toward his truck. "She's coming with me."

I paced closer. Ten yards away. I raised the Glock, steadying it with both hands.

"Let her go," I said. "I'm not going to tell you again."

Cascade turned and looked at me, his grip tightening around the gun. His face was twisted, but his eyes, those eyes, were those of a man who had nothing left to lose.

Then, he raised the gun and fired.

The first shot was aimed at Wallace—wide, wild, cracking into the pavement near his feet.

The second one was coming in my direction.

I squeezed the trigger of my Glock.

The round caught Cascade in the shoulder. He jerked but didn't fall. Emma reeled forward. Shots fired from elsewhere, tearing into his ribs, and he dropped. The pistol clattered out of his hand and on to the pavement.

Emma stumbled, her knees giving out as she collapsed into Granddad's arms. She was crying now—hard, shaking. I ran, gun still up, heart in my throat.

Cascade lay on the pavement, blood soaking through his jacket, gasping for air. His mouth opened like he wanted to speak, but no words came.

I dropped to my knees beside Emma, pulling her into me, holding her close.

"I've got you," I whispered, my voice breaking. "You're safe. It's over."

She nodded against my chest, her breath coming in sharp, painful gasps. "I thought—I thought I was going to—"

"You're okay," I said, my voice low, again and again, like saying it enough would make it true.

The officers stood over Cascade with their guns drawn. The EMTs arrived seconds later, cutting open his shirt, shouting out vitals.

"He's alive," someone shouted. "Get him loaded up!"

I stood, helping Emma to her feet. Granddad Lincoln steadied her on the other side, his hand on her arm like he was afraid to let go.

"Are you hit?" I gasped at Emma.

"No." She shook her head and looked at me. "Bub and I are okay."

CHAPTER 67

Five days after the shooting, five days after the verdict, we celebrated.

The small Italian place had seen its fair share of celebrations—graduations, anniversaries, quiet wins, all over pasta and red wine. Tonight, it felt different. Tonight, the Holt family had something real to toast—freedom.

The owner of the restaurant, round in the middle with an apron and scuffed dress shoes, piled our plates high, poured the wine himself, and clapped me on the back like a man who understood what we'd risked, and what we'd won.

Holt couldn't stop talking. His voice boomed louder than usual, words slurring just enough to tell me the wine was doing its job. "You should've seen their faces," he said for the third time, grinning like a kid. "Dean had them on their heels the whole time. It was like watching a heavyweight title fight."

His wife, Michelle, sat beside him, one hand resting on his shoulder like she wasn't sure it was real. The kind of grip that said, "Don't vanish on me now." She hadn't stopped smiling since we walked through the door.

Bruce and Kayla sat next to me, eating and drinking and enjoying the merriment.

I let the joy wash over me. There were no speeches. No grand reflections. Just the satisfaction of knowing I'd kept an innocent man out of prison, torn down a bogus case, and dragged the corrupt into the light.

Holt raised his glass again, toast number five, by my count. "To freedom," he said, clinking glasses all around. "To justice. And to this man right here, Mr. Dean Lincoln."

Bruce added, his voice warm but carrying weight, "To justice, and to not screwing with our Dean Lincoln."

We all laughed, and for the first time in a long time, it didn't feel forced. It was easy.

Someone spilled wine across the red tablecloth, but no one cared. The room hummed with low voices, silverware clinking gently. In our little corner of it, time had loosened its grip.

"So, what happens now?" Holt asked, finishing off his glass.

I leaned back, took a slow sip, and nodded toward him. "All charges are dropped. You're free to get back to your life."

"And Wayne Cascade?"

"He survived the shooting, and he's been charged with a range of offenses in relation to his stunt at the courthouse."

"And in relation to Judge Newton's death?"

"They'll push him and see what they can get out of him, but right now, all they have is Paul's testimony that he drove there that night. That's not enough to charge him."

"Think Cascade will talk to the police for a reduced deal?"

I shrugged. "He doesn't seem like the type of man who wants to live his life in a cage. He may talk once he's recovered from the shooting."

"Or he might escape," Bruce quipped.

The night continued on, and we ate, talked, and laughed. The laughter grew harder as the wine kept flowing. At one point, Holt broke into a song, and to everyone's surprise, Kayla knew the second verse. They sang, badly, and without an ounce of shame.

Eventually the night wound down, and we spilled out on to the sidewalk, with stomachs full of food and hearts full of love. Holt pulled me in for a hug, strong and steady, and held on longer than I expected.

"You gave me my life back," he said as he patted my back. "I will never forget what you've done for me."

I nodded. "Take care of yourself, Malcolm."

They piled into a cab, and I watched the taillights fade. Kayla stayed at my side. She didn't say a word for a long time.

Then she broke the silence. "What is it, Dean?"

"Sorry?"

"I know that look," she said, arms crossed. "I've seen it too many times. Something's still chewing at you."

"It's the link between Cascade and Judge Newton." I stared down the block, hands shoved deep in my pockets. "This isn't over yet."

CHAPTER 68

Bruce and I stepped out of the Clerk of Court's office. The filing had gone through, and the case was completed. It was done. Over.

Bruce was beside me, mid-sentence about the weather, when I spotted Stephen Freeman ahead of us.

He stood casually at the edge of the courthouse lot, one boot resting against the curb, arms folded across his chest like he owned the ground he stood on. He wasn't smiling, but the arrogance was still there—in the way he leaned, in the way his eyes tracked me.

We made it five steps before he moved.

"I guess you think it all worked out for you," he said, stepping into our path.

I stopped cold. "Justice worked out for the city of Beaufort."

He laughed. "You don't know a thing about justice, boy. You think courtrooms and verdicts are what keep this place standing? I keep this city running. Me. Not you. I run this city."

I stepped forward. My voice was low and steady. "You're the reason the system keeps failing. You don't run this city. You poison it."

His jaw tightened. He took a step closer, so close I could see the sheen of sweat on his temple. "Don't test me, Lincoln. If you and Emma want that picture-perfect life for your baby, you'll pack up and leave Beaufort while you still can."

My hand was on his collar before I registered the motion. I gripped it tight, squeezing my fist against the underside of his chin.

"Don't you ever talk about Emma," I said, my face inches from his.

Freeman tried to laugh, but his jaw was pinned.

Behind me, I heard Bruce's voice. "Dean. Dean, not here."

I held Freeman another second, then let go. Freeman stumbled back and straightened his coat like nothing had happened. His face was flushed, but he didn't flinch.

"You think this is a win?" he said. "You've made enemies you don't even know exist."

"I'm not afraid of you," I said.

He leaned in, eyes cold. "Then you're a fool."

I stared at Freeman. "I'm coming for you. Not with threats, but with the truth. And when it lands, you won't be able to buy your way out."

Freeman didn't respond. He didn't have to. He gave one last smirk, turned, and walked off without another word.

I stood there, fists clenched, pulse still hammering in my ears.

CHAPTER 69

Five days later, I walked into Blessington's office, a slight pressure in my chest.

The thick carpet muffled my footsteps, the dim overhead lights making the space feel more like a bank vault than a law office. Blessington was behind his desk, sorting through papers, glasses perched low on his nose. When he saw me, he gave a nod, indicating the chair across from him.

"Sit down, Dean. This won't take long."

I hesitated, then sat, folding my hands together. "You wanted to meet about Julie Steinberg's case?"

Blessington sighed and leaned back in his chair, his fingers rubbing the bridge of his nose like he had a headache. "Julie's case is all but over, I'm afraid."

I sat forward. "What do you mean?"

Blessington glanced up, a flicker of resignation crossing his face. "Casper Remington has decided he won't testify. He's pulling out. And without him on the stand, without his testimony, there's no case. We have no choice but to drop the charges. The Remingtons are leaving town. They're headed to the Cayman Islands, setting up shop there with some new hotel development."

"The Cayman Islands?"

"They've got investments there. The type of developments that take a lot of cash and very little oversight." He paused, his eyes glinting with something almost smug. "Paul Freeman's testimony really shook them up, you know? Feathers have been ruffled. People are spooked."

"By what?"

Blessington chuckled, a short, dry sound. "Paul's testimony made a lot of people nervous. The Freeman name carries weight in this town, but when you start talking about dirty dealings, well, some people don't want to be tied up in that. The Remingtons are trying to clear out before anything gets worse."

"The Remingtons are leaving because Paul Freeman knows something?"

"I don't know the whole story, but between you and me, it was never about the case against Julie Steinberg. I think John Remington wanted to buy her bar, knock it down, and build some new townhouses. I wouldn't be surprised if his son set her up. But now, with Paul's testimony on the record, things are too complicated. And you'll be happy. You're getting rid of Stephen Freeman as well."

"Why?"

"Rumor is he's about to move to the Cayman Islands with them. The Freeman family has been investing in Remington's real-estate developments for years now. Stephen's business dealings are long and many. The Freeman family have got their hands in all sorts of things, if you look hard enough."

I didn't respond as a thought tracked through my mind.

Blessington leaned back in his chair, clearly enjoying the unfolding drama. "I don't think you're as slow as you seem, Dean. There were rumors that Robert Newton's fishing business was a money-laundering front, but nothing was ever proven. I guess that was the Remingtons' escape plan." He wiped his palms on his suit, then met my gaze. "But I'm glad John Remington is gone. He was always so angry. He used to be around these halls a lot."

"Why?"

"Meeting various people." He exhaled. "The angriest I saw him was around a week before Judge Newton's death. I remember walking past his office and hearing Freeman and Remington yelling at him. They were screaming and swearing, but Judge Newton was giving it back to them. It was very intense and the only time I heard Judge Newton swear."

"And you've never mentioned this before?"

"I have." He shrugged. "I told my superiors, but they told me not to get involved."

"Judge Newton had a falling-out with Stephen Freeman and John Remington," I muttered to myself, barely above a whisper.

Blessington squinted as he looked at me. "I don't know what you're thinking, but it's a wild thing when the people who appear to be the ones pulling the strings find themselves tangled up in their own mess."

I stood up, my mind reeling with what Blessington had revealed. "Thanks for the information," I said. "I've got everything I need."

As I turned toward the door, Blessington's voice called out. "Don't do anything stupid, Dean. I was just beginning to like you."

I didn't turn around. I left the office, the door clicking shut behind me. My mind was already racing. Paul Freeman, the Remingtons, the Freeman family's connections to the real-estate developments—it all added up.

I took out my phone and called Julie with the good news. She was happy, thanking me many times, but my mind was elsewhere. I agreed to join her for a drink and then hung up. Then I called Bruce, then Sean Benning, and then Terry Wallace.

CHAPTER 70

"He could be armed," Wallace said, keeping eyes forward as the cruiser rolled to a stop at a red light on the edge of Beaufort.

I glanced up from my phone. "If he is, he's outgunned," I said. "Five to one."

Wallace gave a single nod and didn't say anything else.

My phone buzzed again. "He's at home," I relayed the message to Wallace.

He grunted, turned the wheel, and ten minutes later, we were in the Ashdale neighborhood. Wallace stopped across the street from the Freeman residence. Out front of the house, Sean Benning was already leaning on the hood of his truck.

"I've been flying the drone high over his house," he said. "Freeman is sitting outside on his porch with a glass of whiskey. We can go in via the side gate and he won't notice us." Benning looked at the crumpled driveway. "His driveway is a hell of a mess."

"That it is," I commented. "Someone took a compact excavator to it. And I don't blame them."

Two uniformed officers from the Beaufort Police Department arrived. Under direction from Wallace, we moved quickly. Wallace led the way, advancing along the side of the house, and then unclipping the back gate without a sound. He approached Stephen

Freeman, who was lying on a sun lounger in his yard, flicking through information on his cell phone.

His head snapped toward us as he sensed our presence. He stood, whiskey in hand. "Terry Wallace. Can I help you? This is private property."

Wallace didn't answer. He stopped about fifteen feet from Freeman, fingers resting on his weapon.

I stepped forward into view for Freeman. His eyes narrowed when he saw me.

"The city lawyer?" he said. "What's this about?"

"This is about the truth," I told him. "And it's coming for you."

He smirked, but it didn't touch his eyes. "What are you talking about?"

"You're the missing link between the Remington arrests and Judge Newton," I said. "You're the person who asked law enforcement to make the arrest, and encouraged Court Administration in Columbia to put it in front of Judge Newton."

"That's a nice story. Pity it's not true."

"I've got proof."

"Proof?" He laughed. "What proof?"

"You're 'TLM.'"

"What?"

"You're 'The Liberated Man' in the documents obtained by a journalist."

"What are you talking about?"

"Freeman . . . The Liberated Man. That's your code name in the communications that Marsha Reynolds uncovered."

"Nice theory, but you can't prove it."

"I've spent the past day researching the investments into Remington Red Rock Inc. Digging into their financials, I found a million-dollar investment you made in 2005. The first return from that investment was then transferred to a company named Ashdale

Liberated Enterprises, which is registered in the Cayman Islands. That was the only payment made directly to Ashdale Liberated Enterprises, but Remington Red Rock has made millions of dollars in payments to Newton Fishing, which in turn has made millions of dollars in payments to Ashdale Liberated Enterprises in the Cayman Islands. Those payments were disguised as docking fees, and nobody would question the docking fees of a fishing company. It's a textbook laundering loop—local investments make profits, the profits are then washed clean through the fishing company and transferred offshore, and not a dime is paid in taxes."

"You can't prove any of that."

"We will." Wallace's tone was firm. "But more importantly, in an attempt to avoid the death penalty, Wayne Cascade has agreed to talk about your involvement in Judge Newton's death."

Freeman's face went blank.

"You have no idea what you're doing," he said.

"Judge Newton wanted out of the game, and he was going to talk to Marsha Reynolds. He was going to tell her all about Remington's illegal behavior. And the more she found out about Remington, the closer she came to exposing Ashdale Liberated Enterprises. You had to stop Newton before he could expose you. Your motive is clear."

"Cascade is not a reliable witness. He's trying to save his own skin. His testimony won't stand up in court."

"No." I stepped closer. "But Paul's testimony will corroborate it."

Freeman snarled. "You leave my son out of this."

"You're done, Stephen. Your corrupt reign over this city is over."

"Corrupt? I'm not corrupt! I keep the peace here. I make sure everything works. I'm the glue that ties this community together."

Wallace made his move. "Stephen Freeman, we're asking you to come in for questioning regarding your connection to the murder of Judge Newton."

Freeman didn't budge. His eyes flicked to Wallace, who gave the faintest nod.

"No," Freeman said, almost laughing. "No, it doesn't work like that. I'm your superior, Wallace. I'm a former circuit solicitor. You know what that means, don't you? It means I'm well above your pay grade. You don't just walk in here and flip the script. Turn around now and I'll forget this happened." His hand twitched, and he looked straight at me. "I make this community safer. I brought order. I brought justice."

"There was no justice for my sister," I said.

Freeman was cornered. There was nowhere to go.

And he did the thing that most cowards do when it's over. He ran.

He turned and ran toward his boat at the end of his dock. He was fast for his age. But I was faster. Within a few strides, I'd caught up to him. I reached out my right foot, clipping the back of his heel, and sending him tumbling forward. His face planted on the ground, his shoulders pushing into the grass.

I stood over him as he rolled over.

"That's assault," he said. "I have witnesses."

"You've got bigger problems than that." Wallace walked up behind us. "Mr. Freeman, I tried to be polite. I tried to do this the right way, but you didn't want that, so this time, I'm not asking you." Wallace reached down and dragged Freeman to his feet. "Stephen Freeman, you're under arrest for conspiracy to commit murder and for actions impeding a criminal investigation."

CHAPTER 71

It took another week for the dust to settle.

Statements were taken. Files opened. Names jotted down. One after another the dominos fell. What started as a single murder charge unraveled into something messier. Bigger. Something with teeth.

I spent most of that week bouncing in and out of Beaufort PD, giving the same answers to different people wearing different badges. I told the truth. No shortcuts and no cover-ups.

Wayne Cascade was getting a firsthand education in how brutal South Carolina's laws could be. He was charged with a wide range of offenses, from assault to felony firearm possession to murder. After several weeks in hospital under police guard, the reality of his new life was setting in. In exchange for the death penalty being dropped on the charge of murdering Judge Newton, he gave up everything he knew. Some of the crimes had gone cold years ago and Cascade flipped them back to life. He gave the kind of confession that made prosecutors create new calendars and gave law enforcement a reason to skip sleep.

He admitted Stephen Freeman had paid him fifty thousand dollars to shoot Judge Newton, claiming the judge was about to expose Freeman's money-laundering operations to impress a pretty journalist named Marsha Reynolds. Cascade suggested that the judge was also going to assault Reynolds, and tried to get off on manslaughter, but law enforcement didn't buy it.

Cascade made the news five days in a row. He just kept giving up information. Once he opened his mouth, he couldn't stop. "From Investigator to Informant," one headline read. Another read, "PI Breaks the Code." People ate it up—a dishonest investigator exposing the depths of local corruption made for a good story. Cascade hadn't realized it yet, but he'd signed his own death warrant. I doubted if he'd make it a year inside.

Five days after Freeman's arrest, I found myself back in the Beaufort County Courthouse for an arraignment hearing. This time, I sat in the front row. The benches behind me were packed. Cameras weren't allowed, but that didn't stop the press from lining the walls.

Kane Newton sat in the second row. I made eye contact with him. He mouthed something. It was hard to make out, but it wasn't friendly. His brother, Robert, was under investigation for money laundering and had been told not to leave the state. I didn't respond to Kane. I wasn't here for him.

John Kirkland, a defense lawyer from Charleston, was at the defense table.

Everyone stopped talking when the side door opened.

Stephen Freeman walked in, chained at the wrists and ankles, flanked by two deputies. Orange jumpsuit. Black letters across the back: SCDC INMATE. His hair had been buzzed to nothing, and he had a fresh bruise under his left eye.

He looked shorter than he had before. Deflated. Gutted.

He hadn't pulled the trigger, and he wasn't present at the scene of the crime, but in South Carolina, that didn't matter. Section 16-1-40 of the South Carolina Code of Laws was as harsh as it was clear. The law stated that a person who was an accessory before the fact must be punished in the manner prescribed for the principal felon. Freeman was the architect, the one who had planned Judge Newton's murder, and that meant one thing—he was responsible. He had tried to set up Holt to shoot Judge Newton, he had tried to encourage Holt to defend another innocent girl, but when Holt didn't show up in time, Freeman sent in Wayne Cascade to do the job instead.

When the clerk read the charge of murder, Freeman cracked. "I'm innocent!" he shouted. "This is my courtroom!"

The judge told him to be quiet, but Freeman wasn't done. When asked for his plea, he shouted, "Not guilty! I'm not guilty! This court is a sham!"

Due to the very real flight risk, the judge denied bail. Freeman yelled some more, but fifteen minutes after it started, it was over.

The bailiffs led him away, and the door shut behind him with a hard, final clang.

CHAPTER 72

A week after Freeman was charged, I stood next to Rhys, staring at the marshland behind his house. The tide had gone out, leaving long stretches of mudflats and a familiar trace of salt floating on the breeze. I stood on the back deck, cold beer in hand, watching egrets pick their way through the shallows. Rhys leaned on the railing next to me, eyes distant, gazing out at nothing.

We hadn't said much. We didn't need to.

"You hear about Wayne Cascade?" he asked, voice low, still not looking at me.

"Died late last night." I gave a slow nod. "He was transferred to the medical wing of Kirkland Correctional, and a lifer stabbed him on his second day there."

"Karma doesn't wait forever, I guess," Rhys muttered. "And I heard Newton Fishing has closed down."

"They're under investigation for offshore money laundering. Robert has been told not to leave the state." I took a sip. The bottle was sweating in my grip, and the condensation was slick on my fingers. "The Freemans are finished now. Paul's back behind bars for his involvement in Judge Newton's murder. As an accessory. Stephen's locked up and awaiting trial for murder. That chapter's closed."

Rhys nodded, eyes locked on the water. "Terrible men. All thought they were untouchable."

I didn't respond.

"They built their family wealth on the pain of others," he said. "And I'm glad they got done. I'm glad they've crumbled."

I waited a moment before speaking. "I don't know how I feel about Paul. I'm glad he's repenting for his past, but forgiveness is a big ask."

Rhys's jaw tightened, but he didn't look at me. "I'm not there yet, and I don't know if I'll ever get there, but I'm trying to find forgiveness in my heart. I can't hate a man who tries to right the wrongs of his past. I respect that. It shows maturity, but man, it takes some time to get to forgiveness. I've still got a long way to go, but I'm working through it."

The wind stirred the palmettos at the edge of the marsh. Somewhere off in the distance, a boat passed, a silhouette on the open blue.

"I want to honor her somehow." Rhys sighed. "Not with a plaque or sign somewhere, but something real. Something living. Something that can be loved."

"Any ideas?"

"I don't know." He shrugged. "The world tends to throw surprises when I put ideas out there like that." He looked at the horizon for a long time. "Heather was the best person I ever knew." His voice didn't break, but it had a raw edge. "And she didn't deserve to be a footnote in someone else's recklessness. Her name and spirit deserve to live on."

"Amen to that." I raised my drink, and we clinked bottles.

We fell silent again and just stood there, watching the light shift over the marsh. The tide had started creeping back in.

"You doing okay?" I asked.

"Better now. It's not closure, but it's a start." He shrugged. "Thanks, Dean. Thanks for all your help."

I nodded.

We stayed there a while longer, not talking, but listening to the water, the wind, the quiet hum of a world. We were two men tied by grief, standing still while the tide moved on.

CHAPTER 73

When I stepped through the door, I could feel every eye turn to me. My hair was a mess, shirt half-untucked, and there was a smear of something across my shoulder.

But I couldn't stop smiling.

The fluorescent lights in the hospital waiting room buzzed overhead. Rhys was near the window, elbows on his knees, eyes fixed on nothing. Granddad Lincoln stood by the vending machine, hands behind his back like he was still presenting a closing statement to a jury. Grandma sat beside Jane, her hand resting gently over hers.

Jane looked thinner than she used to, but her cheeks had color again. Her hair was coming back soft and silver, and there was strength in her spine that hadn't been there the last time I had seen her. The remission had held.

And now they were waiting for me.

"Well?" Grandma Lincoln asked, already halfway out of her seat.

I didn't keep them waiting.

"She's here," I said. "Emma's good. She's doing okay. And the baby's healthy."

There was this soft, relieved sound—like laughter and tears crashing into each other in the same breath.

"It's a girl," I added, still barely believing it myself.

I ran a hand through my hair, my eyes finding Rhys across the room.

"We named her Heather."

He froze.

"For my sister," I said, quieter now. "For your wife."

The room went still. The only sound was the hum of the hallway and the breath catching in Rhys's chest. Jane dabbed her eyes with a tissue that looked like it had already been through a few rounds.

Rhys stood up and crossed the room in long strides. He wrapped me in a hug—tight, fast, and strong.

"Thank you," he said as his eyes filled with tears. "That's so beautiful. She would've loved that."

Granddad Lincoln shook my hand next, grip steady even if his fingers trembled at the edges. Grandma Lincoln reached up and cupped my face like I was still a boy and kissed my cheek.

"You've done her proud," she whispered.

Then I turned to Jane. She was smiling, eyes bright and wet. She took my hand in both of hers, warm and steady.

"You're a father," she said.

I nodded. My throat was too tight to say anything back.

We all stood there for a moment. Years of pain and healing, of grief that never fully left but had softened enough to let something new grow. The past was still with us—but it was quiet now. Settled.

"She has Emma's eyes," I said, wiping at mine. "But the rest, she's all Lincoln."

Granddad chuckled. "Then the world better get ready."

The laughter came easy after that—gentle, warm, and real.

A nurse stepped into the room and gave us a smile. "We're ready for visitors."

I turned to them, the grin finding its way back to my face.

"Come meet Heather Jane Lincoln."

And one by one, they followed me down the hall.

Grief may have shaped us, grief may have pushed so hard to break us, but love, with all its beauty and joy and ecstasy, still filled us with hope.

ABOUT THE AUTHOR

Peter O'Mahoney is the author of the bestselling Joe Hennessy, Tex Hunter, and Jack Valentine thrillers. O'Mahoney was raised on a healthy dose of Perry Mason stories, and the pace and style of these books inspired him to write, and he hasn't stopped since. O'Mahoney loves to write fast-paced stories filled with exciting characters, thrilling legal cases, and mind-bending plot twists. His thrillers have entertained hundreds of thousands of readers around the world.

O'Mahoney is a criminologist, with a keen interest in law, and is an active member of the American Society of Criminology. When not writing or spending time with his family, O'Mahoney can be found in the surf, on the hiking trials, in the boxing gym, at home reading, or staring at a beautiful sunset in wonder.

Follow the Author on Amazon

If you enjoyed this book, follow Peter O'Mahoney on Amazon to be notified when the author releases a new book!

To do this, please follow these instructions:

Desktop:

1) Search for the author's name on Amazon or in the Amazon App.
2) Click on the author's name to arrive on their Amazon page.
3) Click the "Follow" button.

Mobile and Tablet:

1) Search for the author's name on Amazon or in the Amazon App.
2) Click on one of the author's books.
3) Click on the author's name to arrive on their Amazon page.
4) Click the "Follow" button.

Kindle eReader and Kindle App:

If you enjoyed this book on a Kindle eReader or in the Kindle App, you will find the author "Follow" button after the last page.